Fiona Leitch is a writer wit ... written for football and mot... illegal raves and is a stalwa... commercial, even appearing as ...alasian face of a cleaning product called 'Sod Off'. After living in London and Cornwall, she's finally settled in sunny New Zealand, where she enjoys scaring her cats by trying out dialogue on them. She spends her days dreaming of retiring to a crumbling Venetian palazzo, walking on the windswept beaches of West Auckland, and writing funny, flawed but awesome female characters.

Her debut novel, *Dead in Venice*, was published by Audible in 2018 as one of their Crime Grant finalists. Fiona also writes screenplays and was a finalist in the Athena Film Festival Writers Lab, co-run by Meryl Streep's IRIS company.

www.fionaleitch.com

 twitter.com/fkleitch
 facebook.com/fionakleitch

Also by Fiona Leitch

The Nosey Parker Cozy Mysteries

Murder on the Menu

A Brush with Death

A Sprinkle of Sabotage

A CORNISH CHRISTMAS MURDER

A Nosey Parker Cozy Mystery

FIONA LEITCH

One More Chapter
a division of HarperCollins*Publishers* Ltd
1 London Bridge Street
London SE1 9GF
www.harpercollins.co.uk
HarperCollins*Publishers*
1st Floor, Watermarque Building, Ringsend Road
Dublin 4, Ireland

This paperback edition 2021
1
First published in Great Britain in ebook format
by HarperCollins*Publishers* 2021
Copyright © Fiona Leitch 2021
Fiona Leitch asserts the moral right to be identified
as the author of this work
A catalogue record of this book is available from the British Library

ISBN: 978-0-00-852535-4

Printed and bound in the UK using 100% Renewable Electricity
by CPI Group (UK) Ltd

MIX
Paper from
responsible sources
FSC™ C007454

FSC
www.fsc.org

This book is produced from independently certified FSC™ paper
to ensure responsible forest management.

For more information visit: www.harpercollins.co.uk/green

For Lucas, whose arrival was like all my Christmases at once

Chapter One

'Wow!'
        'Bloomin' 'eck!'
'Holy guacamole!'
'Woof!'

The exclamations of my companions as we drove through the wrought-iron gates and chugged painfully up the snow-covered driveway echoed my own thoughts. The house that was still some way ahead of us, framed by an avenue of bare, skeletal trees silhouetted blackly against a pale sky, was undoubtedly impressive.

'Yeah, it's all right, innit?' I said calmly, as if I was used to working in great big, fancy country mansions. But, truth be told, I was hugely excited about this job. This one was going to be fun.

The gears on the Gimpmobile, my ancient but well-loved (and inappropriately decorated) catering van, ground nastily as I shifted down to second, slowing down as we approached the front of the house. I assumed my employers for the day would not want my knackered old Transit parked there, where their guests would see it, but in this weather I wasn't wholly convinced that, once parked, the van would start again. I leaned on the horn, hoping for a jaunty *Toot! Toot!* to alert the inhabitants that we'd arrived, and was rewarded with a sort of strangled whine that reminded me of the year I'd had to sit next to Colin 'Thunderpants' Dobson in Maths. The combination of the school's hard plastic chairs and the weird diet that his mother fed him had resulted in many similar noises, and had left me unable to attempt any type of mathematical equation without my eyes involuntarily watering.

As I'd hoped, the grand wooden door opened and Lily Swann, an old friend of mine from the same school (but with a better digestive system), rushed out, waving me on and pointing around the back of the house. The Gimpmobile groaned but made it around the corner of the house before I took pity on it and parked up, leaping out as soon as the engine was off.

Mum climbed creakily out of the van on the passenger side, stopping to stretch and trapping my teenage daughter, Daisy, who was trying to follow her out.

'Hurry up, Nana,' said Daisy. 'Germaine's been crossing her paws since Launceston.'

'She's not the only one,' muttered Mum, jigging about. 'It's the cold weather.'

Our Pomeranian, Germaine, who we'd 'temporarily' inherited after her owner had died and who had wormed her way into the family for ever just by virtue of being more cute and floofsome than was strictly legal, couldn't wait any longer and climbed over both of them before jumping down into the snow. She yelped; her little legs meant that her fluffy tummy was only inches away from the cold stuff. I'd bought her a cute little coat, not that I'm a sucker, or that I treat her like my baby or anything (ahem!), but that wouldn't keep her feet warm. She trotted round to the back of the van, picking up her paws in a highly exaggerated fashion to avoid them being in contact with the ground for too long, and peed up one of the wheels. I could almost hear her sigh with satisfaction.

I bent down to pick her up, then thought better of it at the sight of the snow under her paws, which was yellow and still steaming slightly. Instead I clicked on her lead as the fifth member of my ragtag band of helpers, Debbie, followed me out of the driver's side of the van. It was a bit of a squeeze up front – the van's passenger bench-seat was only really meant for two passengers, not three and a dog – but given how cold it was, the journey from our homes in the seaside town of Penstowan, across Bodmin

Moor to Kingseat Abbey, had been more cosy than cramped.

'Blooming heck, this is some house, innit?' said Debbie, her Mancunian accent showing unaccustomed signs of awe. She had a dry sense of humour and was usually quite hard to impress, probably a result of her years as a nurse back in Manchester where she had, as she was proud of telling us, seen everything. She'd only been living in Cornwall for about three months, and as much as she didn't really regret moving, I knew she still occasionally hankered after the shops and big-city lifestyle she'd left behind. If her husband Callum (Penstowan High School's Class of 1996 Top Stud Muffin, although – bless him – that was kind of hard to believe when you saw him now) had found them a house like *this* down here, I don't think she'd have given her home town a second thought.

'Jodie!' Lily had gone back indoors and reappeared at the rear door, which was a much less grand affair; what I assumed had once been the servants' entrance. She wore a smart suit, trouser legs shoved hastily into a pair of wellies, with a pink puffer jacket slung incongruously over her shoulders. She stamped her feet against the packed snow and ice in the courtyard, trying to keep warm. 'Thank you for doing this at such short notice. I wasn't sure you'd get here in this weather.' She stepped forward and we hugged.

I'd spoken to her on the phone and made most of the arrangements for today by email, but we hadn't actually seen each other for several years. I'd moved to London to join the Metropolitan Police when I was nineteen, almost twenty. I had always made a point of looking up my old friends on my regular visits home, but Penstowan was the kind of place where people regularly moved away, and every time I came back there'd be fewer and fewer of the old gang. Lily was one of those who had moved, working overseas and raising her family away from Cornwall.

After my dad had died seven years ago I'd toyed with the idea of coming back for good, but I'd only taken the leap earlier that year. I'd returned to set up my catering business and have a quiet life with Daisy, away from the dangers of my previous career and the irritation of having my useless ex-husband and Lifetime Holder of the 'Crappest Dad in the Universe' award, Richard (aka That Cheating Swine), living just round the corner. Lily had also only recently returned herself.

Lily smiled as she stood back and looked me up and down. 'Tony said you hadn't changed a bit. You haven't.' Tony Penhaligon was my oldest friend in the whole world. He knew everyone in Penstowan and everything that they got up to, and he was almost as big a gossip as my mum. 'Shirley, you're looking well. Daisy, you were a baby the last time I saw you! And you must be Debbie?

Come in, I'll show you where the kitchen is and you can get warm before you unload everything.'

We followed her inside, glad to get out of the cold. The snow that had started falling as we left Penstowan had stopped as we crossed the moors, but it was starting again now in earnest and I was already dreading the drive home. But that was hours away. Hopefully the weather would sort itself out. We didn't normally get snow this close to Christmas, with the day itself usually being grey and miserable rather than white and pretty.

'This place is *amazing*,' I said.

'A bit different to Singapore, though,' Lily laughed.

'Yeah, and a lot colder.'

'You used to live in Singapore?' Daisy's eyes widened. We'd watched a programme on the telly about the world-famous botanical gardens in Singapore, and she was now obsessed with going there. I hadn't told her, but I had this dream of saving up and taking her there for her eighteenth birthday. It was just as well that was some years away.

'Yes, we lived there for eight years. I worked in hotel management—'

'Did you work in that *amazing* one with the swimming pool on the roof?' Daisy had done her research. I wasn't sure my budget would ever stretch to us staying in that particular hotel, though…

'No, although I knew people that did, and I used to

sneak in and use the pool,' said Lily. 'Have you heard of Raffles? I used to work there.'

'Wow,' said Debbie, impressed again. I made a mental note to tell Callum to start saving up so they could come to Singapore with us, although I doubted we'd be staying at Raffles either. 'I've always wanted to stay there.'

'How on earth did you end up back here?' said Daisy, which could have sounded rude – I mean, the house we were standing in was hardly slumming it – but then, living and working in one of the most beautiful and historic hotels in the world was definitely not an easy thing to live up to.

'It just felt like time to come home.' Lily smiled at me. 'You know how that feels.'

The house was every bit as impressive on the inside as it was on the exterior, even in what would once have been the servants' domain. The stone floors were polished and smooth with hundreds of years' use, but still felt sturdy and reassuring underfoot. The walls were at least a foot thick; massive slabs of the local granite keeping the cold at bay. The windows were small and mean, and didn't let in much light; but then this was the business end of the house, and I assumed the more ornate arched windows and carved stone lintels that I'd spotted as we'd slowly crawled past the main entrance would have been saved for the bits the aristocracy saw.

At least it meant the draughts had trouble finding their way in.

Lily slipped off her wellies and jacket, hanging them in a cupboard in the rear entrance lobby, then led us down a corridor towards a lime-washed hallway, with several doors leading off. She pointed to one.

'There's a toilet just there, if you need it—' she started. Mum rushed off without a word. We all stopped and waited for her, Germaine taking the opportunity to sniff at Lily's trouser pockets. You never knew where a doggy treat could be concealed, and she lived in constant hope.

'Thanks for letting me bring the dog, by the way,' I said. 'She won't be any trouble. All my usual dog-sitters have come with me.' I gestured to Debbie and Daisy, who were both having a good gawk at the house.

'That new bloke of yours not able to look after her?' Lily said with a grin, and I knew that Tony really *had* been gossiping. He was such an old woman.

'Nathan's working,' I said, feeling a little warm glow in my tummy that DCI Nathan Withers, once of the Royal Merseyside Constabulary but now firmly ensconced in the Devon and Cornwall Police (and my heart), was indeed my 'new bloke'. To say it had been love at first sight would be a massive lie – I had muscled in on his first big investigation down here, and in return he had threatened to arrest me at least three times – but once he'd realised that it was better to work with me than against me, because I wasn't backing down, and I'd realised that what I'd mistaken for arrogance was actually him trying to find his place in a new town, it hadn't taken long for it to develop. It was still early days for us as a couple – it was our two-month anniversary in five days, on Christmas Day – but I thought it was going well.

'All right, Shirl?' asked Debbie, as Mum rejoined us. 'You can stop crossing your legs now.'

'It's the cold weather,' said Mum. Germaine yapped in agreement.

'Is there somewhere we can put down her bed, and some water?' I asked. 'For the dog, I mean, not Mum. Although…'

'There's the old butler's pantry.' Lily pointed to a doorway up ahead next to the kitchen. 'We use it as a kind of mud room. That should do.'

We reached the kitchen and went inside, me clutching tightly onto Germaine's lead. Bringing a dog on a catering job was hardly ideal, and normally I'd have let Daisy stay at home and look after her with her best friend Jade, who lived a couple of doors down. Jade's mum, Nancy, was always happy to keep an eye on Daisy and as for the dog, she felt almost as at home at their place as she did at ours. But they'd gone up country, visiting relatives for Christmas. I could usually ask Tony, seeing as he was the one who'd initially suggested we look after the dog, but he was away too, enjoying a summer Christmas with his sister in New Zealand. Lucky beggar. I knew from her photos on Facebook that it wasn't always sunny at Christmas over there, but it sure as hell wouldn't be snowing. But Tony had had a pretty tough year and I could hardly begrudge him the chance to escape for a bit.

And then there was Nathan, *my* Nathan, who was stuck at work trying to solve a spate of burglaries that had hit Penstowan and the surrounding villages. Cornwall may be beautiful, but it can be a tough place to find work, and nothing brings poverty home to you like Christmas time. Theft always seemed to rise during the height of summer, when tourists came to enjoy our beaches and sometimes relaxed a little too much, leaving expensive phones, watches and wallets in unguarded backpacks on the sand while they went for a swim, and at Christmas, when the lure of other people's presents became too much.

I wasn't sure what I'd been expecting in the kitchen – maybe an old-fashioned range, and a big scrubbed wooden table in the middle to work on – but it wasn't what confronted me. It was love at first sight.

'Wow,' I breathed. Lily looked at me anxiously.

'Is it OK? Trevor just had the whole thing refitted.'

'It's perfect,' I said, running a hand along the

stainless-steel worktop as I took in the two large ovens and the eight-burner gas hob, all of which gleamed. 'This is a proper professional kitchen.'

'I'm glad you like it.' Lily smiled brightly. 'This'll be the first big event Trevor's held since he bought the house. I told him the first thing he needed to make this a luxury hotel was a decent kitchen to cater for the guests with.'

'So this Trevor fella, he's your new beau, is he?' asked Mum. Honestly, and they say *I'm* the nosy one.

'Nana!' Daisy rolled her eyes at Mum, who tried to look all *Who, me?*

Lily blushed. 'No, no, he's my boss.'

'Well-heeled, though? And I heard from your mum that you and Nick split up a couple of years back—'

'Mum!' I hissed. 'Any more of that and I'll be dropping you off at a nursing home on the way back to Penstowan.'

'It's all right,' laughed Lily. 'I remember how the village gossip thing goes. OK. Trevor is forty-eight, divorced, has three children and shares custody with his ex-wife, who's actually really nice and they still get on. He was a property developer up in Yorkshire, residential stuff mostly, but he decided he'd had enough of flipping houses and wanted to settle down. He found this place and decided to turn it into a hotel. Have I missed anything out?'

'How big's his—'

'Oh my God, Nana, will you just stop?'

'—bank balance? How big's his bank balance, is all I was going to say!'

'How did you get the job?' asked Debbie. I gave her a *Don't you bloomin' start* look, but she just shrugged.

'I was part of the team who moved Raffles—'

'Wait, what? You *moved* a whole hotel?' Oh God, now I was questioning her.

'Yes. They took the hotel down and rebuilt it in another part of the city, back in 2019,' she said, like we should all have known that. Because I do like to keep abreast of developments in the overseas luxury hotel industry, obviously. 'We rebuilt it and renovated it back to its former glory. So Trevor could see that I knew a thing or two about setting up a hotel from scratch, although the budget here's a lot lower, of course.'

'So he's not your—' Mum shut up abruptly as I glared at her, but I couldn't help but notice Lily blushing again.

'So will you be doing weddings here, that sort of thing?' asked Debbie, changing the subject with a quick grin in my direction.

'That's the plan.'

'Ooh, this would be a lovely place to get married, wouldn't it?' said Mum enthusiastically. She looked at me with a glint in her eye. 'Don't you think so, Jodie, love?' I gave Debbie a *Thanks for setting her off!* glare, but at least Mum had stopped badgering poor Lily, who was looking slightly bemused. If this was what Mum was like after I'd been seeing Nathan for a couple of months, God help me on our actual anniversary.

Lily looked at the clock on the wall above the door, and assumed a business-like air. 'Right, make yourself at home. Help yourself to tea and coffee to warm up first. Will you need a hand unloading the van? There's only me and Pippa, and Trevor of course, but if you need us...'

I could tell she was hoping we'd say we could do it ourselves – she probably had a lot to organise still – so I said we'd be fine on our own. Lily hurried out, a busy woman with a lot on her plate. I tied Germaine's lead to a table leg, well away from the main prep area, rubbed my hands together in anticipation and said, 'Right, first things first, who wants a cup of—' then stopped as I spotted that Mum had already filled and switched on the kettle, found mugs and located the teabags. That woman was like an airport sniffer dog when it came to PG Tips. Give her another couple of minutes and she'd have found the biscuits, too.

We had a cuppa to warm ourselves up and rehydrate ourselves (as an English person, there is nothing I fear more than allowing my tea levels to fall below a certain point and risk dehydrating), then got on with unloading the van. I'd brought along extra pots and pans, and even baking trays, as I wasn't sure what equipment the abbey would have, but the new kitchen was so well equipped, I left most of it in the van.

The day's event wasn't a big posh sit-down meal. It didn't require cordon bleu-type recipes or fancy ingredients. The guests, although possibly a bit fussy and unlikely to eat anything green on the grounds that it might be a vegetable, probably weren't too discerning, as long as there was enough sugar in everything. We were catering a massive children's Christmas party.

The abbey had been hired by the multi-millionaire entrepreneur and philanthropist, Isaac Barnes. Barnes was originally from St Austell, where he'd grown up in quite severe poverty and deprivation. You know the picture-perfect, pretty little villages and harbours that populate the postcard stands when you're on holiday? The pristine but rugged beaches, the golden sands, the tiny fishing fleets? Yes, the tourist spots are just like that, but when you live here, Cornwall is not all pasties and cream teas and doing things 'dreckly'. Towns like St Austell, where the locals had relied on the tin mines rather than holidaymakers, had suffered when the natural resources started to run out, or when it just became too expensive to extricate it safely to be financially viable. Even the holiday hotspots were hard areas to live in, with little year-round work. Places like St Austell and Penzance had high unemployment rates and, with that, the sort of problems faced by most deprived areas: rising crime, a dwindling population, and one of the highest rates of heroin use in the country. No wonder young Isaac hadn't stuck around. At the age of sixteen he'd left home and gone off to seek his fortune in the world, and, unlike most of us, he'd actually found it. He'd blagged his way into a small tech firm and, despite having no formal training but an extremely quick, creative mind, had been taken under the founder's wing and worked his way through the ranks to take over as CEO. The company had become a massive success, and Barnes had first appeared on the *Sunday Times'* Rich List when he was just thirty-five.

But after personal tragedy struck – his wife dying in childbirth – he'd taken a step back from the business side of things and had set up a charity foundation, doing a lot of work with young people from disadvantaged homes. He was now just as (if not more) famous for his incredible backstory and subsequent charity work as for his business dealings. Everyone knew and loved Isaac Barnes. He was universally (in England, at least) deemed to be 'a good bloke'.

Every year he threw a big Christmas party for disadvantaged kids in different parts of the country, and this year he was back on home turf. Which was where me and my only-slightly-press-ganged group of glamorous assistants came in, providing Santa cake pops, meringue snowmen, chocolate reindeer muffins – anything sweet and sugary that could be festiverised (totally a word) – as well as the usual sandwiches and sausage rolls. I'd already baked all of the cakes and biscuits, but I hadn't dared ice or decorate them, worried that the unsteady suspension of the Gimpmobile could not be trusted and that by the time we reached Kingseat, Santa's beard would have migrated to his knees, the snowmen would have melted, and the Yule Log would look more like an 'accident' Rudolph had left on the carpet.

I gulped down my second cup of tea and said, 'Let's do this.'

Chapter Two

'Thank the Lord that's over,' said the man in red, as he stomped into the kitchen. 'It's so hot next to that fire, and these trousers really chafe.' He fiddled with the rough material, pulling it out of it his bum crack without even trying to hide what he was doing.

Never meet your heroes. That's what they say, isn't it? Although Santa wasn't exactly a hero of mine, and even Daisy hadn't believed in him for a few years now, this behind-the-scenes glimpse into the man himself did dispel the magic of Christmas somewhat.

'Don't you like kids?' asked Mum, shoving a mug of tea into his hands. He nodded his thanks to her.

'Oh no. I love kids, but couldn't eat a whole one.' He rubbed his beard gingerly. 'Do you know how many of the little angels thought this was false and tried to get it off? Five. Five of the little bleeders, tugging at my hair. I should've charged more. God knows, Barnes can afford it.'

Debbie and I exchanged glances – there really are some people who shouldn't play Santa, and this bloke, Steve from Plymouth, was probably one of them, even if he did naturally look the part.

From my point of view, the party had been a massive success. Three coach-loads of kids had turned up and run riot around the abbey. The owner, Trevor (who I'd been briefly introduced to but hadn't really chatted with, as we'd all been so busy getting everything ready), had looked in turn shell-shocked, then horrified at the small, sticky, excitable humans galloping around and touching all of his lovely soft furnishings, and at one point he'd been forced to bark at a couple of them as they attempted to open a glass display cabinet in the hallway, which housed a long, ancient but still sharp sword. The children had been firmly shepherded away from the potentially deadly (but fun) weapon, while Pippa, a tired-looking woman in her mid-forties who cleaned and did odd jobs around the house, carefully lifted the sword out and hid it in the butler's pantry.

The kids had enjoyed party games, passing the parcel, pinning the tail on the reindeer (not a live one, thankfully) and ODing on sugar. After that they'd gone to visit Santa in the snug, been asked what they wanted to do when they grew up, told to stay in school, and then been given a generic but not cheap present from the big man's sack. Halfway through the local press had turned up, to take some photos of Isaac and his charity foundation's manager, James – a smiley, terribly well-spoken old Etonian in his thirties – pressing the flesh with the leaders of the local kids' clubs who were here today, and presenting them with a massive cheque.

I'd been concerned that Daisy would be a bit bored, but she too had had a good day. I'd thought that she could roam around in the grounds with Germaine during the party, keeping our fur baby away from both tiny grabbing hands and sausage rolls (which both of them had a taste for), but the snow meant the dog preferred to stay indoors, only going outside once or twice to relieve herself or stretch her little legs. Germaine had been happy to curl up on her dog bed in the butler's pantry for most of the day, although she did have an impromptu run around upstairs, away from the party, after Pippa accidentally let her out. Debbie had found her just as she was about to curl up on a huge carved wooden four-poster bed in the owner's private apartment, the door to which he'd foolishly left open. Germaine had not been happy about being turfed off it, and, to be honest, I couldn't blame her; I have always wanted to sleep on a four-poster bed.

Daisy had grabbed her camera after the kids had

arrived – Mum and I had clubbed together to buy her some decent photography gear for her thirteenth birthday a few weeks ago – and had gone to explore the house, both inside and out. I got the impression that part of her really wanted to join the party, but it was for kids and she was basically a grown-up (according to her), so how could she go and see Santa, and get a present, and eat all that yummy food...? One day, I thought, she'd realise that there was no hurry to grow up, and that you could miss out on a lot of fun if you did it too quickly.

Mum sat in the kitchen (she always managed to find a chair from somewhere, and whenever she helped me on a job I would always walk in to find her comfortably settled next to the kettle, gossiping with the client if they were female, or flirting outrageously and embarrassingly with them if they were male), chatting to Santa Steve, while Debbie and I went out to the dining room, where the kids' buffet had been set up. It looked like a cross between the Last Supper and Armageddon; a long table, covered in plates and serving trays, scattered with the remains of a thousand devastated Rice Crispy Christmas tree bites, Rudolph cookies and pigs in blankets. All that had survived of the yule log was a smear of chocolate frosting across the serving platter, suspiciously smooth, as if someone had picked it up and licked the plate. Which was flattering – it obviously tasted *that* good – if slightly disgusting.

Debbie picked up a fruit kebab from a tray that was almost untouched. 'These went down a storm,' she said. I laughed.

'I liked them, but they were far too healthy for most of my guests.' We whirled around to see Isaac Barnes standing behind us, a big grin on his face. He was an attractive man of around forty-five, forty-six. His light-brown hair was fairly long and a bit shaggy, giving him a slightly bohemian air, and he was casually (but, I thought, expensively) dressed; he looked more like an out-of-work theatre actor than a businessman. Next to him stood his son, Joshua, who looked about eight or nine. He was red-faced, flushed with excitement and sugar. 'What did you like best, Joshy?'

'The pigs in blankets,' said Joshua, shyly. I nodded.

'Good choice! They're my favourite too. My dog was hoping there would be some left for her, but they're all gone. Probably just as well.'

Isaac smiled. 'Thank you for your hard work today. The food was excellent. Even the fruit kebabs.'

'They didn't stand a chance next to the Santa cake pops,' I admitted. He laughed.

'No, probably not. Do you do a lot of events like this?'

'Oh yes...' I said, not wanting to admit that this was only my sixth paid job, and that three of those had been gatecrashed by dead bodies in one form or another. 'I'm relatively new to the industry and I'd love to do more like this.'

'Interesting… You've obviously got a good team around you, too.' Isaac looked at Debbie, and I could tell by the smirk on her face that she was debating curtseying or something. My team consisted of a sarky (but loveable) ex-nurse who was more used to stitching up wounds than cutting up veg; a geriatric whose idea of fine dining was a non-ironic prawn cocktail served in half an avocado; and a reluctant teenage pot washer who was quite possibly even now taking an arty photo of a bit of potato peel.

'They're crack kitchen commandos,' I said, crossing my fingers behind my back. He nodded.

'Email your contact details to my assistant,' he said, patting at his pockets. He pulled out a business card. 'I've got some more events coming up in this neck of the woods, so I might be able to put some work your way.'

'Oh, that's brilliant, thank you!' I said, aware that I was gushing a bit too much, but also aware that my savings were steadily dwindling and that I really needed business to pick up after Christmas if I was going to make a go of it. Isaac smiled and reached out for a fruit kebab, then winked at me as he walked away, nibbling at it.

'Hark at you, getting the millionaire's digits,' said Debbie. 'Rich *and* good-looking.'

'Is he?' I asked, but I couldn't deny he was. She laughed.

'Oh, you are SO loved-up, aren't you? Not even a millionaire could tempt you away from Nathan.'

'Not even a *billionaire*,' I said. 'But don't tell Mum that or she'll be buying a new hat and booking the wedding celebrant.'

We started to clear everything up. Some of it, like the fruit kebabs and boring stuff like sandwiches, looked untouched, but the rest of it had the slightly icky appearance of food that had been poked and prodded in an attempt to work out what it was. It all went in the bin. I hate throwing food away, but small children are not the most hygienic when it comes to helping themselves to buffet food, and there was no way I was going to let anyone eat the leftovers.

'I'm starving,' said Debbie, and I had to admit I was too.

'We'll stop for a takeaway on the way home,' I said. 'If the snow's bad we'd best go through Bodmin and join up with the A39, rather than go across the moor. There must be a McDonalds or a Dominos or something in Bodmin.'

'I would *kill* for a Meat Supreme with extra cheese,' said Debbie, dreamily. I moaned.

'Oh my God, *yes*. Come on, let's hurry up and get out of here.'

But getting out of there was going to be a problem. As we finished packing up in the kitchen, my phone rang. I went to answer and saw it was Nathan, but it stopped ringing almost immediately. Lily, who had just come into the kitchen, smiled at my confused expression.

'Our mobile phone reception here is rubbish at the best of times, but in bad weather like this it's practically non-existent,' she explained. 'I'm surprised it even rang. You're welcome to use our landline. Or if you go up in the tower, you can usually get a couple of bars there. Enough to at least send a text.'

'The tower?' Daisy was picking at a plate of Christmas treats I'd put aside for her, and I could almost see her ears prick up at the words. Lily laughed.

'Yeah, we've got a tower. A mini one, anyway. You want to come and see it?'

Daisy grabbed her camera and the two of us followed Lily out into the main part of the house.

I hadn't had much time to admire the house, apart from the well-equipped kitchen and the dining room, which according to Lily was too 'informal' at the moment to be used for the fancy dinner parties, banquets and wedding receptions they were hoping to hire it out for, although I had to say it looked pretty fancy to me and I would have been happy to have my wedding reception there. Not that I had any intention of getting married again... The house was a bit of an architectural hotchpotch, with the earliest parts of the abbey standing cheek-by-jowl with much later additions. There was fine plaster cornicing in many of the rooms, from (I guessed, wildly inaccurately) the Regency period, while in others there was wooden wall panelling, which made it feel very warm and cosy, if quite dark. It was in just one such room that a massive Christmas tree had been put up, lights decking its branches and wreaths of holly and ivy draped around the windows. Daisy and I peeked in as we passed the doorway, over which hung a sprig of mistletoe. A roaring fire glowed in a large brick fireplace, next to a big, very comfortable-looking, squashy armchair which still bore the impressions of Santa's butt cheeks. No wonder he'd been feeling overheated, sitting that close to the flames in his thick red uniform. But it looked lovely, and very, very Christmassy; far more Christmassy than I could ever hope to achieve in my 1930s three-bedroom semi-detached house overlooking a sheep field.

Lily led us through the grand hallway, to the sweeping staircase that led to the upper floors, where another huge Christmas tree had been set up. It was decorated with beautiful glass baubles and vintage-style ornaments, ceramic gingerbread men, candy canes, and a whole choir of angels. On top of the tree was a very shiny silver star, guiding the way not to the Baby Jesus in his manger, but to the foot of the stairs.

'It's a shame today's been so busy,' Lily said, 'or I'd have given you the grand tour. You'll probably be wanting to head straight home in this weather, won't you? You don't want to get stuck on the moors in the snow at night.'

'Definitely not,' I said. We followed her up the stairs, onto a landing with a wide corridor and doors leading off – the bedrooms, I assumed – then up another flight of stairs, smaller and less grand than the big staircase below.

'This would have been the servants' quarters,' explained Lily. 'Trevor's been renovating them.'

'Turning them into guest bedrooms?' I asked, stepping around Daisy as she stopped to take a random photograph of a bit of flaking plaster. Art. I don't know much about it but I know what I like.

'Yes. The floor below's got six rooms, all big suites with proper fancy bathrooms, four-poster beds in some of them, and lounge areas overlooking the grounds, whereas these would just be ordinary rooms with an en suite each. We – Trevor – wants to appeal to the wedding market.'

'Downstairs for the happy couple and immediate family, up here for the dodgy uncles and distant cousins you've only invited because otherwise there'd be a feud?' I said, thinking of my own wedding years ago to

Richard. It certainly hadn't taken place anywhere as grand as this. Lily grinned.

'That's exactly what we're thinking.' We followed as the corridor curved gently round to the left, where almost immediately the atmosphere changed. The walls went from smooth, lime-washed plaster to cold, thick, grey stone slabs. I shivered and Daisy, who was still tagging behind and taking photos of bits of plaster and architectural details that interested her, caught up with us, reaching out to take my hand. When your thirteen-year-old grabs your hand, something is definitely up. Lily looked at both of us keenly.

'You can feel it, can't you?' she said. We both nodded. 'What is it?'

She smiled grimly. 'The ghosts.' Daisy drew closer to me, and Lily laughed. 'Oh, don't worry about them, they won't hurt you. Let me introduce you to them.' She stopped outside a heavy wooden door and turned the handle. Daisy and I both held our breaths...then released them as Lily reached out and turned on a dim light.

'We discovered this room during the renovations,' she said. 'The doorway had been bricked up. Trevor doesn't really know what to do with them.'

'Holy— Look at them all!' I gasped and stepped forward.

The small room had no windows, and looked like a cell. It was cold, although considering the bad weather outside, not as cold as you might expect, and there didn't appear to be any damp present at all – something of a miracle for such an old, and unheated, room. The walls were built of the same big stone slabs as the corridor outside, not that you could see them; because they were lined with bookshelves, each one full of very old books.

'Wowsers...' breathed Daisy, gazing around in wonder. She lifted her camera, almost an instinctive, automatic move, and put her eye to it. Lily put out a hand to stop her.

'No flash,' she said. 'Apparently bright light could damage the spines, spoil the colour or something.'

'Blimey,' I said, walking over to one of the shelves and reaching out a hand, then stopping myself. I really, *really* wanted to take down a book and flick through it, but if these were as old as they appeared to be, then I shouldn't even touch them. 'Where did these come from?' I peered closer; many of the titles seemed to be written in old English, to my very untrained eye. 'Are they as old as they look?'

Lily watched Daisy carefully, ready to stop her touching anything, but my daughter had been brought up to respect both books and other people's property, and she could tell that this wasn't the sort of library where you could casually read the first (and last, if you were a monster) chapter before deciding whether or not to borrow the book. 'We're not sure. There's a real

28

mixture of books. Some don't look *that* old, maybe a hundred years or so? We sent some photos of the really ancient-looking ones to a book expert and he reckons they're probably Elizabethan, if not a bit older. Trevor thinks the shelving looks like it's early 1900s, maybe late 1800s, so either this whole room was a later addition to the house, or the owners at that time just decided to put new shelves in. This part of the building is from the original abbey, built in the thirteenth century, but it was given to the Devereaux family by Henry VIII in 1539 after the dissolution of the monasteries—' She stopped as she saw me smiling at her. 'What?'

'Is this the same girl that got thrown out of History for telling Miss Peat that she couldn't give a monkey's chuff about the Tolpuddle Martyrs?'

She laughed. 'It's a bit different when it's linked to your job, innit? In a roundabout way, history pays my wages these days. Anyway, until we know what to do with them, we thought we'd just leave them here. They've survived this long, so...' She looked around and shivered. 'Let's get out of here and go and see the tower. I know it's just cold and dark, but this place gives me the willies.' She stepped back to let us out of the door.

'That was amazing,' I said, 'but you're right, a little unnerving. Are there any real ghosts here?'

Daisy rolled her eyes in a show of bravado that wasn't fooling anyone. 'Ghosts aren't real, Mum.'

'Don't say that, they'll hear you,' I hissed dramatically, and Lily laughed.

'I don't know if they're real, but there are definitely a few legends about this place,' she said. 'They say the ghost of a grey lady walks this corridor...' Daisy snorted.

'It's always a grey lady, isn't it?' she said, but she looked around a little nervously nonetheless.

'Ha ha ha, yes. They say it's the spirit of Lady Francesca Devereaux. And, downstairs, the ghost of Thomas Dyneley stalks the house, unable to rest after betraying his master...' Lily's voice took on that *Woooooooooo, tremble at my feet, puny mortals and avenge my death* kind of tone that everybody uses when they're talking about ghosts, but stopped when she saw Daisy's face. My cynical teenager maybe wasn't quite as cynical as she liked to make out. 'That's what "they" say, anyway, but I can't say I've ever seen or heard anything, and neither has Trevor, and he lives here all by himself when Pippa and I aren't around.'

We left the hidden library and all its secrets behind us, and carried on along the corridor until we reached a steep stone staircase, spiralling upwards. A cold breeze blew down it.

'That's the tower?' I asked. 'Is it open to the elements?'

'No, but at the same time, it's not particularly weathertight. And, of course, we only come up here when the phone reception's bad, so the weather's always delightful when we're up here...'

The staircase was steep, but thankfully quite short. The tower was more of a rotunda than anything else; any wicked witches with long-haired princesses they were hoping to imprison there would have felt quite short-changed. Small leaded windows all around the room gave an almost uninterrupted 360-degree view of the grounds.

I glanced at the view; very nice, but, I was alarmed to see, getting really dark, and currently very snowy. More snowy than I'd realised, having been stuck in the kitchen most of the day. I took out my phone and, sure enough, there was a very weak signal. And missed calls – lots of missed calls, all from Nathan.

'Thank God!' Nathan sounded relieved. 'I was getting worried.'

'Sorry, the reception here is terrible,' I said. 'You would not believe where I'm having to stand right now, just to get a signal. Everything OK?'

'Are you still at Kingseat?'

'Yeah, just finishing up. We'll be leaving in about half an hour, I reckon.'

'Is there any way you can stay there?'

'What? Why, what's happened?'

Nathan sounded amused but a little exasperated. 'Have you looked out of the window recently?'

'Yeah…the snow's bad there as well, is it?' I looked out at the garden again, more closely this time. The trees and shrubs were shrouded in a thick blanket of snow, and the darkening sky was full of low clouds that looked pregnant with the promise of more.

'It's not too bad around Penstowan, but they've shut all the roads around and across the moors. There are already people getting stuck in vehicles, and no one's going anywhere.' Nathan sounded very concerned. 'Honestly, if you can stay there it'd be much safer. I don't want you starting out and getting stuck all night in the snow.'

'No, I don't want that either. Spending the night in the van with Mum and the dog is not my idea of a good time…' I looked at Lily, and I could see she'd already guessed the gist of Nathan's side of the conversation.

'There's lots of room here, if you want to stay,' she said, and I smiled at her gratefully.

'Lily's here, she just said we can stay…'

'Good!' Nathan let out a sigh of relief, and I felt warm in spite of the draughty room. He worried about me. Bless him. 'I was really worried you wouldn't know how bad it was and would have already set out. Sergeant Adams is on duty tonight so I've asked him to keep checking in with the Highways Agency and let me know if the situation changes. If I get any updates I'll let you know. If the signal's bad there, it's probably better if I just text you rather than try and call...'

'Yes, that might work better. I'll call you in the morning from their landline and let you know what we're doing.'

'Good.' He hesitated. 'Well, I'll leave you to it, then...'

'Yeah. I'd better see if Lily will let me raid the pantry. Debbie needs feeding and you know what she's like when she's hungry.'

He laughed. 'Oh God, yes. All right, talk to you tomorrow.' He hesitated again. 'I...'

I waited. 'Yes?'

'You know, take care and that.'

'You too.' I disconnected the call, not even noticing the big smile and goofy expression on my face until I saw Daisy and Lily grinning at me. 'What?'

'Nothing, nothing...' said Daisy.

'Sweet,' said Lily. I hurriedly wiped the loved-up look off my face and we headed back downstairs, into the warm.

Chapter Three

We reached the bottom of the stairs to find Trevor, James and Isaac deep in discussion. Nearby, Joshua played with a small toy truck, running it along the top of a wooden wall panel, making engine noises and occasionally crashing into things.

'Everything OK?' asked Lily.

'I was just telling Mr Barnes—'

Isaac interrupted Trevor, good-naturedly, 'Isaac, I told you.'

'Sorry – Isaac – the radio says the roads are blocked across the moors.'

'My boyfriend, Nathan, just rang and told me the same thing,' I said, and Lily nodded.

'Jodie and her gang are going to stay, if that's all

right? Isaac, I think the three of you should all stay, as well.' James looked doubtful.

'We really need to head back,' he said, turning to Isaac.

'Where are you staying?' I asked. 'You're weren't planning to drive back to London this evening, were you?'

'No, we're staying at Fowey. It's only about forty minutes away,' said James.

'According to the radio, the A390's blocked around Lostwithiel,' said Trevor. 'And if that's blocked, the roads round Fowey will be impassable too.'

'I really think we'd be OK...'

Isaac ignored his colleague and spoke instead to Lily. 'Can you put us up? I don't want to be any trouble, but then I don't fancy the idea of being stuck in the snow with Joshua. This cold weather isn't good for his asthma.'

Lily smiled. 'Of course we can, if you don't mind sharing a bed with him. We're still renovating several of the rooms, but there should be enough beds.' She looked around. 'What about Santa? Has he left yet?'

'He's in the kitchen, polishing off the mince pies,' said Pippa. I hadn't noticed her before, as she was lurking in the background.

'He'd better stay too,' said Lily. She looked at Trevor. 'That's OK, isn't it? I'm here so much, I sometimes forget it's not my house.' He gave an almost shy, boyish grin.

'I sometimes forget it's not yours, too,' he said, and I thought, *Oh hello there...* What with Lily blushing at my mum's clumsy questioning about her love life earlier, and now this, was there festive romance in the air? Maybe I should attempt to 'accidentally' get them together under the mistletoe or something... I looked at Trevor properly for the first time – I really had been too busy to notice him earlier, but if he had designs on one of my old friends then I should really give him the once-over.

His salt-and-pepper hair was cropped short, and he had neatly trimmed facial hair – not really long enough to be a beard, but a bit more than stubble; kind of the missing link between the two. That was also salt and pepper, dark brown flecked with grey. It made him look distinguished; kind of like a shorter, slimmer George Clooney. He was smartly dressed, but still casual; nice trousers, and a shirt with a crew neck jumper over the top. No tie. A George-Clooney-popping-out-for-an-informal-meeting-with-his-agent type of outfit.

It might sound like I was standing there staring him up and down for a good couple of minutes, but after twenty years in the police I'm adept at taking in people's appearances in seconds. I'm also pretty good (I think) at judging people's characters, and, from what I could see of him, I was happy to give Trev my seal of approval.

Trevor turned to look at Pippa and she shuffled her

feet, looking down as we all followed his gaze. I'd noticed that she'd tended to keep out of everyone's way during the party, staying in the kitchen as much as possible; she must be quite shy. 'Can you make up some guest rooms?'

'I'll give you a hand,' said Mum, who had wandered into the hallway munching on a mince pie. I was mortified to see that she was leaving a trail of crumbs behind her.

'Thanks, Shirley, that's really nice of you,' said Lily, and I thought, *Don't you believe it, she just wants a nose around the house.* She turned back to Trevor and looked at him meaningfully. 'We need to work out what rooms to use…'

'I'll call the hotel,' said James, resigned, already bustling away, holding up his phone to get a signal. *He'll be lucky,* I thought. I wondered why he was so eager to leave; did he think staying at Kingseat would be slumming it or something? How posh must their hotel in Fowey be? To be fair, if it was in Fowey, it probably was *very* posh.

'Dad…' Joshua had stopped making revving engine noises as his toy truck idled next to the empty glass display case.

'Oh yes,' said Isaac. 'Joshy saw the sword in there earlier and wanted me to ask you about it. What's the story behind it?'

'Funny you should ask,' said Lily, smiling. 'It belonged to an ancestor of yours, Joshua.' Joshua looked at her, and then at his dad, his eyes wide, his mouth forming a silent *Woah!*

'Thomas Dyneley?' asked Isaac. She nodded.

'Who's Thomas Dyneley?' asked Daisy. 'You mentioned his ghost earlier…'

'He was a very, very distant relative,' said Isaac. 'He used to own this house. I had no idea when I was growing up in a council house in St Austell that I was part of the aristocracy.' He laughed, but there was a hint of sadness in it. 'My mum would've loved that.'

'We looked at the genealogy of the previous owners after we bought the house,' explained Trevor. 'When we found the link with Isaac, I contacted him.'

'That's why I chose Kingseat for the Christmas party,' he said. 'But I don't think my ancestors were a very nice bunch, were they?'

'No,' said Lily. 'Thomas Dyneley was a steward here. He worked for the Devereaux family, who had been gifted the house by Henry VIII. The Devereaux family were devout Catholics, which Henry didn't really care about, but when Elizabeth I came to the throne she basically declared war on the religion. Devereaux had a priest hole built, a secret room where the family hid outlawed priests and celebrated Mass. Thomas Dyneley decided to dob the family in, and in return he was given this house as a reward. The queen's most infamous priest hunter, Sir Richard Topcliffe, gave him his sword as a reminder of the great service he'd rendered. It was the very sword used to, um...' she stopped and glanced at Joshua, who was listening intently, '...um, *dispatch* Edward Devereaux.'

'Niiice...' said Daisy.

'Innit?' Lily laughed. 'Actually, it turned out to be a curse on the Dyneley family, because Thomas Dyneley saw it as a reminder of his betrayal of his old master, who had treated him well by all accounts, and eventually he was driven mad by it.'

'Serves 'im right,' said Mum, still masticating her mince pie. 'Snitches get stitches.'

So we were all going to spend the night in a posh country house. Dammit. It was a beautiful building (although I still hadn't seen much of it), and I could only imagine how romantic it would be to wake up in one of those gorgeous suites on the first floor, a fire roaring in the ornate grate, a view across the snow-covered grounds... At least, it would be with Nathan next to me. It wouldn't be quite so romantic with my teenage daughter.

It was nearly six o'clock by now, and most of us – not

having eaten much of the buffet – were getting hungry. Lily gave me carte blanche to rifle through the pantry and see what I could rustle up for nine adults, one teenager and one small person for dinner. Mum went to help Pippa and Lily make up bedrooms for all of us, Daisy and Germaine entertained Joshua, who was a sweetheart, and Debbie went off to phone Callum, her husband (or 'big chunk of love', as she was fond of calling him), to let him know she wouldn't be home and to say goodnight to her kids.

And where were the men all this time? Where, indeed. My search of the pantry concluded, I wandered out to the hallway and followed the sound of voices. Isaac, James, Trevor and Santa Steve were having a very jolly time. They were in the room where Santa had met the children earlier – the snug, Lily called it, although to my mind it was far too spacious to be called 'snug'. As the fire was still blazing, it was lovely and warm in there. Santa had changed out of his red suit and was very much just Steve now. He was eyeing a bottle of brandy, having clearly already drunk a fair bit of it, as Isaac and Trevor talked about the hotel business and James listened, occasionally adding a witty remark. So the men were enjoying themselves while the women did all the work. Typical. I stood in the doorway, noticing the sprig of green foliage over my head, and thought, *If only Nathan was here to take advantage of the traditional Christmas kiss under the mistletoe.* But maybe I could persuade Lily and Trevor to utilise it instead…

'Ahem!' I cleared my throat and they all stopped and looked over at me. 'While you lot have been emptying the drinks cabinet, I've started thinking about dinner. Does anyone have any allergies?'

'I'll eat anything,' said Steve, slurring slightly.

'So will I,' said Trevor, looking guilty. 'Whatever you cook will be wonderful, thank you. I'd better go and help Lily…' He scuttled out. Isaac grinned.

'I'm not a great cook, but I can peel potatoes,' he said. 'And James is great at laying tables and washing pots.'

James smiled and gave a little bow. 'At your service, madam.'

'Great! You're both hired.'

———

Now night was falling, it was starting to feel a bit chilly even inside the house, so I decided we needed something warm and hearty to eat. There were four large chicken breasts in the fridge, along with lots of root vegetables – carrots, potatoes and a couple of sweet potatoes – and a big head of broccoli, tucked away in the pantry.

'What are you thinking?' asked Isaac, watching me closely. I got the feeling that he was treating it a little bit like an impromptu job interview – a test to see if he'd been right to mention the possibility of me doing future catering jobs for him. Could I perform under pressure? Of course I could.

'Let me see…' I double-checked the store cupboard again. Lots of spices, which gave me options; cumin, coriander and turmeric. Fresh root ginger, tomato purée and a tin of coconut milk… 'Chicken and vegetable curry,' I said. 'Will Joshua eat that?'

'Only if there's naan bread to go with it.' Isaac gave me a hopeful grin, and I laughed.

'I'm sure we can rustle some up for *Joshua*,' I said. 'There might even be enough for you to have some…'

I set Isaac to work, peeling and chopping a couple of large carrots, some potatoes and a huge sweet potato. I chopped garlic and ginger, then threw it into a pestle and mortar with the spices and a pinch of salt and pepper.

'You are as cool as a cucumber,' said Isaac. I grinned.

'What makes you say that?'

'All these people to suddenly cook for, and it hasn't fazed you at all. I'd be hyperventilating about now.'

'I'm used to keeping calm in difficult circumstances.'

'I see – you've catered a few parties that have turned bad, have you?' He was joking, but he was right. Tony's wedding, the arts festival, even catering on the movie that had been shot in Penstowan two months ago. I laughed in a way that sounded extremely false to me, but there was no way he could have known about them.

'You could say that. Actually it's more down to my previous career.' He raised his eyebrows. 'I was in the Met for twenty years.'

'You were a copper? Wow, that's a change of career. Why did you leave?'

I nearly said, *I didn't lose my nerve or anything*, which was my automatic, knee-jerk response when anyone asked me that question, but I stopped myself in time. I hadn't lost my nerve, but Daisy had. She'd had more than enough of saying goodbye to me when I left for work, and then spending the rest of my shift worrying about whether or not I'd make it home again.

'I left because it wasn't fair on my daughter.'

'Daisy?'

'Yeah. I got involved in a terrorist attack a few years ago, one outside a Tube station—'

'The one where that madman drove a van at people? God, I remember that. I'd been in the area the day before. Scary stuff.'

'Yes, it was. I helped to disarm him – he had a knife and he jumped out, waving it at everyone. I played it down to Daisy, of course, but one of her friends found a video of it online and showed her. She was only a couple of years older than Joshua at the time.'

'Oh God, that's terrible. I can imagine how upset she would have been.'

I remembered the absolute panic attack that had overtaken her, the crying and not wanting me to leave the house. Every time I missed being a police officer, I remembered that, and I remembered why I'd stopped.

'Yes. I couldn't put her through that again, so I quit and retrained. I was all she had. I couldn't put myself at risk.'

'No. I get that.'

James came into the kitchen, whistling. His earlier bad mood over staying at Kingseat seemed to have completely evaporated.

'I spoke to the hotel, they know not to expect us,' he told Isaac. 'And I spoke to Gloria back at the office, told her we'll probably get back later than planned.'

'Here, James, you'll never guess who our chef here is,' said Isaac. I waved him away, modestly, but I had to admit it was nice being recognised as someone who wasn't 'just' the cook. 'Police hero.'

'You're a police officer?' James spoke politely, but I recognised that look. The one that every copper gets when they socialise with people who don't know them very well. The one that shuts down conversations, because the rest of the group are suddenly very conscious of incriminating themselves or saying something that could be used in evidence against them.

'*Ex*-police officer,' I said, lightly. 'These days you could confess to hiding Lord Lucan or plotting to steal the Crown Jewels and I wouldn't give a monkey's.'

Isaac laughed and slapped James on the back. 'Your secrets are safe with me and Jodie. As long as you set the table.'

James smiled. 'Phew! That's a relief. I'll put back the family silver before we leave, honest, Officer.'

We got back to cooking. I ground everything down, then dumped it into a very shiny food processor (which I suspected had never been used before) with equal amounts of oil and tomato purée to make a tikka masala paste. It wasn't exactly authentic, but it would be tasty.

Isaac caught me watching him chop, and laughed. 'What?'

'Nothing... I'm just impressed. I wouldn't have thought you knew your way around a kitchen.'

'Well, admittedly I do have someone who comes in and cooks for me sometimes...' He brushed his hair away from his face. 'I'm trying to bring my son up in as normal a way as possible. So no nanny or anything like that, only if I have to go away for work. And I don't go away now unless I really, really have to.'

'That must be nice for Joshua,' I said.

'Yeah...' I looked over at him. He was staring down at a carrot, wistfully – at least, his expression was wistful. I'm pretty sure it had nothing to do with the carrot. He shook his head. 'It's mad, innit?' For the first time that day I heard a hint of his Cornish accent. 'If tragedy hadn't struck – if Joshy's mum hadn't died – I wouldn't be here today. I'd be off somewhere hot, probably without the two of them. I'd still be a real dick.'

'I'm sure you wouldn't...' I said soothingly, but what did I know?

'No, I would. I wasn't a nice person before my son was born, you know.' He finished chopping the carrot and put the pieces in a pan before moving on to the next one. 'I left home just before my seventeenth birthday. I couldn't wait to leave, because my dad was a right git. He used to moan all the time about how unlucky he was, how we never had any money, then he'd go and drink what little we did have. I hated him.'

'Oh...' I said, thinking, *Oh God, don't go all confessional on me, I'm just here to make a curry...* But sometimes the simple, homely act of preparing a meal reminds people of their families, or makes them think of the past, and their pasts aren't always something they want to remember.

'I had to fight for everything when I started out,' said Isaac, matter of factly, starting to chop again. 'I never gave a damn about the people I ruined when I bought out their businesses. It never even occurred to me that I might be putting their employees out of work. I had this crack legal team who dealt with all the fall-out, so all I ever saw was the bottom line, the numbers in my bank account getting bigger and bigger. I was insulated from real life, even after I married Selina, even after she got pregnant.' He stopped for a moment, remembering, then shook his head again. 'Of course, there's one thing even the best legal team in the world can't insulate you from. Death.'

This is cheery, I thought. *Happy Christmas.* But Isaac clearly felt the need to talk, and I'm a good listener, so I let him.

'I couldn't believe it when the doctor said she was dead. Women don't die in childbirth anymore, do they? I knew he must be wrong.'

'But he wasn't,' I said gently.

'No. She had an undiagnosed heart condition, and the strain was too much. The first couple of months after that, we'd already hired a nanny, so I let her get on with it. I wanted nothing to do with the baby. I'd barely even held him. I drank too much. I was horrible.'

'Grief…' I started, but he shook his head.

'No. I was horrible. Then one day the nanny had a go at me and I fired her. She walked out and left me with Joshua. I was alone with my son for the first time.' He looked at me. 'I can't imagine that now. He's my whole world.'

I smiled. 'That's what being a parent is.'

'He was crying. I ignored him for as long as I could,

but eventually I had to pick him up. And I stood there and looked at this furious little bundle in my arms, who looked so much like me already, and I knew that if I carried on the way I was, he'd hate me the way I hated my dad.'

'And that changed everything?'

He nodded, smiling. 'Yes. It wasn't easy, of course, but it must've been easier for me than some poor single mum on her own, with no money to smooth the way. And that was when I realised that I had to start giving back to people who weren't as fortunate as me.'

'That's when you started the charity?'

'Yeah. I sacked most of my legal team and brought in new people, ones who would go back and tell me exactly what I'd done wrong in the past, who I'd hurt, how I could make it better. It cost me a lot of money. But once you've made enough to live on, why keep accumulating more? What's the point of having it in the bank?' He laughed. 'Don't get me wrong, I've still got plenty in the bank...'

'I hope so,' I said. 'I haven't been paid yet.'

Isaac laughed again and put the vegetables on to boil. Normally, I would let them cook slowly in the curry itself, but everyone was hungry and this needed to be curry in a hurry. I got him to dice an onion for me while I cut up the chicken into bite-sized pieces, glad that the only tears in his eyes were allium-related and nothing to do with his earlier life story.

James and Daisy came ambling into the kitchen, Germaine at their heels.

'James has been showing me how to teach Germaine some tricks,' said Daisy proudly. 'Watch this.' She looked at Germaine sternly, raising her hand, then pointing down. 'Play dead!'

Germaine immediately flopped onto the floor, her corpse impression slightly spoilt by her panting and the look of absolute adoration on her face as she gazed up at her mistress. She was so eager to please Daisy.

'Oh well done, Germaine!' I said, and James laughed.

'You can get a dog to do almost anything with the right form of bribery,' he said. 'We found Germaine's weak spot.'

'Which is…?'

Daisy unfurled her other hand, showing a lump of sausage roll. I laughed. 'To be fair, a decent sausage roll would probably work on me, too.'

'The method works on *everybody*,' said James, grinning at me. 'You just have to find the right bribe. Food, or…other things.' He winked at me. *Cocky little bugger,* I thought, but I kind of liked it. Who doesn't enjoy a mild flirt? Daisy sniffed.

'Oooh, are we having curry?' she asked. I nodded. 'Can we have naan bread?'

'Only if you make it,' I said. 'I saw some yeast in the pantry. You know what to do.'

Isaac watched in admiration as Daisy, with only a few instructions from me, measured out the flour, sugar, yeast and salt, before mixing it with warm water and vegetable oil to make a soft dough. James loitered, watching; he wasn't much use, but he was funny and good company.

'She's a chip off the old block,' Isaac said, watching Daisy knead the sticky dough. She gave a dramatic sigh.

'Honestly, Isaac, I've been brought up to fend for myself. If I didn't make my own dinner some nights, I'd starve…'

Isaac and James exchanged surprised looks, before Daisy and I both burst out laughing.

'She's joking,' I said. 'Little madam. She just gets press-ganged into helping me when she'd rather be watching the telly.'

I heated some oil in a pan and threw in the onions, listening to them sizzle for a while before adding the curry paste. I let it cook through for a couple of minutes then added the chicken. I flicked the pieces over, watching them turn from pink to white, although I knew they would still be raw in the middle at this point. Isaac drained the root vegetables and added them to the pan, while I cut the broccoli into small florets and put them in, too. Then I poured over the tin of coconut milk, stirred the contents so everything was coated in the sauce, and brought it to the boil. Daisy covered her bowl of dough with a tea towel and we put it in the oven, which had been put on a low heat, to prove.

I turned down the pan to a simmer and put the lid on.

'And now we wait?' asked Isaac.

'And now we wait.' But not for long.

Chapter Four

Half an hour later, everything was ready. I cut the naan dough into three pieces and rolled each one out into a teardrop shape, then dry fried them in a screaming-hot pan, watching the air bubbles inside them puff up. Fluffy basmati rice was piled into a big bowl, and the curry, which I'd cooked on the hob in a big saucepan-cum-casserole pan, was carefully carried out to the dining room, where James had already set out places.

I was just about to head back into the kitchen to collect the naan bread when there was a loud *BOOM! BOOM! BOOM!* on the front door. I leaped out of my skin as everyone ran out into the hallway, the noise reverberating around the room.

'Who on earth can that be?' said Trevor, and we all

looked at each other like a bunch of morons instead of opening the door and finding out. There was another loud *BOOM!* as whoever it was outside rapped the big brass door knocker against the heavy wood. It broke our paralysis.

'We should probably let them in,' said Isaac, mildly. Santa Steve, who had ambled out of the snug surprisingly quickly for a man his size, without relinquishing his grip on the brandy bottle, held it up.

'Give 'em a drink to warm up,' he said.

'If it's Christmas carollers, they've definitely earnt one,' I said.

But it wasn't Christmas carollers. It was four extremely cold-looking young Japanese women. Not what any of us had been expecting. They all giggled nervously as Trevor opened the door and beckoned them inside, then stood with their mouths open, looking around the room in awe.

'What are you ladies doing out here, in this weather?' asked Trevor. The girls looked at each other blankly, then spoke rapidly (but quietly) amongst themselves. Then one of them, who had obviously been hurriedly designated as the spokesperson, stepped forward.

'Sorry, my English not good. They not speak any English. We, um, wrong road?' She looked flustered, and I could hardly blame her. Poor thing. James stepped forward and smiled charmingly at her.

'Kon'nichiwa,' he said, giving a little bow. They all looked at him, wide-eyed, and then gave a little bow back, giggling. He then proceeded to go off in a stream of what sounded (to me) like fluent Japanese. The relief on the girls' faces and in their body language was palpable. They chatted back to him animatedly, and he smiled and nodded and generally calmed them down. He finished the conversation and turned round, seemingly surprised to see the rest of us watching him, mouths agape.

'What?'

'How did you do that?' breathed Daisy, and I thought, *Uh-oh, he's far too old for you, missy!* But then I had had a schoolgirl crush on Colin Firth (well, Mr Darcy) when I was her age. James shrugged.

'I had a nanny who was from the Aichi prefecture when I was young,' he said. Over his shoulder I could see Debbie pulling a face and going, *Oooh, I had a nanny from the Aichi prefecture! Get me!* I smothered a grin and looked away hastily.

'Show off,' said Isaac, but jokingly.

'So these young ladies were visiting the Eden Project, but because of the snow there were some detours in place and they got completely lost.' He turned to Trevor. 'And their hire car is now in a ditch at the bottom of your driveway.'

'Oh dear! Are you OK? None of you are hurt, are you?' Lily rushed over to them, concerned, as James translated. Two of the girls burst into tears. The men all looked at each other, bewildered, as Debbie and I went over and gently drew them into the snug to warm up in front of the fire.

The girls' spokesperson, Hina, thanked us, as her friends bowed and smiled and dried their tears. Germaine, who had been held back by Daisy up to this point, decided to act as their Emotional Support Animal and rushed at them enthusiastically, tail wagging. They all shrieked with delight and fell upon her.

'I think they're feeling better,' murmured Debbie. I nodded. 'Good job Little Lord Fauntleroy over there had a nanny from the Aichi prefecture, innit?'

I snorted. 'Stop it!'

'I didn't have a nanny, I had a babysitter from Moss Side.'

'You had it easy, I didn't even have a babysitter after the age of four. I was too busy working down the tin mines.' Debbie guffawed loudly and that set me off. Then her tummy rumbled really loudly, making us laugh even harder.

'Ooh stop it,' she gasped. 'I need curry.'

We headed back to the kitchen, passing Trevor and Lily deep in discussion.

'Food's ready when you are,' I said. 'Everything all right?'

'Yeah, just working out where to put everyone,' said Lily. 'It might take a bit of juggling, but we'll find somewhere to put them. No one's going to come and rescue their car tonight, and they can hardly sleep in it.'

'We'll be fine as long as no one else turns up,' said Trevor, his words hanging in the air. Debbie and I looked at each other, thinking, *Ooh, you've jinxed it now!* We both glanced at the heavy wooden front door, as…it stayed resolutely shut and silent. I relaxed.

'Let's eat.'

———————

In the kitchen, Pippa was pulling on a long, padded coat and thick scarf.

'Aren't you staying for dinner? I've made enough for all of us,' I said. 'Even with the newcomers.' Lily came in and began to fill a large jug with water.

'You're not going home, Pip? Stay and have dinner with us. It's the least we can do to thank you for your hard work today.'

'Thanks, but it's been a long day and I'd really rather just go home,' she said, awkwardly.

'Will you even get home?' I asked. 'If the roads are closed…'

Lily shook her head. 'Pippa lives in the gatehouse,' she said, and I remembered the tiny but characterful building, like a stonemason's vision of a gingerbread cottage, that we'd passed on our way in that morning.

'Still, it's dark, and it's snowing, and you've quite possibly got a crashed hire car as a garden ornament now...'

'It's stopped,' said Pippa, and I knew we wouldn't be able to persuade her. 'I'll be fine. Don't let me hold you up, your dinner'll get cold.'

I looked at Lily, who shrugged. We bade Pippa good night and carried our (tasty but completely inauthentic) Indian feast into the dining room.

But we didn't even get a chance to sit down before a loud shriek rang out from the hallway. We all looked at each other, no doubt thinking, *What NOW?* before rushing out of the room.

Pippa looked round at us.

'Sorry,' she said, sheepishly. 'It was just a surprise. I opened the door and there they were.'

'They' were a bewildered-looking couple, who were still standing in the open doorway letting the cold air in.

'Come in, for goodness' sake!' said Lily, rushing forward to shut the door. 'Who are you?'

'I am *so* sorry,' said the woman. She was in her fifties, grey-haired but with piercing blue eyes that spoke of a lively, intelligent mind. The man beside her was younger, and I got the impression that he was probably used to taking a back seat and letting her do the talking. 'We were visiting some friends who have just moved down this way, and we'd just left when the snow got really bad and we got lost. We've been driving round for an hour, trying to find the road back to their house, but it's so dark and everywhere is so blocked...' She smiled. 'I'm afraid I was starting to get slightly hysterical at the thought of being trapped overnight in the car, so when we saw your lights through the trees we just headed up here.'

'Well, you're welcome to stay the night here,' said Lily, although one glance at Trevor's face was enough to tell us that anybody else knocking on his door was going to be out of luck. 'There's quite a gang here now.'

'Thank you so much!' said the woman. 'I'm Bea, by the way, and this is Liam.' Liam nodded to us all in greeting, but didn't speak.

'We were just about to eat,' I said, hoping they'd say, *Oh no, that's fine, we had a big lunch,* or something, because I'd cooked for eleven people (including two children but not counting the dog), and at last count we were up to seventeen and I wasn't sure it would stretch. At least

Pippa hadn't changed her mind and decided to stay. But they both smiled, hungrily.

'That's great, thank you!'

After a delicious if rather stretched dinner, during which Germaine sat under the table with her cold nose pressed against my leg, reminding me she was there and happy to take any unwanted bits of chicken off my hands (just to help me out, like), Lily stood up decisively.

'Who wants a tour of the house?' she asked. It was only about 8.30 p.m., but we'd moved into the snug and the combination of full bellies, a long day and the roaring fire was conspiring to make several of us yawn and feel sleepy. I knew that if I stayed sitting down for much longer I wouldn't get up again.

'Me,' I said. Daisy nodded. James was sitting in front of the fire, talking to the Japanese girls, who were all gazing at him with rapt attention. He looked up and saw me watching them, and winked. Debbie 'Eagle Eye' spotted it, of course, and rolled her eyes.

'He's a right cocky one, ain't he? Full of himself.'

'I know. I might not have had a nanny from the wherever-it-was prefecture, but I can tell a flirt in any language.' I laughed. 'He's harmless enough, and they're lapping it up.'

'I take it you ain't joining us then, James?' called Debbie, in her most strident Mancunian accent. 'Got your hands full.'

He just grinned and turned back to the girls. Isaac laughed.

'You've got the measure of him.'

'Anyone else coming?' said Lily. Bea and Liam shook their heads and stretched out in their armchairs. Santa Steve looked like he was already half asleep and didn't react either way. Joshua, whose eyelids had been getting very heavy, sat bolt upright in his chair.

'Can I go, Dad?' he asked. Isaac smiled.

'Of course, Joshy. I just need to have a chat with Trevor...'

'We can keep an eye on him if you've got stuff to do,' I said. 'If that's all right with you, Joshua?'

It was fine by Joshua, who had taken quite a shine to Daisy, and to Germaine in particular. I wasn't sure about taking the dog with us, but she whined as we got up to leave.

'She can come,' said Lily. Trevor looked dubious but said nothing. Isaac clapped him on the back.

'Let's leave the ladies to their expedition while we do the dishes,' he said.

'Good looking, a millionaire, *and* knows his way around a pair of Marigolds and a dish mop,' murmured

Debbie next to me. 'You can keep James, but if you don't want Isaac, can I have him?'

'Your chunk of love might have something to say about that. And no, I still don't want either of them.'

Chapter Five

Lily was a great tour guide. She knew all the ins and outs of the house, and for someone who'd been so bored by History at school, she was really passionate about the abbey's past. She proudly showed us the priest hole on the ground floor, the secret room where the Devereaux family had celebrated the forbidden Mass and hidden outlawed priests. Disguised by a wall of wooden panelling, the entrance was completely invisible unless you knew what you were looking for – a very slight depression in the corner of one panel, which, when pressed down upon, caused it to pop open, revealing a low, narrow entrance. Priests in those days – the ones who survived long enough to need a hiding place, anyway – had obviously been short and skinny, or at least not too dignified to bend over when entering.

Lily had grabbed a torch at the start of the tour, which we were glad of after we'd squeezed into the room after her, but the torch's beam was weak, and the room was still almost pitch black. There were no windows, so no light, not even from the full moon above us, could penetrate the cell. That was exactly what it felt like: a prison cell, rather than a sanctuary. Lily reached out and turned on a floodlight on a stand, all of us squinting at the sudden brightness. The room wasn't completely spartan. The walls were panelled in the same rich, dark wood that the main room had been, and there was a large, ornate cross on the wall opposite the entrance, its gilding glinting in the glare of the floodlight. A small, functional and unadorned fireplace had also been built into one wall, and I guessed that it shared a chimney with the grand stone fireplace in the main room.

Daisy was fascinated. 'Did people actually live in here?' she asked, looking around the room. Lily nodded.

'If they had to, yes. It wouldn't have been very comfortable, but with the fire and a couple of candles, some food supplies and a few sticks of furniture they could hole up in here for as long as they needed to. It beat getting caught.'

'What happened to the ones who did get caught?' asked Joshua, wide-eyed.

'Hung, drawn and quartered,' said Mum behind us with relish, making us all jump. I thought we'd left her out in the main room; goodness knew she complained about her back enough, so I hadn't expected her to crouch down through the entrance.

'What's that?' Joshua didn't know, but he had obviously guessed that it wasn't good. I glared at Mum; the last thing we wanted to do was freak the poor kid out and give him nightmares.

'It wasn't very nice,' said Debbie quickly. 'They put you in prison for a long time.'

———————————

Lily showed us our rooms after that. We were up on the second floor, the one that would once have been the home of the domestic staff and would one day (with any luck) be reserved for the less-popular members of future wedding parties. Daisy and I would share one room – it had a double bed, but we'd shared before in a pinch, and at least if we got cold in the night we could snuggle up (no doubt with Germaine adding her own doggy and rather hairy body heat to the mix). Mum and Debbie would be in a twin room next door. I pitied Debbie, having to spend the night listening to Mum's snoring, but at least they had separate beds. Lily apologised for making us share, but they were still in the process of renovating and there weren't enough rooms for everyone to have their own. I was slightly disappointed not to be getting a fancy suite on the floor below, but apparently several of them were being redecorated too, and weren't really ready for guests. I would just have to come back one day with Nathan. Only for a night, not for a wedding or anything... I noticed that Lily did not show Joshua where he and his father would be sleeping, and I had the sneaking suspicion that there would definitely be a posh suite available for the multi-millionaire.

'Where are you staying?' I asked Lily. 'Are there enough bedrooms ready to use?'

She shook her head. 'Not with all the newcomers. There's four up here, and two on the floor below us, one of which is Trevor's apartment, but we've still got some of the old beds stored in one of the suites, so I'll probably drag some of the mattresses down into the dining room or something. Everyone else will just have to make do with the sofa or an armchair. We've got lots of blankets, luckily.'

'Is there anyone waiting at home for you?'

'No. The kids are pretty much grown up now, so they're fine on their own. Luke's twenty-one now! Can you believe it?'

It was around 9 p.m. now, usually bedtime for Daisy and well past it for Joshua, but it had been an exciting day and, after our tour of the house, we were all more awake again.

'Are there any more secret rooms?' asked Daisy. Her

imagination had really been caught by the hidden rooms, and I couldn't blame her. I'd always wanted to have a library with a hidden door, activated by pulling on a particular book, or a candle sconce on the wall or something, and all my adult life I'd been forced to live in normal boring houses without one. Lily shook her head.

'Sadly not. There's a passage that leads from the butler's pantry up to one of the bedrooms, but the previous owners used it as a conduit for new electrics and plumbing. It was already narrow, but not even Joshua could fit through it now.' She smiled. 'But then, no one knew about the secret library until we started renovating up there, so who knows? Keep your eyes open and let me know if you find another one.'

Daisy laughed and shook her head to signal that she knew Lily was joking, but I couldn't help noticing her eyeballing the wooden panelling in the other rooms or discreetly tugging at a metal cleat that had been set into one wall for no immediately apparent reason in the butler's pantry, where we'd left Germaine's food bowl, when she thought no one was looking.

We headed back to the room with the Christmas tree and the roaring fire, but as we approached I could hear raised voices from the nearby lounge. It sounded like Santa – I mean Steve – and Isaac were having what Mum would euphemistically call a 'heated debate', but to me sounded like they were only seconds away from having a punch-up. Debbie and I exchanged looks over Joshua's head as we heard Trevor's voice, trying to keep the peace, but this time it was Mum who saved the day.

'I wonder if Lily has any hot chocolate in the kitchen, Joshua? What do you think?'

'Oh yes,' said Lily quickly. 'I'm sure we can find some. Let's go and see, shall we? Everyone?' She gave me a meaningful glance, which I took as *Please use your police training and magnificent people skills to step in and calm them down*, but which could equally have meant something completely different – I'm very good at interpreting things the way I want them to be – and I nodded. The others headed off to the kitchen and I made my way into the thick of it.

'All right, fellas?' I said. I may have had a little bit of a confident swagger in my step. God, I missed being a copper sometimes. 'Sounds like things are getting a little bit heated in here.'

Trevor looked at me gratefully. Isaac gave a big false smile as Steve, who really did not look like Santa at this precise moment, scowled and knocked back the drink in his hand in one go.

'We were just having a chat about my old business dealings,' said Isaac brightly. Steve scowled again and went to toss back his drink again, but then stopped as he noticed his glass was empty. He looked around, presumably searching for more alcohol. Who would have pegged Santa as an alcoholic? What with his ruddy complexion and beer belly... I reached out for his glass and tugged it from his fingers.

'Oi!' slurred Steve.

'I think maybe you're taking advantage of our host's generosity, don't you?' I said, and he stared at me combatively. Like a lot of men – particularly older, well-built ones – when confronted with a woman he probably expected them to back down or mumble an apology or something, but that really is not and never has been my style. I smiled at him. 'Trevor has been the perfect host so far. We should probably try and be the perfect guests, don't you think? Which means not getting legless and having a fight. Especially when there are children in the house, and one of them is young enough to think you've got a hotline to Santa.'

He stared at me again for another couple of seconds, and then dropped his shoulders and I knew he was calming down.

'Now, you can either take your chances and go and sober up out in the snow, or you can sit there, have some coffee and be civil.' I smiled at him again. I am *so* friendly when delivering an ultimatum. 'What's it to be?'

He looked at Isaac, who looked relieved that the argument was over, then turned to me and mumbled, 'Black with two sugars, please.'

'Good choice.'

The kitchen was warm and had a far nicer atmosphere than the lounge, so I stayed in there with Daisy, Debbie, Mum and Lily, where we drank hot chocolate and made a big fuss of Joshua, who had been looking a bit anxious. Then I took Steve a mug of coffee and, would you believe it, he had calmed down enough to actually laugh at something Isaac was saying. I shook my head. *Men*. Sometimes they acted like children, and you just had to treat them like they were.

I popped my head round the door into the snug. The Japanese girls had all zonked out on the sofa, and someone had covered them up with throws and blankets. The fire was still smouldering, but it would be out by the morning and they'd need them then.

I wondered where James and the latest newcomers, Bea and Liam, were. I wouldn't have been at all surprised if James had ended up sleeping in there, with his adoring audience from earlier gathered around him. He totally struck me as the type of bloke who enjoyed being gazed at in adoration, his flirtatious nature and witty remarks pointing to someone who had a pretty good opinion of himself, although I wouldn't necessarily have gone as far as calling him arrogant; he still seemed like a nice enough person. I'd known a few ex-public schoolboys in the Met (always, *always* in the higher ranks), and they all had this air of supreme self-confidence about them. It was inbred. To me, it had something to do with the knowledge that their families (and, by extension, they themselves) were wealthy enough that they never had to really worry about anything. If they failed an exam, or didn't get as far in their chosen career as they'd hoped, it didn't matter that much. They'd never be facing homelessness, or the choice between feeding their kids or paying the power bill. And because they never had to stress about anything and always came across as being so self-assured, they invariably did well in life anyway. Confidence builds careers, sometimes even when competence is lacking… Still, I couldn't help liking him. And my dog and daughter liked him, too, and they were both excellent judges of character.

There was something I didn't like about Bea and Liam, however, but I couldn't put my finger on it. I totally believed that the Japanese girls had got lost in the snow and crashed in a panic, but Bea and Liam… I wasn't so sure. She'd said that she'd been getting hysterical at the thought of being stuck in the car overnight, which was a totally reasonable reaction to the situation – only she did not strike me as the sort of person who ever gave in to hysteria. I wasn't sure what I was basing that on, other than my instincts. My suspicious police officer sixth sense was tingling about them, but why?

For starters, they seemed like unlikely travelling companions. Bea had said they were visiting friends who had just moved down from London, and she made it sound like they were a couple visiting another couple; she hadn't said as much, but that's what she seemed to be hinting at, and equally it didn't sound like it was a work trip. But then, although they obviously knew each other well – I'd seen them exchanging meaningful looks during dinner, although meaning what exactly I didn't know – they didn't feel like a couple to me. There was no softness or warmth between them, not the sort you'd expect from lovers, anyway. Maybe they really were a couple, but the tension of driving round and round in the snow and the dark, down twisty country roads that all looked the same, had led them to have a falling out. They would hardly be the first couple to have a massive argument on a road trip. I shook my head. It didn't matter. We'd all be on our way home in the morning.

Daisy and I went to bed soon after that, but not before I'd made my way up the tower again, braving the cold wind that found its way in through the gaps in the old masonry, to send a good night text to Nathan. Bless him, he'd already sent me one, and it came through just as I was typing.

Hope you're having a good night in that big posh house! I'll
try and call you in the morning with an update on the roads.
Keep warm and have sweet dreams xxx

Spending a night in the big posh house really would
have been more fun with him there, I thought. I sent him
a reply that ended in far more *xxxx* than were strictly
necessary, then went to bed.

———————

I fell asleep quite quickly, and dreamed of the secret
library. I reached out to take a book from the shelf, then
whirled around as I felt someone watching me. Across
the room stood a woman, dressed head to foot in grey.
Her face was young, but lined with care, and her eyes
were full of a great sadness. Aren't they always? I was
slightly disappointed to be dreaming in such clichés, but
my subconscious obviously wasn't as subtle as I'd hoped
it was. I knew she was a ghost, by the way her feet
hovered above the ground. That and the fact I could see
through her skirt to the books on the shelf behind her. Bit
of a giveaway, that.

I opened my mouth to say something, but she just put
her finger to her lips and said, *Shh.* Clearly she'd been a
librarian when she'd been flesh and blood. *I only wanted*
to have a look at the books, I tried to say, but she lifted both

hands, like a Vegas magician about to do a conjuring trick. Her fingers trembled.

OK, I think I'd like to wake up now, I thought, but I didn't. Something bad (or weird, knowing my dreams) was going to happen.

With a twitch of her fingers, the books on the shelves began to vibrate. *Ah,* I thought, *she's going to—*

The books exploded off the shelves, flying through the air around me. I ducked and dodged, but one very heavy-looking book was on a direct collision course with my face. It was like a heat-seeking missile, and I couldn't shake it off, no matter much I bobbed and weaved and twisted. I heard it whistling through the air as it came towards me, and as it got near I saw the front page of it; not an Elizabethan book at all – Lily and her book expert had been wrong. No, it was a copy of *Advanced Sugar Craft and Cake Decorating Techniques*, one of my old textbooks from catering college, a book that had been the bane of my life the whole time I was learning to be a cook. I never passed that bloody cake decorating module, and I never would now.

The book descended rapidly, and then it was only centimetres away from me. I could feel the wind of its passage, the air parting before it. Closer and closer, it was right in front of me and any minute now—

I snapped awake, gasping, as Germaine's tail brushed across my face. I wriggled her away from me, not wanting to wake her up, but all she did was lift her head sleepily as if to say, 'What are you doing, Mum?', and then went straight back to soft doggy snores.

Next to me, Daisy was also thankfully still fast asleep. Her face looked so peaceful, and so beautiful, illuminated by the shaft of moonlight that had found its way in through a gap in the curtains. I rolled over to watch her, going all maternal and soppy for a moment; she really was the best thing that had ever happened to me (sorry, Nathan). But then my legs started to get restless and I couldn't get comfortable, no matter how much I stretched out or scrunched up or rolled around. I didn't want to disturb my sleeping companions – God knew, Germaine could quite easily wake the whole house up if she started barking or whining at being shut in this room – so I gently slipped out of bed, shivering at the cold.

I knew from past experience that the best way to settle my legs down was to give them a bit of exercise; I'd actually gone for a walk around the block at midnight a couple of times in the summer, taking a surprised Germaine with me for company, but I was hardly going to do that now. The house was big enough for me to walk up and down the corridor a couple of times (although if there really was a Grey Lady up there, maybe not…), or I could just head for the kitchen and make a cup of tea. Yes, tea. I'm British, OK? Tea at – I checked my phone – just after midnight is definitely not a weird thing if you're British.

I tugged my jeans and jumper on, stuffed my phone in my pocket and quietly turned the door handle. It creaked slightly, but neither Daisy nor Germaine stirred. I tiptoed out into the corridor. It was dimly lit, only one of the overhead lights working; they really were still in the middle of renovations up here. It was just the sort of atmosphere in which I could imagine a grey female wraith floating towards me... So that settled that; the kitchen it was.

I'd just turned towards the stairs when I heard the sound of footsteps, coming up them. I froze, then fled back up the corridor, God knows why; I had as much right to be out of my room as anyone else at this time of night. But maybe it was the Grey Lady? *Would ghostly feet make a noise?* I asked myself. I didn't really want to find out. I headed up the corridor, where it bent round towards the secret library. There were no other bedrooms there, so I should be safe. Why I should be *un*safe, I didn't know. But it was late and I was tired.

I listened as the footsteps approached, shrinking back against the wall. *They're coming this way*, I thought, cursing myself for not just going back to my room; but then, I hadn't wanted to wake Daisy. Then the footsteps stopped, and I heard knocking, the rap of knuckles on wood.

Silence.

The knuckles (ghostly or otherwise) knocked again. After a few seconds, I heard a door opening, and a man's voice.

'What the – what are you doing here? It's midnight, for God's sake. Just leave me alone.' James. His voice was befuddled and thick with sleep, but I could still hear an edge of anger to it. There was a quiet lull, and I strained my ears to hear James's nocturnal visitor answer him, but I couldn't; maybe just the hint of a voice, possibly female? Or was I imagining that? James hissed, 'All right, all right! Come in before you wake everyone up.' I heard the door shut, waited for a second, then stuck my head around the corner; the corridor was empty. I tiptoed back and stood outside the door to the nearest bedroom, my ear pressed against the wood. I hoped that James and his unexpected (and unwanted) guest were loitering just on the other side; if they'd gone as far into the room as the bed, I probably wouldn't be able to hear what they were talking about.

'I've told you, no, I won't do it.' It sounded like James was struggling to keep calm, his voice barely controlled, that edge of anger threatening to overwhelm him. 'How many times do I have to tell you?'

There was a pause as (I assumed) his visitor

answered. I pressed my ear harder against the wood in frustration, but I still couldn't hear the other side of the conversation.

'Or you'll what?' spat James, his voice low with contempt. Another pause. Then – 'Get the hell out of my room now – I don't care, just get out!'

I leaped away from the door and bolted back to my hiding place, keen to peer out and see just who had upset James so much. I stayed out of the way as I heard the door shut, then waited a couple of seconds, to make sure they would be heading away towards the stairs and wouldn't spot me, peeping out at them. I poked my head around the corner and, sure enough, there was a real person heading away from me. Not a ghost. But it was so dark down that end of the corridor, they might just as well have been, because I couldn't make out who it was. For all I knew, it could have been the Grey Lady herself, only I doubted James would be arguing with her in his bedroom. The only person I could say for certain that it *wasn't* was Santa Steve, because he was twice the size of everyone else in the building.

I yawned. Whatever was going on, it had nothing to do with me. James was a big boy, and he could sort it out himself. And now it was time for me to get back to bed, before I pushed my luck and ran into a real ghost.

Chapter Six

I was woken the next day by Germaine scratching at the door of our room. Daisy, who unlike me was able to go from fast asleep to wide awake in about three seconds, leaped out of bed and grabbed Germaine's collar, pulling her away from the door before she scraped any of the paint off the freshly decorated wood.

'She needs a wee...' I murmured, awake but not even willing to admit it to myself yet.

'I know, but it's still dark,' whispered Daisy. 'I don't want to go out there on my own.'

I shook my head to clear it and sat up. I picked up my phone and checked the time: just gone six, so not *that* early, particularly as we'd been asleep before ten the night before and I'd managed to nod straight back off after my nocturnal wanderings, but it was lovely and warm in bed and I didn't want to go out in the snow. On winter mornings I sometimes wished I didn't have a dog.

As if reading my mind, Germaine gave a pathetic whine and immediately made me feel guilty. I sighed and turned on the bedside lamp.

'Come on, then,' I said, bracing myself for the cold. But it was actually quite warm – these rooms, not subject to the same restrictions as the oldest parts of the house, had been allowed to have heating installed in them, and it must have been set to come on early in the morning – and I was able to throw my clothes on without risking frostbite. Daisy quickly got dressed too, then we padded downstairs as quietly as we could. A couple of steps on the first staircase creaked loudly and we froze, not wanting to wake our fellow guests; but with Mum snoring in the room next to ours, we could have stamped our feet and sung show tunes and *still* been quieter than her rhinoceros-with-sinus-trouble impression. I felt a pang of guilt for poor Debbie, sharing with her. I carried Germaine in my arms just in case she got any funny ideas about exploring the house; she was partial to a four-poster bed, after all. We'd left our coats in the kitchen the day before, and as we got into them I tried to open the back door, where Lily had let us in yesterday, out into the yard; there was no way Germaine was getting a proper walk in the snow, this early, so she'd have to make do with a quick nip outside and a toilet break. But the door wouldn't budge; it was firmly locked, and I couldn't see the key anywhere.

'Out the front,' I said to Daisy, and we tiptoed through the hallway to the grand entrance. Our footsteps still echoed on the stone floor, but I thought that was probably more down to the fact that everywhere else was so silent, rather than us actually making a lot of noise. A gentle snore reached us from the direction of the snug, and we relaxed; the girls at least were still fast asleep together.

The big wooden door also refused to budge at first, but then I noticed that it was secured by heavy iron bolts which slid back smoothly, and we managed to get it open before the dog peed on anything. A blast of cold air chilled us, but once outside we acclimatised to the frigid air fairly quickly. By which I mean we were so cold, we went numb after a few minutes and didn't feel a thing.

It was absolutely silent outside, the blanket of snow muffling the sound of Germaine's panting breaths. It felt unnaturally still, eerily quiet; no birdsong, not even the rustle of the breeze in the trees and bushes. There was no wind. It was like the rest of the world, everything outside the abbey, had died. I shivered.

Germaine barked. Daisy, who seemed to be as unnerved by the stillness as I was, gave a little shriek.

'What's she barking at? What's that?' We peered through the dark. This time of the morning, this far into winter, the sun hadn't even started to think about coming up yet, and the lantern above the front door served only to show how dark it was outside that small pool of artificial light. Shapes loomed ahead of us as we followed the dog further into the garden. She barked again. I reached down and caught her collar, then peered up at the figure in front of us.

'Holy sh— Oh my God,' I laughed.

'What? What is it?' said Daisy, still anxious. 'Is it the Grey Lady?'

'It's the fountain. I noticed it from the driveway when we got here yesterday. It's a bloody great metal dolphin, look.' Daisy let out her breath and squatted down in front of Germaine to tell her off for barking and scaring the bejesus out of us.

I looked around at the garden, stamping my feet and blowing on my hands while Germaine did her business. At least it wasn't snowing. With any luck there hadn't been any fresh falls overnight, so hopefully the snow, which looked just as deep here as it had yesterday, hadn't got any worse. I hoped the Highways Agency had cleared the roads and we would be able to go home today. As if on cue, my phone (which I'd tucked in my pocket from sheer force of habit) pinged with a text message. Either the weather was getting better, or this was the best spot on the whole property for a phone signal.

Nathan:

Morning, gorgeous.

And suddenly the snow didn't feel quite as cold.

Hope you slept OK. Just heard that the A30 across the moors is being cleared now, they reckon it'll be open again at 9 but I'd leave it a bit longer. Tell me when you're on your way xxx

I was glad it was too dark for Daisy to see my cheesy grin.

You're up early! The dog just woke us up. Am outside in the snow waiting for her to go... We'll probably leave about 10, will go via Bodmin and the A39 instead of the moors, might be clearer.

I wanted to type in something soppy about missing him, but we'd only been away one night and I might not even have seen him had we got home when we were supposed to.

Will text you when we leave xxx

Germaine satisfied, a pile of snow left thawing in her wake, we went back inside and up to our room, where we had a nice hot shower to restore the feeling to our extremities. We could hear movement in the rest of the house, so we went downstairs and I helped myself to tea and made hot chocolate for Daisy while we waited for everyone else to get up.

Mum and Debbie joined us, Mum looking bright-eyed and bushy-tailed, her roomie not so much.

'Sleep well?' I asked. Debbie grunted.

'I had a lovely sleep!' trilled Mum brightly. 'Lovely comfy bed, and it's so quiet here.' Debbie grunted again, the dark circles under her eyes proof that not everyone had had such a restful interlude.

'Good night?' I asked Debbie, as Mum flicked on the kettle. She looked at me for a moment, as if she was trying to decide whether I was trying to be funny or not.

'It took me a while to fall asleep,' she said, glancing towards Mum for a second, 'and then when I did I had this really weird dream that I were in this forest, and there was this bloke coming after me with a chainsaw, one of those really loud, petrol-driven ones.'

'What a funny thing to dream about,' said Mum, pouring hot water into a mug. 'I wonder what made you think of that?' She snorted loudly as Germaine chased her tail in front of her.

Debbie looked at me darkly. 'I wonder...'

Pippa arrived, cheeks and the tip of her nose red with the cold as she shed her thick coat and woolly hat. Lily joined us soon after, looking almost as tired as Debbie but in a rather better mood. 'Did you sleep well?' she asked, not waiting for an answer. 'I hope you had everything you needed. Did you find the toiletries I left in your room? They were samples from potential suppliers for the hotel.' She rubbed her hands together, in a 'Let's get cracking!' gesture. 'OK, who's hungry?' she asked, dancing over to the pantry. 'Let's get some breakfast going!' Debbie was too busy staring into the bottom of her coffee mug, but Mum and I exchanged looks. Lily was in a *very* good mood…

I carried a tureen full of scrambled eggs into the breakfast room and set it down on the table, alongside a covered dish full of bacon. The eggs were soft and creamy, with a twist of black pepper and a pinch of sea salt to give them extra flavour. Eggs were one of the first ingredients we'd been let loose on in catering college, and *everybody* had overcooked theirs the first time. Our tutor had gone ballistic and accused us all of being nothing more than microwave cooks (the biggest insult he could come up with). It was drilled into us that scrambled eggs should at least still have a *hint* of a runny yolk, rather than a texture that was a cross between rubber and those polystyrene packing peanuts you get (which was exactly how Mum made them, unfortunately, and I hadn't been able to persuade her otherwise). At least that meant more eggs for everyone else. On the sideboard stood a toaster and a loaf of bread, so everyone could help themselves to toast. Daisy was waiting for two slices to pop up.

I looked around. Mum, seated at the table, had immediately begun helping herself to some eggs (which she would be sadly disappointed by), and Trevor was pouring Debbie a cup of tea. James sat at the foot of the table, away from the rest of us, looking like he'd barely slept, his usual good humour seeming to have deserted him. Perhaps his unwanted room guest the night before had really disturbed him. Or perhaps he just wasn't a morning person.

'Cup of tea, James?' I asked. 'Or do you want some coffee?'

He looked up and gave me a big, false smile that didn't reach his eyes. 'Oh, tea for me, please. Best way to start the day.' Trevor poured another cup and I passed it to him.

'Sleep well?' I asked, but he obviously hadn't.

'Oh – you know – it's not the same when it's not your own bed, is it?'

'Morning, everyone!' Bea and Liam had just entered the dining room. 'Wow, this looks great! I'm so glad we found this place last night, aren't you, Liam?' He nodded.

'Yeah, we really lucked out there, didn't we?' He pulled out a chair next to James, who stared moodily into his tea cup. Bea smiled.

'Persistence pays off,' she said, which didn't seem to make any sense to me, but I assumed she meant that they'd carried on driving until they found somewhere, rather than just pulled over and slept in their car. She pulled up a chair on the other side of James, and suddenly I had the strongest suspicion that I knew the identity of James's nocturnal visitor.

The Japanese girls came in, all looking freshly made up, hair nicely done, clothes straight... I ran a hand through my hair, which was still wet from the shower, suddenly aware of how dishevelled I must be looking. They all smiled and said, 'Good morning,' in their best English accents, then gave little bows. I found myself doing it back. James looked up and gave them a brief, tight smile, then concentrated on his tea again. The girls didn't seem to notice, as they were too busy trying to work out what we were eating for breakfast.

Lily brought in a plate of sausages and put them down.

'Are Isaac and Joshua not down?' I said. She shook her head.

'No. I expected them to be the first ones to wake up,

to be honest,' she said. 'Kids are normally up at the crack of dawn, aren't they? Steve's still not up either, but he was really putting away Trevor's brandy last night, so I'm not entirely surprised. I sent Pippa to wake them. If they're going to try and go home today they should probably get on the road sooner rather than later.'

'Yes,' I said. 'Nathan sent me a text earlier and he reckoned the emergency services are out clearing the moors now.'

I felt a bit bad about not waiting for the others to come down – I thought the chances of the bacon lasting until they joined us were not terribly high, not with Germaine under the table begging for some – but it was their own fault if they were sleeping in. I'd just picked up a plate and begun assembling a bacon sandwich when a blood-curdling scream reached us.

I looked at my fellow diners and leaped up. 'Stay there,' I commanded Daisy and Mum, my police instincts kicking in. I raced out into the hallway, followed by Lily, Trevor and Debbie, in time to see Pippa rushing down the stairs. Mum and Daisy (and the dog) had ignored me as usual and followed me out of the room, although slightly more sedately.

'What on earth…?' began Trevor.

'He's dead!' cried Pippa. She reached the bottom step and swayed slightly. I could see something clutched in her hand. A key.

'What? Who? What are you talking about?' said James, joining us. But before Pippa could answer, Isaac and Joshua came bustling in from outside, wrapped in their coats, shaking snow off their boots and laughing.

'Did we miss something?' said Isaac pleasantly. Pippa swayed again, her eyes rolling back into her head, then began to fold up in a heap.

'Catch her!' I cried. Trevor and James both rushed forward and caught her, stopping her from hitting her head on the stone floor. I took the key from her hand and rushed up the stairs.

'Jodie—' Trevor called after me, but I heard Isaac stop him.

'She can handle it, she used to be a copper. Let's get this poor woman moved somewhere more comfortable, she's had a shock.'

I bounded up the stairs, then stopped on the landing and looked down at the key. The tag on it read, *The Dyneley Suite*. On the wall in front of me was a sign, directing me to the different suites and room numbers on that floor. An arrow pointing right directed me to the Dyneley Suite, and I could see that it was in the oldest part of the house, beneath the secret library Lily had shown us the day before.

'Mum?' Daisy had followed me upstairs, Lily close behind her. 'What's going on?'

'Go back downstairs,' I said firmly. Until I knew what we were dealing with, I didn't want anyone else getting involved. And if someone – Steve, it could only be Steve – had died, I didn't want everyone gawping at him. 'Now.' Daisy looked mutinous, but Lily could tell I was deadly serious; she nodded and herded my unruly daughter away.

Like the secret library, the suite was down a long stone corridor, but this one was heated by big art deco-style iron radiators that had obviously been installed before the building had officially been listed by the Heritage Committee – I couldn't imagine them being allowed to install anything quite so 'modern' now. There was thick carpet underfoot as well, and although the historic charm and character were still evident, it also felt more luxurious and hotel-like than the floor above where we'd spent the night.

At the end of the corridor was a very grand, imposing, heavy wooden door. With its big iron hinges and reinforcement, it looked like the sort of door that would keep out all kinds of intruders – even nightmares would have trouble penetrating it, I thought. But it now stood slightly ajar, and I wondered if it had been like that when Pippa had come across it, or if she'd unlocked it and then fled.

I slowed down as I neared the door. The thick walls and heavy carpet muffled all sound except my heartbeat, which was starting to get faster and louder in my ears. The silence felt sinister, foreboding. But (I asked myself), what was there to be nervous of? Steve was an older man, very overweight, who had drunk a lot last night. His red face and nose might suit his career as a Santa Claus impersonator, but they were also testament to someone who did not look after himself terribly well, who could have had any number of health problems: obesity, diabetes maybe, probably some kind of heart condition. That was it. The poor man had probably had a heart attack in the night, and Pippa had found him when she'd opened the door that morning. It would be enough to give anyone a turn. Poor Santa.

But then there was the smell; faint at first, but unmistakeable.

One of the first calls I was sent on as a young copper was a fight outside a night club. There had been multiple participants, most of whom were so drunk they could barely stand up, let alone land a punch, and they were pretty easy to round up. While the more experienced officers I was with took their names and loaded them all into the back of a police van, I was left to move the small, equally drunk crowd who had gathered to watch away from the scene and back into the club. Until one of them said, 'What about the bloke with the knife?'

The bloke with the knife had run away the minute he heard sirens, and was no doubt streets away by the time we got there. A senior officer had rolled his eyes at me and told me to get a statement and a description, but by then I'd spotted the trail of blood, leading away down an alley behind the club.

I'd found the victim propped up against some bins at the back of a kebab shop. God knows why but, I guessed, he'd limped away too at the sound of the sirens, blood oozing steadily from a deceptively small and innocuous-looking wound in his thigh. By the time he'd reached the shelter of the bins his jeans must have been stiff with it, the deadly puncture in his femoral artery pumping out more and more blood. If the silly sod had waited for us to get there, we could have saved him. But by the time I got to him, he'd lost consciousness and so much blood that there was nothing I could do but yell for back-up and helplessly, uselessly put pressure on the wound. I knew he was as good as dead, but I had to try.

The smell had lingered in my nostrils for days afterwards, even after I'd scrubbed myself in the shower several times. I knew it wasn't really there, it was just my imagination, but it took a long, long time to go. And I could smell it again now, a rusty, metallic odour that made my heart pound even more. I read somewhere once that it's an evolutionary thing; that while blood attracts some animals, hunters like wolves, it repels others – animals who would be more likely to be preyed upon. And until modern times, that had included humans. Had it included Steve?

I took a deep breath and immediately regretted it, inhaling the scent more than I really wanted to, then froze at a sound behind me.

'I thought I'd best come and see if I can help,' said Debbie, walking up behind me. I unfroze in relief and turned to look at her. 'He might not be dead, he might just be unconscious. A ripe candidate for a heart attack, that one.' She frowned. 'Uh oh…'

'You can smell it too, can't you?' I said. She nodded. 'Still want to come in?'

She laughed, a deep throaty laugh that reminded me that we'd both dealt with some pretty bad things in our professional lives and we could handle it. 'Love, I were a nurse for nineteen years. You would not *believe* the stuff I've seen. Blood's the least of it…'

We gingerly stepped inside. The room had been built out of that thick, grey stone, the doorway opening out onto a wide, spacious room that nonetheless felt quite dark; instead of the large casement windows overlooking the grounds that the downstairs rooms had, the exterior wall here, in the older part of the house, had a row of small windows hung with thick tapestry curtains, which blocked out the weak sunlight. An internal wall had been added to partition off what I assumed was an en suite bathroom or dressing room. It was painted a rich, dark red – *blood red,* I thought. The floor was more of the grey stone, but covered in a thick rug that felt soft and warm underfoot. The overall effect was surprisingly warm and cosy, a perfect romantic winter retreat – but for the shape of the body on the beautifully carved, wooden four-poster bed. I reached out and flicked on the light.

'Ooh bloody hell,' said Debbie. 'I think we can rule out natural causes.'

Santa Steve lay on his front, his naked bottom sticking up in the air, head (and beard) buried in a pile of pillows, legs hanging limply over the side of the bed. With half his torso on and half of it off the bed, I was surprised that his dead weight hadn't dragged his body down and into a heap on the floor.

Around Steve's immobile face, stuck to his beard, were lots of small, white feathers – or rather, once-white feathers; most were now mottled with red. They came, I guessed, from the pillow beneath his head. It must have been slashed during the attack on him. His body was lying on top of the flat sheet covering the mattress. The sheet had once been identical to the one on the bed in mine and Daisy's room: brilliant white, starched, good quality. But a massive stain had soaked into it where it lay under the late Santa's bulk, and now it was dark red, almost black with blood. I swallowed hard, feeling slightly nauseous. Not a heart attack, then.

The cause of death was pretty easy to work out. It no doubt had something to do with the bloody great sword sticking out of his back, pointy end up. The sword that, until yesterday afternoon, had been safely under lock and key in a glass display cabinet in the hall, but since then had been stashed in the butler's pantry downstairs.

The hilt of the sword was hidden by Santa's bulk, which was itself surrounded by more pillows or bedding of some sort. Weirdly, there was a large, leather belt wrapped around the post nearest to his head, but it just hung there, limply; I couldn't work out what it was doing there. Was it part of some sordid sex game? Or did the fact that that was the first thing that sprang into my mind say more about me than the victim?

'What the hell—' Debbie took a few steps towards the body, unable to tear her eyes away from it.

'Stop!' I said. 'Don't get too close or touch anything. We don't want to contaminate the scene.' She stopped and pointed to the side table next to the bed.

'There's some pills here.'

The bottle of pills was lying on its side, lid off, and a couple had spilled out. Maybe he'd taken a couple before bed, and had been too drunk to get the lid back on. I looked at the label: Zopiclone.

'What are they?'

'Sleeping pills, really strong ones.' Debbie shook her head. 'Not under any circumstances to be taken with alcohol. A couple of them, on top of all that brandy – that'd be enough to turn you into a flipping zombie. He'd have been lucky to wake up after that lot, even without the sword through his chest...' She pointed to the leather belt. 'And what the hell is *that* all about? Some kinky sex game?' We both looked at the unfortunate (and naked) Santa on the bed, then at each other, and shuddered.

'I'm glad it weren't just me who thought that,' I said.

A door key sat on the table next to the bottle: so the one I had in my hand must be a spare, used by the abbey staff. I looked around the room but there didn't appear to be anything unusual, or anything obviously out of place, but of course I'd never been in there before so I couldn't say for certain.

'Everything all right?' said a voice behind me. *Daisy!* Debbie and I both whirled round, taking care to shield the grisly sight on the bed from her eyes. I was thankful that she hadn't made it further than the doorway.

'What are you doing in here?' I cried, shooing her away. 'I told you to go downstairs!'

'I was worried about you,' she said, which would have been sweet had I not noticed that she'd gone back for her camera before finding me.

'Out! Now!' I shoved her (gently, because she's my daughter and I love her) back into the corridor, as Debbie turned off the light switch and followed me, pulling the door closed behind us. I heard the lock click shut. 'Sweetheart, I know you're interested and you want to help, but there are some things you do not want to see.' She opened her mouth to protest, but Debbie stopped her.

'Your mum's right, love,' she said. 'Thirteen is far too young to see a dead body.'

'He is dead, then? What happened? Did he drink too much and choke on his own vomit?'

'What the— No, he didn't choke on his own vomit. Or anyone else's, for that matter. Look, it's not just that you're too young, although you do need reminding of that occasionally... Believe me, there are things I saw when I was in the Force that I really wish I hadn't. And I bet the same goes for Debbie, working in a hospital. Don't go looking for trouble, OK?'

'If I'm anything like you, it'll find me anyway,' she muttered, turning to trudge away dejectedly.

'She's got a point,' murmured Debbie, and I couldn't really deny it. I put the room key in my pocket, took a deep breath, and followed my daughter away from the horrible, horrible scene that lay beyond the heavy wooden door.

Chapter Seven

When we got downstairs, Trevor was waiting anxiously in the hallway for us.

'What's the news?' he asked quickly. 'Was Pippa right?'

'Yes,' I said quietly, looking around. No point broadcasting the gory details and sending everyone into a panic. 'Santa – Steve – is dead.'

'Heart attack?'

Debbie and I exchanged glances. I shook my head gently at her: *Don't tell anyone anything just yet.*

'I think we can rule that out as cause of death,' I said. 'Can I use your phone?'

'Of course. Use the one in the lounge, it's more private.' Trevor indicated a door on the other side of the hallway, and I remembered the room where the late

Father Christmas had nearly got into a punch-up with Isaac the night before.

I left him and Debbie to check on Pippa, then made my way into the lounge. I hadn't really had a chance to admire it the night before, being more concerned with preventing a bout of fisticuffs, but it was beautifully decorated, full of furniture that looked old and expensive but well-loved and looked after, and surprisingly comfortable. A big-screen TV looked out of place against one wall, but then Trevor did actually live here, and future guests would no doubt want to be able to watch TV. I wandered over to a big mahogany sideboard by the window, where a telephone sat, another incongruous reminder of the modern world in amongst all the antiques.

There was no dialling tone. The phone was dead. Hmm... Maybe the snow had brought the line down? Or maybe it had been cut by the murderer...

I put the phone down and followed the telephone cable – there was always the possibility that the cable had just come out of the wall socket – but no. There was a phone in the kitchen too, so I went and tried that, but that was also silent when I held it to my ear. The WiFi modem, sitting next to it, blinked the sad, solitary blink of the turned-on-but-not-connected-to-the-Internet. The line was definitely dead. I slowly wandered back out to the hallway, deep in thought.

'I'm taking Germaine for a walk,' said Daisy, making me jump. Germaine sat back on her haunches and looked up at me, keen for me to join them.

'OK...' I said. 'Do me a favour, take Debbie or Nana with you?'

'Why?'

Because it's just struck me that there could be a murderer loose in this house. 'I just don't want you going anywhere on your own, OK?'

'I'm not on my own, I've got Germaine—'

'For once in your life, will you just do as I tell you?' I snapped at her angrily, then felt bad. She looked annoyed for a second, but my daughter is one smart cookie (too flipping smart by half, sometimes) and her expression changed to one of shrewd calculation.

'You're worried, aren't you?' she said.

'Of course I am. It's freezing cold out there and I don't want you catching pneumonia,' I said carefully.

'Not about the snow. Santa didn't die of a heart attack, did he?' I didn't answer, but I didn't need to. Why was my daughter so blooming clever? *Takes after me*, I thought, which made me proud, but I had to admit it was also a pain in the backside. 'Santa was murdered, wasn't he? And you don't know who did it. And that means—'

'That means *possibly* someone in this house murdered him, although it's unlikely. To be honest, if I'd topped someone in the night I wouldn't be hanging around here,

I'd be miles away by now, even if I had to go on foot because of the snow,' I interrupted, with more confidence than I actually felt. 'If I was snowed in here, the last thing I'd do is murder someone, because it would immediately make me a suspect along with everyone else trapped here. So it's more likely that someone broke in, killed him and then left again.' Except as I said it, I knew that wasn't the case at all; because the back door had been locked, and the front door had been bolted from the inside. 'But don't you go repeating what I just said to anyone else.'

'Not even Nana?'

'Oh God no, *especially* not Nana. Now please, if you're going outside just take Nana or Debbie with you, like I asked. I don't want you going off on your own and poking your nose into things that might get you into trouble.' The irony that it was me saying this – the undisputed queen of poking my nose into things that routinely got me into trouble – wasn't lost on me, but I wasn't backing down, and Daisy knew it. She sighed and went into the dining room, where the sounds of breakfast were still going on. Not everyone had just seen a sight that was fit to make them lose their appetites. I turned and made my way back up the stairs. I needed a mobile phone signal.

'What the hell's going on?' Nathan was aghast. At least, I think he was – the signal kept cutting in and out and I could barely hear him. I was amazed he'd got through to me at all.

I'd climbed the stairs up to the tower, feeling the cold wind bite at the exposed skin on my cheeks and hands. I'd dialled 999 but my phone had resolutely refused to connect, and despite holding it up at increasingly high and bizarre angles (which was pretty pointless as I wouldn't have been able to talk into it if it *had* got a signal), I'd only managed to get enough bars to send Nathan a text message.

There's been a murder. Phone line is down, can you call 999 for me?

In retrospect I probably should have explained the situation a bit more. Anyway, he rang me straight back and actually got through, and now I was filling him in on what had happened, aware that we could be cut off at any moment.

'We're OK. Santa's been stabbed clean through the torso with an historic sword, and as the house was securely locked, it must've been someone who was here.' I swallowed. 'Someone who's *still* here, because no one's left yet.'

'Don't let anyone leave,' he said promptly. 'Have you told them what's happened?'

'Not yet. I wasn't sure what to do. They know he's dead, but I think at the moment they're just assuming it was natural causes. Unless the poor woman who found him has said anything, but she was pretty shocked, and I think they've taken her off somewhere quiet on her own to recover.' Maybe she shouldn't be on her own. Maybe she'd spotted something that would give the murderer away. I made a mental note to keep everyone together as much as possible, without giving rise to panic, hysteria and wild accusations, preferably. 'What should I do? About telling people, I mean?'

'What's your gut feeling?'

'To say as little as possible. If no one but me and Debbie know what's happened, the more likely it is that the only other person who knows – the murderer – will say something to incriminate themselves.'

'That's exactly what I think,' said Nathan. 'If everyone starts getting impatient to leave, then tell them it was murder – it'll shock them into staying put, hopefully. But otherwise keep it to yourself if you can. I'll call Carricksmoor, I think that will be your nearest station with CID officers. They're good.'

'Not as good as you, though,' I said, loyally, and he laughed.

'I dunno about that, the last few big cases I've solved,

I've had a bit of help, haven't I?' His voice suddenly became serious. 'Don't do anything…'

'Anything what? Stupid?'

'Anything Jodie-ish, I was going to say. Don't poke your nose in, just sit tight and wait for them to get to you.'

'That's all I intend to do,' I said haughtily. 'I've got my daughter and my mum here, remember. My priority is keeping them safe.'

'Good. Keep yourself safe too, OK?'

'I will.'

He paused for a moment. 'Seriously, be careful. If anything happened to you, I'd…' his words were lost in a rumble of static, '…you.'

'What? I can't hear you.'

'I said, stay safe because I—' And then the phone went dead. I could have screamed with frustration. Instead I went downstairs to tell everyone that Santa had uttered his last 'Ho ho ho' and would not be coming down any more chimneys.

By now, most of the abbey's reluctant overnight guests had finished breakfast and moved into the snug – everyone except Daisy, Mum and Germaine, who I assumed were outside stretching their legs and risking hypothermia, and Bea and Liam.

Lily beckoned me over into the corner of the room, where she and Trevor were looking white and pensive.

'Trevor told me what you said,' she said in a low voice. 'Does that mean you don't think it was natural causes? Do you think someone murdered him?'

'It's looking that way, I'm afraid,' I said, thinking of the sword sticking out of his back. 'I've locked the room. I'll keep hold of the key until the police get here, if that's OK.' It was sort of a question, but not really. Lily nodded anyway.

'Of course.'

'The victim's key was on his bedside table, and I've got the one that Pippa used to open the door. Are there any more copies?'

She shook her head. 'No, there's just one guest key and one staff key for each room.'

'Good, we don't want anyone going in and disturbing the crime scene.'

'Fine,' said Trevor. 'Did the police say how long they'll be?'

'No, I had to text Nathan and get him to call them. Because that's another thing. The phone line's not working.' They looked at me in shock.

'Do you think – whoever did this…?'

'The snow might have brought the line down,' I said. 'There's not much point cutting the lines these days, is there? Everyone's got their own phone. Even with the poor reception here, I still managed to call for help. I think it's probably just a coincidence.' I don't really believe in coincidences, not when it comes to crime, but it did seem like a pointless thing to do.

Lily and Trevor exchanged looks. 'It might not have been done to stop us calling the police,' said Lily slowly.

'What do you mean?'

'We have a really good security system here,' said Trevor. 'There was a string of robberies just after I bought the house, really nasty home invasions, so I invested in a monitored alarm system.'

'Which uses the phone line to alert the monitoring company?' I asked. He nodded. 'What about the alarm itself? If someone broke in, would it still make a noise in the house?'

'No,' said Trevor. 'If someone broke in at night, either through a window or one of the doors, the security company would be alerted straight away and a message would be sent to my phone. Because the signal's bad, they also know to call me on the landline. If there's no answer they call the police.'

'So maybe it was cut deliberately to allow someone to break-in, rather than to stop us calling for help afterwards?' I said thoughtfully to myself. I'd told Daisy that was what I thought had happened, but I'd only really said it to stop her worrying about being in close proximity to a murderer – not that she had been. I hadn't spotted any signs of a break-in when I'd taken Germaine out for her early morning constitutional, but then I had been half asleep and not looking out for anything suspicious.

'The front door was bolted from the inside...' I said. Lily nodded. 'What about the back door? I tried to open it to take the dog out earlier but it was locked. Could someone have come in through there, then locked it behind them again as they left?'

Lily shook her head. 'No. It's got an ordinary Yale lock, which you can unlock from the outside with the key, and that's all we use during the day. I've got a key, so has Pippa, and Trevor, obviously. But once everyone's left for the day I always use the deadlock as well, and there's only one key. And that was still in the kitchen where I left it, when I came down this morning.'

'Who knows about this alarm system? You two and Pippa, I take it?'

'And Isaac,' said Trevor. 'He spotted the alarm monitor by the front door and said he used the same company. We talked about it last night.'

'Hmmm...' I said. Would a multi-millionaire really do something as clumsy as murder someone he'd been seen arguing with earlier that evening? And he was already inside the house, so even if he did know about the alarm system, why cut it off? I had the feeling I was heading into a dead end with that train of thought, so I changed track.

'The sword...' I said. 'Who knew it was in the butler's pantry?'

Lily frowned. 'Everyone, I think. Isaac saw Pippa take it out of the display case, and we were talking about it later that evening, remember? Why?'

'Because it's not in the butler's pantry anymore,' I said. 'It's in Steve.' Trevor and Lily both gasped and looked at each other, horrified. 'Why didn't you put it back in the case after the kids left?'

'With everything else that was happening – making up rooms for everyone – I didn't even think about it, did you?' Lily's face was pale as she turned to Trevor, who shrugged.

'It did cross my mind, but then I noticed that the glass case was covered in sticky handprints where the children had been trying to get it open, so I asked Pippa to give it a good clean before she put the sword back. I thought she might as well give the sword itself a polish while it was out.' He sighed. 'I didn't think there was any hurry. If only I'd just locked it away again...'

'The murderer, whoever they are, would have found something else,' I said. 'A knife out of the kitchen would have done the job just as well.'

Lily shuddered. 'That poor man...'

'So what happens now?' asked Trevor, putting his arm around her shoulders.

'No one leaves,' I said. 'Everyone stays here until the police arrive. No one disturbs the crime scene. In fact, try and keep everyone together, down here, if you can, without making them alarmed.' They looked at me quizzically. 'Don't let anyone go off on their own. Just in case.'

'Just in case what?' asked Lily, wide eyed.

'Just in case there's another murder.'

I wandered back out into the hallway, not really sure what to do next. Doing *nothing* wasn't really my style, but the police were on their way and they wouldn't want me trampling all over their investigation; they weren't Nathan, who (it had taken me some time to realise) had had an ulterior motive for letting me poke my nose into things. He fancied me. I smiled and gave myself a little hug, and then realised that if anyone saw me they'd think I was bonkers, so I stopped. My phone, which was tucked uselessly in my pocket, vibrated. A text message had actually come through, my phone managing to connect just long enough to download it while the mobile signal paid a fleeting visit, before buggering off again. It was from Nathan.

Spoke to Carricksmoor CID, lots of staff struggling to get in because of the snow, will get to you asap but it could be as long as an hour, roads still blocked in surrounding villages. Be careful xxx

An hour? Dammit. My fellow snow refugees would be beginning to get impatient soon, eager to get on the road, even those of us who hadn't killed anyone. Unless they lived here, in which case they would probably be very keen to get everyone out of the house and back to some semblance of 'normal'. So where did that leave us? Well, I knew it hadn't been me or Daisy. Mum had been snoring loud enough to wake the dead all night (a poor and inaccurate choice of words, now I thought of it, because Steve's bucket had stayed resolutely kicked despite her cacophonous nostrils), and besides that she wasn't a killer. Occasionally irritating and a bit batty, yes, but not homicidal. And she was my mum and I knew her. Debbie – why would Debbie have killed a Father Christmas impersonator? Was there some deep-seated childhood trauma – the memory of a department store Santa who had refused to give her a train set, on the grounds that it was a 'boy's toy', and forced her to take a Barbie doll instead – that caused her to fly into a homicidal rage at the sight of a red suit and white beard? I mean, I didn't know much about Debbie's childhood, but I was guessing the answer to that was a resounding 'no', and anyway she'd said that he'd been a likely candidate for an early (but natural) death as it was, particularly mixing alcohol and strong sleeping tablets. If she'd wanted him dead, all she had to do was wait…

Who did that leave? The Japanese girls. OK, they *could* really be a crack team of undercover ninjas, sent to assassinate grumpy Santa impersonators in the depths of Cornwall, but it seemed unlikely. Bea and Liam – well, there was something off about them, but they'd barely exchanged two words with Steve, which either meant they had very cleverly made it look like they didn't know him and therefore wouldn't have a motive to kill him before doing him in or, most likely, they genuinely *didn't* know him and therefore *didn't* have a motive. And hadn't killed anybody.

James… Now, James *had* been a bit moody this morning, and there'd been that conversation in his room the night before; he'd refused to do something, something that the mere suggestion of which had made him furious. But he was an old Etonian for goodness' sake. Not that they didn't have the capacity to murder someone, but James and Steve would hardly have moved in the same circles and again, where was the motive?

Lily. I'd known Lily for most of my life, even if we hadn't stayed in close contact when I'd left Penstowan. I couldn't imagine her being a killer, which didn't mean she *wasn't*, but – she'd practically had a nervous breakdown when, at the age of sixteen, Tony and I had persuaded her to go and watch *Scream* at the cinema – not just over it being scary, but over the fact that it was rated 18. She'd been convinced the houselights would come up halfway through the film and the cinema manager would chuck us out for being underage. She didn't have the nerve or the stomach for murder. Trevor seemed like a nice bloke, a bit stressed out, but what possible motive could he have for bumping off Santa? Pippa – well, Pippa had gone home, which probably put her out of the picture (although she still feasibly could have come back later to do the nefarious deed), but even without that, why would she kill Steve?

Why would *ANYONE* kill Steve? What motive would anyone have for brutally stabbing an overweight, middle-aged, borderline alcoholic Father Christmas from Plymouth? As far as I was aware, no one in the house even really knew him – he'd been hired specially for the party.

Except one person seemed to have known him well enough to have had an argument with him. Isaac…

Chapter Eight

Just as I was wrestling with myself, trying to decide whether or not to go and have a chat with Isaac and find out exactly how well he'd known the victim, Daisy and Germaine dashed into the hallway, bringing a blast of freezing-cold air with them and, following rather more sedately, Mum.

'It's cold enough to freeze the doo-dahs off a brass donkey,' said Mum, rubbing her hands together to get some warmth back into them.

Monkey, not donkey, I thought, but I didn't correct her because I knew from previous experience that that way madness lay.

'Mum, Mum, I've been doing some detecting!' said Daisy excitedly. Germaine yapped and leaped up at me, her four-legged excitement reflecting her owner's. I shook my head at Mum.

'You're supposed to be keeping her out of trouble!' I said, and she laughed.

'Am I? I thought it was the other way round…'

'I've found some clues,' said Daisy, tugging at my arm. 'Come and look.' I wasn't dressed for the snow, but I followed her outside, Germaine keeping us company.

'OK, what have you found?' I asked, stamping my feet to keep warm. I would quite possibly die of exposure while I was humouring her.

'It didn't snow overnight,' she said.

'How do you know that?'

She pointed to a bird table that was just off to the side of the path. 'When we brought Germaine out here for a pee before bed, it had just finished snowing, yeah? I went over to the bird table and wiped the snow off so the birds could get to the nuts underneath.'

'And there's no new snow on it,' I said. 'OK. So what?'

Daisy rolled her eyes. 'So look at the footprints in the snow.' She pointed to a set of footprints encompassing two pairs of fairly small feet and one set of cute little paws, leading away from a mess of prints around the front door. 'That's me and Nana, just now. We had a walk round the outside of the house.' She pointed to another set that also included pawprints. 'That's you and me this morning, when we brought Germaine out. There's another set like it there. I think that lot's from last night, because there's mine, leading to the bird table, see?' I nodded. 'It was snowing when Hina and her friends turned up, so you can't see their trail, but there're two people's tracks heading for the house there – that weird couple.' So Daisy thought Bea and Liam were weird, too? That was interesting. I wondered why she felt like that.

'Yes... And there's another lot here, one person on their own, leading away from the house and down the path...' I pointed.

'That's what's-her-face, when she left last night,' said Daisy.

'Pippa? Yes. And here's where she came back this morning, following the same path.' I spotted another trail, one large set of footprints accompanied by a small one. 'Isaac and Joshua, this morning?'

Daisy nodded and led me around the corner of the house, where the prints milled around next to a magnificent snowman. 'Joshua told me he had a dream about building a snowman, so when he got up he asked his dad if they could make one before they went home.'

'I see...' I turned my head, looking this way and that. 'You walked around the whole building?' Daisy nodded. 'And there were no more footprints?' She shook her head.

'No. You know what that means? You were wrong

about someone breaking in, killing Santa and then leaving again. After Pippa left, no one else came to or from the house, apart from us walking Germaine, and the snowman builders this morning, after he was already dead. And Pippa coming back, of course. Otherwise they would have left footprints.' She gave me a satisfied smile. 'The murderer is still in the house.'

I looked at her for a moment and sighed. 'OK, you might be right. Although I can't for the life of me think why anyone would want to kill Santa.'

'Oh, Mother...' Daisy shook her head sadly, like I'd bitterly disappointed her. 'You're looking at it all wrong. No one killed Santa. Steve was only pretending to be him.'

'Yes, all right, Missy, I do know that!' I said, irritated, but her words awakened something in the back of my brain. I'd been thinking of Steve as only a Santa impersonator, but why would someone kill a Santa impersonator? They wouldn't. Steve was not just a man who went to work in a red suit for one month of the year. Steve was impersonating Santa. He was used to pretending to be something he wasn't. So the question was, who was he really? And why had that led him here?

Daisy looked at me expectantly. I pulled her towards me for a hug.

'Very good detecting. I am actually very impressed.' She preened. I took her face in my hands and peered into her eyes, so she knew I was serious. 'But no more, OK? If you're right—'

'I am.'

'*If* you're right, if the person who killed Steve is inside that house, then they're not going to take very kindly to you poking your nose in. And yes, I know I do it, but I'm a professional. Ex-professional, anyway. And even I know to stop when it could be dangerous.'

She rolled her eyes. 'You sound like Nathan.'

'Maybe I do. On this occasion, Nathan would be absolutely right. No more looking for clues, *please*. Stick with me or Debbie or Nana, keep the dog with you, and just stay where everyone else is until the police get here. We'll tell them about the footprints, OK? Now let's go inside before we both freeze.'

I fully intended to take my own advice and keep my nose out of the murder. All I had to do was stall people until the police got there. They'd take statements from everyone, and then we could finally go home. If the Gimpmobile started in this cold weather. I had my doubts.

But back in the hallway, I could hear a few rumblings of dissent coming from the snug. Debbie came out and saw me, heading towards me with a concerned expression on her face.

'Your mum and James are winding each up into a frenzy,' she said. I groaned.

'What are they saying?'

'She wants to go home and she can't see why we all have to wait for the police. And James agrees with her, he says him and Isaac need to get back to London.' She gave me a rueful grin. 'I haven't said anything to them about the murder, so they still think it was natural causes. But maybe we should say something?'

'Yeah, I think we might have to. But we'll keep the details to ourselves.' I frowned. I had been trying to keep it quiet, but if it meant quelling an uprising and stopping everyone rushing for their cars, I would probably have to come clean. Lily and Trevor knew about the murder weapon, of course, but at the moment only Debbie and I (and the murderer) knew all the gruesome details. Maybe revealing a little more about Steve's death would prompt a comment from the murderer; maybe they would give themselves away by revealing some snippet of information that no one except me and Debbie should have known.

Round and round my train of thought went, a perpetual circle of *if* and *why* and *who* that showed no signs of actually getting anywhere. It had seemed to me when I was on the Force that most murders are spur-of-the-moment things, a sudden rush of blood that leaves a trail of evidence in its wake. It might not be obvious, but it's there, and all you have to do is find it, follow it and *voilà!* There's your murderer. But this was like a Sherlock Holmes locked room mystery; more than that – a locked room in a locked house. That was another thing: I hadn't even *thought* about how the murderer had got into the room yet, too busy trying to work out how they'd got into the house – if they hadn't already been there. But if they *had* already been there, they must be some kind of idiot to murder someone when suspicion would be sure to fall on everybody who'd been trapped in the house overnight...

'I know that look,' said Debbie.

'What?' I came to with a start.

'Oh my God, and you just told me to keep my nose out!' Daisy shook her head.

'I'm not—' I was interrupted by my phone vibrating again. The weather must be getting better if text messages were coming through. Nathan said:

Everything OK? Just spoke to a contact at Carricksmoor CID and they admitted they don't know when they'll get to you. It's so cold the diesel in their 4x4s keeps freezing and their smaller cars can't get through.

Well that's just marvellous, I typed back, although it

wasn't his fault. He wasn't to know that I was struggling with that familiar urge. *What am I supposed to do?*

NOTHING!

Maybe he did know.

I mean it, just keep everyone there, tell them the roads are still blocked across the moor – to be fair, they might be where you are. Stay together. I'll see what I can do.

I wasn't sure exactly what he would be able to do from Penstowan, but I couldn't answer him because the signal disappeared again. I looked up at the expectant (and a bit too smug, for my liking) faces of my daughter and my friend, and said, 'Ah crap.'

Inside the snug, things were coming to a head. The Japanese girls watched nervously, trying to follow the conversation, while James and my mother tried to convince the others it was OK to leave.

'They said on the news this morning that they've cleared a lot of the moors,' said Mum. 'And there's more snow forecast for later, so you don't want to be too late setting off.'

'You're right,' said James. 'We have to head back to the hotel first as it is, so God knows how long it will take to get back to London.'

'You should really stay until the police get here,' said Trevor, but James shook his head.

'I don't see why. Look, I'm sorry for the man, but what has his death really got to do with any of us? It's not like the police can't come and find us if they want a statement.'

'What do you think?' Bea asked Isaac. He shook his head.

'I don't know. Of course I want to get home today. It's three days until Christmas, I've got things to do before the big day. But someone's died. His family won't get to spend Christmas with him ever again. It won't hurt us to wait for a little while longer.'

'I think you're right,' said Bea. She turned to smile calmly at James. 'You should wait here with us. Why not? It's not like you'll have no one to talk to.' James gave a big impatient huff.

'The traffic—' he started.

'I'm sorry, but no one leaves until the police get here,' I said. Everyone whirled around to see me standing in the doorway.

'What?' James sounded exasperated. 'No offence, but I'm not taking orders from the caterer. Joshy wants to go home, Isaac. We should take him.'

'No one leaves, because the victim didn't die of a heart attack. It wasn't natural causes.' I glanced at Joshua, but he was completely entranced by the dog, and Daisy, bless her, was making sure it stayed that way while the grown-ups talked. 'Santa – I mean, Steve – was murdered.'

Everyone gasped. Isaac's mouth dropped open in horror. 'What? But we...' He stopped and glanced over at his son, but Joshua was still oblivious.

'Blooming 'eck!' said Mum. 'That's a bit of a shocker.' She wobbled slightly and Lily immediately guided her into a nearby chair. I wondered if it was uncharitable of me to notice Mum eyeing up the brandy bottle (not that it had much left in it, after Santa's attack on it the night before) on the table next to her, but then she was getting on a bit and, to be fair, most Christmas house parties don't end up with Father Christmas decomposing in a guest bedroom. Years of being married to my dad, Chief Inspector Eddie Parker of Penstowan police and the surrounding areas, had hardened her to a lot of things, but murder had been a very rare occurrence during his days on the Force.

'Can I get you a drink, Shirley?' Lily looked concerned.

'Ooh yes please, just a small one, as it's so early,' said Mum. Lily looked surprised but reached for a glass anyway.

'I think she meant a cup of tea, Nana,' said Daisy. 'And anyway, you said to me outside that Mum was being a bit shady, and that you thought she thought someone had bumped him off.' Mum murmured something about not knowing what she was talking about, as she accepted the proffered glass of brandy.

Isaac was still staring at me in shock. James was staring at me too, but with a more hostile expression on his face. 'So no one is leaving,' I said.

'Who put you in charge?' he protested.

'Jodie used to be in the Met,' said Debbie, with a hint of pride. 'And now she's a consultant for the local constabulary, *and* a private detective, *and* you haven't lived until you've had one of her saffron buns.' I grinned to myself; she was laying it on a bit thick, but it was true about my buns.

'I told you before.' Isaac gave me a small smile. 'She's a police hero.'

'Look, I know it's a pain, but the police can't be much longer.' I decided I wouldn't tell them about Carricksmoor CID's current transport woes. 'I think it's best if everyone just sits tight in here for now,' I said, looking around. 'Hang on, where's Pippa?'

'In the kitchen,' said Lily. 'Washing up the breakfast stuff.' I'd forgotten about breakfast. I'd left a bacon sandwich behind when I'd gone to look at the body. My tummy rumbled. 'She said she was feeling better but she just wanted to keep busy, take her mind off it.'

'OK. Maybe I should check on her, make sure she's OK…' *Make sure no one's bumped her off as well*, I thought.

The kitchen was empty. *Uh-oh…* I thought, but there was a noise behind me and there she was, bringing the last of the plates in from the dining room including, my stomach was pleased to note, my bacon butty.

She looked surprised to see me. 'Oh! You made me jump. I thought you were all busy in the other room.'

'I wanted to make sure you were OK. You had a nasty shock there.' I took the plates from her hands (not purely a selfless gesture of help, as I wanted to grab my breakfast before she scraped it into the bin), then set them down on the side and smiled at her. 'You didn't have to do all this, you know.'

Pippa gave me a tight smile. 'I know, I just needed to do something.'

'To stop you thinking about it? I get it. But don't overdo it. Here, sit down.' I gestured to the chair that Mum had brought in from the butler's pantry the day before and Pippa sat down, stiff and unwilling. Nearby, there was a big drum of cooking oil that Daisy had been using as a stool yesterday, so I dragged that over and perched on it, next to her. I smiled, trying to set her at ease. I'd thought she was nervy and shy yesterday, but now she was so tense, I was amazed she'd managed to bend enough to sit in the chair. Hardly surprising. The scene that had greeted her that morning had been particularly grisly – bad enough to make both Debbie and I feel a bit queasy, and we were used to icky dead bodies – so I could only imagine what was going on in her head. She must see the blood-stained sheets and the lifeless Santa, naked bottom uppermost, every time she closed her eyes.

'Why don't you have a rest and I'll wash up? Better still, go and sit with the others—'

'No!' she said. 'No, thank you. I'd honestly rather just be on my own. Everyone would try and talk to me, and I know they're just trying to be nice but, really, I just want some peace and quiet. I'll finish this and then go home.'

'Yeah... I think it would be better if you stayed here, with us. Even if you don't want to sit with everyone else, if you want to stay in here where it's all a bit calmer. I don't think you should go home.'

Her eyes filled with tears. 'I just want to be on my own.' I reached out and took her hand. I needed to impress upon her the importance of her staying close by, without terrifying and upsetting her even more.

'I know, but the police will be here soon and they'll want to talk to you.' Her eyes widened in alarm, and I squeezed her hand gently. 'It's OK, they'll just want to ask you about finding Steve. So it's much easier if you just stay here and think about what you saw.' I took a deep breath. 'Just in case you saw anything…incriminating.'

'I didn't.'

'You don't know that. And, more to the point, the murderer doesn't know that either.' She looked at me, confused for a moment, and then the truth dawned on her.

'You think – the murderer's still in the house?' I nodded slowly. 'And they might think I saw something in the room that points to them?'

I nodded again. 'Yes. And you might have done, without even realising it. That's why it's important to think about what you saw—'

'You think, if the murderer thinks I saw something, I might be next?' Her eyes widened again, even bigger, and I thought, *I'd better stop talking soon or she'll look like an owl.*

'Well, I don't know, but there's a slim chance of that…'

'You think they'll murder me too, to stop me talking?'

'No, no, nothing like that…'

'I am *definitely* going home.' She stood up, but I still had hold of her hand.

'Pippa,' I said, calmly. 'Pippa, sit down. Is there anyone at home? Or do you live on your own?'

'On my own.'

'Then you're much safer here, with us. You'd be even safer in the other room, with the rest of us—' She opened her mouth but I carried on. 'I know, you'd rather stay in here, and that's fine. We'll just make sure no one comes in here to join you, on their own.'

'You're in here on your own with me,' she pointed out, not unreasonably.

'Well – yeah, but that's different. I'm not the murderer.'

'I don't know that though, do I?' she also pointed out, again not unreasonably. I looked at her for a moment and then stood up.

'I can't really argue with that, can I? OK, look. You stay in here. Hang on…' I rushed out into the corridor and into the butler's pantry next door, looking for something that I'd spotted (and been tempted by) yesterday, when Germaine had been snoozing in there. I carried it into the kitchen and put it onto the work bench next to Pippa, who looked at it in surprise and then gave a small laugh.

'The old dinner gong?' she said.

'Yep. If you feel unsafe, come and find us, but if you can't, grab the beater and bash the gong as hard as you can.' I picked up the small metal beater and brandished it. It was no good, the temptation was far too strong. I swung it back and hit the old, tarnished brass gong with a very satisfying *GA-DONNNNGGGG!* The sound reverberated around the room, much louder than I'd expected, and Pippa looked at me in surprise.

The sound of running feet soon reached us. Trevor appeared in the doorway.

'What the hell's going on?' he cried. 'Pippa, are you all right?'

I smiled at Pippa. 'See? Help will come running.' I handed her the beater, then grabbed the plate with my bacon sandwich on it. It was cold but better than nothing. 'Now we'll leave you in peace.'

Chapter Nine

I followed Trevor back into the snug. They looked a bit surprised at me eating – I don't know why, from the lack of food left on the plates in the kitchen, I guessed that news of the death hadn't put everyone else off their breakfast, but then none of them had actually seen the corpse – but what can I say, I think better when my tummy isn't rumbling.

Lily was talking to the Japanese girls, but seemed to be having trouble making herself understood. I saw her exasperated expression and went over to join her.

'How are you? Everyone OK?' I said, cheerfully. Hina, the designated spokesperson, gave me a worried smile.

'Yes, thank you. But we call for help for our car, yes?'

'The phone line's down,' said Lily, for what I suspected was not the first time.

'Ah, right. The phone,' I said, involuntarily raising my voice and doing a big mime of picking up a phone, 'is not working.'

'They're Japanese, Mum,' said Daisy, rolling her eyes. 'Not deaf.'

'Or stupid,' muttered Debbie. I lowered my hand and my voice.

'Where's James when we need him? Do these girls have any idea what's going on?' I turned to Hina. 'The police are coming. Police? Yes?'

'Yes. For the man who died. The police will help our car?'

'Yes,' I said, although I had no idea if they would or not. At the very least one of their 4x4s should be able to pull the girls' car out of the ditch. With any luck it might still be drivable. I patted Hina's arm. 'It will be OK. Just stay in here with everyone else.'

Mum was sitting suspiciously quietly in the corner while Germaine warmed herself on the rug in front of the fire. I wondered if she'd helped herself to any more of that brandy (Mum, that is, not the dog – Germaine's teetotal) and fallen asleep in the chair with her eyes open. James was nowhere to be seen, or Bea and Liam. I really didn't like the fact that I kept losing track of those two. It definitely felt to me like there was something 'off' about them, but they could hardly be Steve's killers; they'd barely spoken to him the night before, and he'd shown no signs of knowing them. There was also no sign of Isaac or Joshua.

'Where are the others?' I asked. Keeping this lot all in one place was harder than herding cats.

'Isaac and Joshua are in the lounge, watching the telly,' said Daisy. 'Nana said there's a Christmas film on that Joshua might like.'

'*Die Hard*,' said Mum. I hoped she was joking. The last thing I wanted was the multi-millionaire's eight-year-old learning the phrase 'Yippee kai yay, motherf—' – yeah, that one – because of my own dotty mother.

'What's taking the police so long?' said Lily, leaving the four eco-tourists chatting animatedly amongst themselves. 'It's been at least an hour since you called them.'

'Yeah, we could all have been murdered in our beds by the time they get here,' said Mum. She glanced up at the ceiling, genuflecting and making the sign of the cross on her chest. 'Begging your pardon, Santa.'

'You do know Christmas was originally a pagan festival, don't you, Nana?' said Daisy. 'You don't have to cross yourself. I don't think saying "Santa" counts as blasphemy.'

'Well thank God for that.'

Debbie and I exchanged looks and I shook my head. 'Anyway...' I began.

'I watched this true crime programme on the telly the

other night,' said Debbie. 'For some reason, since I moved down here I've got hooked on them. Can't think why.' She grinned at me. 'They said there's this thing called the golden hour—'

'The period just after the crime's taken place,' I said. 'When the evidence is still fresh, there are still witnesses and suspects around, and the case is most likely to be solved. Yeah, I know.'

'Well, they're going to miss the golden hour, aren't they?' She looked meaningfully at me, and I thought, *No, don't encourage me, because I don't take much encouraging.*

'I promised Nathan...' I said, weakly, because yes, I had, *technically* promised not to get involved, but not *actually*, in so many words. I'd promised not to do anything Jodie-ish. 'Jodie-ish' could cover a number of things. Cooking. Walking the dog. Not necessarily poking my nose in. And I hadn't *actually* said the words, *I promise*. I'd just kind of hinted that I wouldn't investigate. Was it my fault if he took that vague hint and assumed it was a promise?

'Oh Nathan, schmathan! He's not here, is he? He's not here, on the ground, in the zone...' Debbie was getting a little bit carried away in her excitement.

'It has only been two months, dear,' said Mum, reprovingly. 'You can't stop being yourself just because your boyfriend doesn't like it.'

'You were getting ready to buy a wedding hat earlier!'

I protested. 'Anyway, he *does* like it. We fell in love over a murder case, didn't we?'

'Are we investigating? I could take some photos of the crime scene.' Daisy held up her camera. Germaine sat up and barked. I shook my head.

'No, *we're* not investigating anything,' I said.

'You can't do it on your own,' said Debbie. 'You need a team. We helped you before, when you were looking for that Craig Laity.'

'Well, yeah, but that was different...' I was starting to realise that I was fighting a losing battle, and, to be fair, I kind of wanted to lose it.

'Come on! We don't need the police! We don't need men blundering in here and taking over.'

Lily had been watching our conversation, head moving back and forth between us as if she was at a tennis match. She looked slightly bewildered.

'They're just as likely to be female officers,' I said. Daisy shook her head.

'You know that's not true, Mum,' she said. 'Women are still under-represented in the CID and in higher positions in the police force in general. You told me that yourself when you quit the Met. And that's not fair when women are much more emotionally intelligent than men and just as good at problem solving.' I'd told her that, too. Dammit. 'So let's do it. Or should we all just go and wait in the kitchen for them to turn up?'

I looked at her admiringly. The little madam knew exactly what buttons to press to get me on her side, and I was really quite proud of that. And she'd actually listened to and remembered something I'd said to her. If you have a tween or teenager, you'll understand that that is a Very Big Deal.

'They *are* taking a very long time to get here,' said Lily. 'And I heard what you did for Tony, when poor Mel died.'

On cue, as if to add more weight to everyone's argument, Germaine jumped up off the rug and pattered over to me, putting her front paws on my legs and gazing up at me, a faithful hound ready to do her mistress's bidding. *Sorry, Nathan*, I thought, as the last of my resolve fizzled out like a damp firework, putting up a pathetic struggle before finally dying away with a little *pffft* noise, leaving behind nothing but a faint whiff of gunpowder (although that might just have been my imagination).

'You have to do *exactly* as I tell you. No going off-piste and wandering around on your own,' I said. They all nodded. 'I'm in charge here. If you find something, or think of anything, come and tell me at once. No putting yourselves in danger at any time. Do you hear me?' Daisy, Debbie and Mum all nodded obediently. A bit too obediently. I sighed. 'All right then.'

'Yay!'

'Sisters doing it for themselves,' said Debbie, high-fiving my daughter.

'Ovaries before brovaries,' said Mum.

So this was my squad. If the murderer really was still in the house, I almost felt sorry for them.

***

So where to start? With the dead man, and the only person who, so far, seemed to have any motive to kill him. The person who'd been arguing with him the night before.

Trevor had joined us. I thought for a moment he was going to slip his arm around Lily's waist, but then he didn't and I wasn't sure if I'd imagined it or not.

'You ladies looked like you were plotting something,' he said.

'Jodie's going to investigate,' said Lily. Trevor looked a bit alarmed, but she patted him on the arm. 'Don't worry, she knows what she's doing. She's the one who cleared my friend Tony.'

'That was you?' Trevor looked incredulous. 'Wow. Good job we hired you, then.'

I laughed. 'I won't even charge you extra for my detective services.'

'Do you need us to do anything?' asked Lily. I nodded.

'Yeah, if you could come and look at the room with me in a bit, make sure nothing's been taken? It seems unlikely to be a robbery gone wrong, but this house is full of antiques and stuff…'

'Not in the bedrooms,' said Trevor.

'No, I think it's unlikely to be that too, but we need to check it out. But I think first of all I need to talk to Isaac. You were there when him and Steve were arguing last night. Can you tell me what it was all about?'

He frowned. 'No, not really. I'd gone out to the barn to get some more wood for the fire, and by the time I got back Steve was halfway through my brandy and having a go at Isaac. He looked really uncomfortable and kept trying to calm him down, but I didn't actually hear what he was so angry about.'

'That's a shame… Did Isaac know who was playing Santa before he got here? Did he have any say in it?'

'No, he left that up to us. We put out a press release in the local paper, advertising that Isaac was going to be holding his annual Christmas party at Kingseat and asking for someone to play Santa.'

'We had quite a few people contact us, but Steve was really insistent that he wanted to do it,' added Lily. 'He said he was going to be in the neighbourhood, and that he'd always admired Isaac and was keen to meet him. He even offered to do it for nothing.'

'We still paid him, of course,' said Trevor. 'Although

admittedly it wasn't much.'

'Hmm...' So it seemed that, although Isaac may not have known Steve, Steve definitely knew him and had made a point of being here to confront him...

———————

I left the snug and ventured into the lounge, where Isaac was sitting quietly in an armchair, gazing off into space, while Joshua was sprawled out on the sofa watching a film on the TV. I was pleased to see that it wasn't *Die Hard* after all (which is a perfectly good movie and definitely a Christmas one, and I will fight anyone who says otherwise, but probably not the best choice for an eight year old). I didn't recognise it, but a round-bellied, jolly man with a beard and a smiling face, clad in a pair of cargo shorts and a Hawaiian shirt, was currently protesting that he wasn't Santa, honest, he was just plain old Nick Festive from Hollyville, Arizona, and he was on his holiday. It all sounded a bit fishy to me.

'Isaac? Can I have a word?' He jumped at the sound of my voice, and I could see that he had been deep in thought. He looked up at me, then glanced at his son; but I'd brought Daisy and Germaine with me to keep Joshua company. Joshua sat up and shuffled along on the sofa to let them sit next to him, only taking his eyes off the screen when Germaine laid her head in his lap and gazed up at him, half in adoration, half in an expression of *Oi, you, give me some attention, I am proper cute!*

'Let's find somewhere quiet to talk, shall we?' I said, and he looked at me, undecided for a moment. 'The police are on their way, and they won't worry about disturbing your son's movie with their questions. I might be able to help you.' After a moment he nodded and rose from his armchair, then followed me out into the hallway. I walked to a door opposite and tried the handle; the old library. Lily's impromptu tour of the house last night hadn't included this room.

James, Bea and Liam were inside. They looked around – James, guiltily – as we entered.

'It's OK, we'll find somewhere else,' I said, stepping back, but James immediately rushed towards the door.

'No no, we're finished in here—'

'What are you doing?' Isaac sounded suspicious. I wondered if he had his doubts about Bea and Liam, too. Bea smiled.

'We were just nosing around,' she said. 'All these books! It's a beautiful room, if you're a keen reader like I am. We probably should've asked Trevor first, but we were bored. We'll leave you to it.' She gestured to Liam to follow her, and the three of them left, James in a hurry.

It was indeed a beautiful room. The walls were lined with books, looking in rather better condition than those in the secret book storage room Lily had shown us yesterday. The shelves were of the same rich, dark mahogany that so much of the wooden panelling around the house was fashioned from, and it looked like the sort of room where, at the touch of the right book, a secret door would swing open (creaking noise optional), leading to a long, dark, hidden passage... At the very least, it had enough books in it to while away a whole winter snowed in there. It was the sort of place I would have been desperate to explore, had there not been a corpse lying upstairs in the room above our heads.

'I can't believe it,' said Isaac, dropping into an old leather armchair. I remained standing. 'Why would anyone kill a Santa impersonator?'

'How well did you know him?' I asked.

'I didn't know him at all.'

'He certainly knew you. In fact, it seems like he was only really here to see you. Why was that? What was the argument about?'

'It was hardly an argument. He shouted at me and I agreed with him.' He looked at my puzzled face and smiled ruefully. 'I had no idea who he was during the party, he was just the Santa bloke. I spoke to him before the kids went in to see him, and he made a point of telling me he was from Plymouth and asking me if I knew the city or anyone there. When I said I didn't, he just nodded, like that's exactly what he was expecting me to say.'

'I'm assuming by that, that you *should* have known someone from Plymouth?'

'Yeah...' Isaac looked at me steadily. 'Fifteen years ago I bought a company in the city who were making mobile phone components. They were a family-run business, not massive but doing all right. They employed about fifty people, some of whom had been with them from the beginning.'

'I assume the takeover was better for you than it was for them?'

He nodded. 'I bought them because they were making one particular component, PCBs—' He noticed my confused look. 'Printed circuit boards. They basically make your smart phone run like a computer, and as smart phones have got more powerful, PCBs have become more complex. This company had just started making a particular type of PCB, and that's why I wanted them.'

'You wanted them to make these PCB thingies for you?'

Isaac shook his head. 'No. I wanted them to *stop* making them, because my own company was about to put out a tender to two of the biggest mobile phone manufacturers in the world to exclusively supply them, and I didn't want the lot in Plymouth coming in and undercutting me. So I stripped them of anything that might come in useful – they had a few bits of machinery that were OK, but to be honest, it was all quite old and outdated – and shut them down.' He looked at me. 'I told you I was ruthless before Joshua came along. As it turns out, I doubt that they would have put in for the tender anyway, because they probably couldn't have produced enough units, but I didn't want it getting around that someone else could make these PCBs to the same standard as us, and cheaper, so…'

'So you ruined someone's company and put fifty people on the dole?'

'Yes. It wasn't personal, it was business.'

'I'm sure that was a great comfort to them when they went and signed on at the Job Centre. And your legal team shielded you from any consequences, so why should you care?' I shook my head. 'Mate, that's harsh.'

'I know. Which is why, after I had Joshua, I went back through all my old business dealings and made things right.'

'But you missed this particular deal?'

'No, actually, they were among the first people I went back and compensated properly. But I did miss one of them.'

'Steve? Or someone connected to him?'

'His son.'

I looked at him, a horrible feeling in the pit of my stomach. 'What happened to him?'

'He was out of work for two years. You know what

the job market is like down here. He lost his house. His marriage was put under a lot of stress. Eventually he found work overseas for a while, which is probably why my charity people missed him when they checked up on all the ex-employees. A few of them had found other jobs and were doing fine, but anyone else who was still in financial hardship got some compensation to help them.'

'So what went wrong?'

'Steve's son came home after the job abroad fell through, and found out that his wife was filing for divorce. He had no money, and he couldn't find anywhere to live so he couldn't share custody of their kids.'

'Oh no. Where is he now?'

'He's living in a bedsit, no work, really depressed, and Steve's worried about him. He wanted him to move back home, but he wouldn't, and Steve only has his pension. *Had* his pension. So he couldn't help him with money.'

'So Steve was having a go at you for ruining his life?'

'Yes. And as I said, I agreed with him.' Isaac looked at me, running a hand through his hair and letting out a deep breath. 'I told him that I would pay off his son's debts, and do what I could to help him find a job – retrain him, whatever he wanted to do. I told him we'd get his son's life back on track, although I couldn't rescue his marriage.' He smiled ruefully. 'He actually laughed at that and said that was fine by him, his ex-daughter-in-law was a right miserable cow. I think he was quite drunk at that point.'

I remembered Steve laughing with Isaac the night before, when I'd gone back in with a cup of coffee to sober him up. 'So by the time everyone went to bed, you were on friendly terms?'

'Yes. I mean, he was horribly drunk and I wasn't sure that he'd remember everything I'd said to him the next day, so I emailed my PA there and then, giving her all the details. I asked her to set up a contract of some sort and get my finance guys to work out how much to pay him.' He looked at me frankly. 'I'm still going to help his son, even without him here, pestering me and threatening to go to the press about it.'

'He threatened you?'

'I think he meant to. He was a bit too inebriated to be very articulate at that point. And by the end of the evening that was all forgotten, anyway.' He stood up. 'If you think I'd kill him and risk losing my son over a few thousand pounds, then you're barking up the wrong tree. I can afford it, and it's worth it for an easy conscience.'

I looked at him thoughtfully, then nodded. If he was telling the truth about Steve and his son, it didn't make sense for him to risk so much for the sake of a sum of money that he'd barely notice leaving his bank account.

'The police will want to see that email,' I said. 'If you

sent it last night and it says what you say it does, then it probably puts you in the clear.'

He laughed, with a hint of bitterness. 'It's karma, isn't it? If I get arrested for his murder, it'll be my punishment for being a selfish git in my younger days.'

'You must have done enough to appease karma by now,' I said. Being a successful businessman, he definitely had that killer instinct in him – but his story sounded pretty plausible to me. And I couldn't help liking him; he was a good dad, and a nice bloke.

'I'd better go and check on my son,' he said, and I nodded.

'Of course.' We headed for the door, but I stopped in front of it. 'One more thing...' I said, doing my best Columbo impression; I'd just remembered something. 'Last night, after dinner – while we were having our tour of the house and you were washing up – you told Joshua you needed to have a talk with Trevor. What was that about?'

'What has that got to do with anything?' he asked. He sounded like he was beginning to get exasperated with me. That happens a lot... I held my hands up, placating him.

'Probably nothing. If nothing else, it'll just help me to completely discount you. Humour me, OK?'

He looked at me, weighing up whether or not to say anything, then laughed. 'What the hell. OK, Trevor asked me if I would invest in this place. He wants to turn it into a hotel and wedding venue.'

'Did he give you the hard sell? Did you know he was going to do that before you turned up yesterday?'

'No, but I sort of expected it. I've had business dealings with him before, and he's a good bloke, so I wouldn't rule out working with him again. You would not believe the places where people have pitched their business ideas to me or asked for money. I had someone pitch me an investment opportunity once when I was sitting on a toilet in a nightclub. Apparently they recognised my shoes through the gap at the bottom of the cubicle door, and they stood outside talking about their business while I, you know...'

'While you did *your* business. Blimey, how rude. Trevor didn't do that, though?'

'No, he wasn't that bad. I got the feeling he asked if I would be interested in investing without actually expecting me to say yes, more because if he didn't take the opportunity he'd regret it.'

'That's fair enough. Are you going to invest?'

He narrowed his eyes. 'Why, if I say yes are you going to want in as well? Or are you just being nosy?'

'I think you know the answer to that,' I said, and he laughed again.

'Reckon I do. No, I'm not going to invest. It's a sound enough business model, and the house and location are lovely, but...there are thousands of places like this out there. I hope they'll make enough to keep ticking over, but it's just not the sort of thing I'm interested in. The only things I back these days are community projects and stuff like that, or businesses that are going to give me a really good return that I can plough back into the charity. This place will never make enough money to make it worth my while.'

'That sounds a bit harsh. I don't suppose Trevor was very happy to hear that.'

He shrugged. 'It's honest. Don't get me wrong, I think they'll do OK, but regardless of how much they invest in the business, there's a limit to what they can charge people. Round here, you can't afford to price out your potential customers. Which means they'd never make enough to satisfy an investor like me and still pay the wages.'

'How did Trevor take it?'

'OK, I think. He was obviously disappointed when I said I wouldn't be investing, but I think he appreciated my insight. Like I said before, we've worked together in the past, he knows it's not personal.' He smiled. 'Now, Detective, can I go and join my son? I'm missing what must be the worst Christmas film ever made.'

I stood back to let him pass. 'Be my guest. I'm just relieved it wasn't *Die Hard*.'

'No, he's seen that one already...'

Chapter Ten

So, where did that leave my investigation? Nowhere, really. If Isaac Barnes was to be believed (and I did believe him), then my for-want-of-someone-better chief suspect no longer had a motive. Of course, he could be lying through his teeth, but then there was the email, sent before the phone line had gone kaput, taking the WiFi with it. Not only would it back up his story, the time it was sent would also prove his claim that, by the time everyone had gone up to bed last night, him and Steve had been on friendly terms. I'd seen evidence of that myself, when I'd taken the coffee in, although the atmosphere in the room had still been a bit tense.

I loitered indecisively in the hallway, wondering what my next course of action should be. I took out my phone, but there were no messages from Nathan, and no signal bars. If he'd been contactable I could have talked it through with him, and then done the opposite of what he told me (which would probably have been to go and wait in the snug and let the police do their job). Blow that.

I could hear voices from inside the snug – not arguing this time, just talking – and a loud blast of Christmas music from the TV in the lounge. Everyone was apparently OK. Maybe I should check on Pippa, make sure no one had smothered her with an antique tapestry or buried her alive in a suit of armour or something… I popped my head round the kitchen door, but everything was fine there, too. Mum had joined her and was currently rummaging through the cupboards, looking for biscuits 'for the kiddies' (yeah, right) and talking nineteen to the dozen, while Pippa sat in the chair with the dazed, somewhat bewildered expression that I quite often saw on people's faces when they were subjected to a Shirley Parker charm offensive.

'And *then* it turned purple and got all swolled up to twice its size, and I thought to myself, Shirley, *that* ain't right…' I quietly slipped away before I got embroiled in whatever disgusting anecdote Mum was currently sharing.

Lily came down the stairs, making me jump.

'Where have you been?' I said, exasperated. These people would just not stay still. 'I told you, we all need to stay together until the police get here.'

'You're out here on your own,' she pointed out. *Don't you start*, I thought. 'Anyway, I had to go to the loo. Or am I supposed to take a chaperone with me for that, too?'

'Sorry,' I said. 'I'm frustrated. I just can't understand why anyone would kill Steve. What can you tell me about him? Apart from him being from Plymouth and desperate to meet Isaac?'

'Nothing. All we knew was that he was a fat bloke with a beard, and he looked like he'd make a great Santa. We didn't need to know anything else, and we didn't ask.'

'No…' We stood in silence for a moment, both deep in thought. I shook myself. 'Anyway, how about we go and have a quick look at the room? Just to make sure nothing's missing.'

'OK.' Lily turned to go up the stairs again. I reached out and put my hand on her arm.

'I do have to warn you, though – the body is pretty nasty.' I looked at her face; it had turned quite white. 'If you want to grab a clean sheet on the way, I can go in first and cover it up. Cover *him* up, I mean.' She nodded. 'OK. I only need you to have a quick look round. It didn't look like anything had been disturbed—' *Other than Steve*, I thought. *He'd been REALLY disturbed…* 'But obviously, I don't know what the room normally looks like. There might be something missing, something the murderer wanted.'

She looked doubtful. 'OK. The room was pretty bare to start off with, but I'm happy to have a look.' Pretty bare? It had been full of antique furniture, and the walls and windows draped with old tapestries, but maybe her idea of minimalism and mine were rather different. I nodded, and we headed upstairs.

On the landing I turned towards the Dyneley Suite, but Lily carried on towards the narrow flight of stairs up to the smaller rooms.

'Where are you going?' I called. She stopped and looked back at me in surprise.

'To Steve's room, where are *you* going?'

'The Dyneley Suite,' I said, pointing along the corridor. She shook her head.

'Why are you going there? That's Isaac's room.'

'No it isn't.'

'Jodie, that's the best room in the house.'

'Maybe it is. It's also the crime scene.' We stared at each other in shock. It made sense now. Lily had said last night that there were four en suite bedrooms and two suites renovated and ready for use. But one of the suites was Trevor's private accommodation, so that only left one fancy room for the impromptu guests to sleep in. Putting aside two rooms for me and my crew, and one for James, who was more likely to get the posh suite rather than the last en suite – the multi-millionaire client who they might still be hoping to tempt into investing in the hotel business, or the borderline alcoholic Santa impersonator they were paying fifteen quid an hour for? Thinking about it now, it didn't make sense that Steve had had that big fancy room all to himself.

'They swapped rooms...' I breathed. That put a whole new spin on things. Lily looked at me.

'But why? I didn't know anything about that. As far as I was aware, Steve was in the room a couple of doors down from you.'

'I don't know...' I shook my head. 'Let's not worry about that now. Let's go and check the room out.'

Lily had stopped off at the linen cupboard and taken out a very large, very white sheet. It wouldn't be white for much longer, I thought, but then it didn't matter; it was better than her seeing the body.

We headed along the corridor, the smell of blood and decay now even stronger. Lily, who still looked pale, blanched even further.

'Breathe through your mouth,' I told her. 'Shallow breaths. You won't smell it so much.' She nodded. I still had the key in my pocket, so when we reached the door I turned to her. 'I'll go in first,' I said. 'I'll cover it – him – over, and then call you in. Don't touch anything, just have a look around. You don't even have to come all the way in if you don't want to. And as soon as you've had enough, just go, don't worry about it, OK?' She nodded again. I unlocked the door and walked in.

Inside, the room was stiflingly hot. My head swam for a moment with the stench, which had got really bad over the last hour or so. The grisly sight on the bed had got no less horrific, so I hurried over and gently draped the sheet over the naked and late Father Christmas. At least he had a little bit of dignity now. With the sword protruding from his back it was impossible to cover his bulk, his head *and* his legs, so I had to leave them uncovered. I shivered, despite the heat of the room; the limp, lifeless way they stuck out from the sheet and hung over the edge of the bed just felt so unnatural. You could easily freak yourself out, staring at them, waiting for the corpse to move. They were pasty and white, and looked like bloated sausages.

I felt the bile rise in my throat and staggered away to the window. It was still quite dark in here, with the curtains shut, so I yanked them open and then unlatched the window, throwing it open wide to let in a welcome blast of cold air. I took a deep breath before turning back into the room.

'It's OK, you can come in.'

Lily gingerly stood in the doorway, her eyes immediately drawn to the figure on the bed.

'Oh my God,' she gasped. I moved over to her and took her hand.

'I know, it's horrible. Don't look. You don't need to see him. I just need you to have a quick look around the room and tell me if anything is missing, or out of place, or just looks weird. Apart from the body on the bed with the big sword sticking out of it, of course.'

She gave me a sickly smile. 'Yeah, that definitely wasn't in here before...' She wandered a little way further into the room, then stopped and looked around carefully.

'It's really hot in here,' I said. 'I think that's why the smell's so bad.'

She gulped. 'Yeah, it's not good. There's a heater on the wall opposite the window, he must've left it on all night.' She swallowed hard. 'We weren't allowed to put radiators in this part of the house, so we got one of those fancy hot-and-cold fan heaters. It's meant to be an air purifier as well.' She swallowed again, and I could tell she was feeling nauseous. 'It doesn't smell very pure to me.'

I looked around and spotted the heater. It was quiet, but as I stepped closer I could feel the heat it was pumping out. In a room like this, the thick stone walls and floor acted like a heat sink, keeping it warm for ages. No wonder it felt so oppressively hot in here. I reached out and turned it off.

'The heat will have speeded up decomposition as well,' I murmured to myself. She shook her head.

'Sorry, I have to get out of here—' She disappeared at speed, probably heading for the nearest bathroom.

Poor Lily. As dead bodies go, this one was pretty gruesome.

I carefully picked my way past the bed and the heater, careful not to touch or knock anything. There was a door set into the red-painted partition wall, and it had been left open, so, without touching the door knob, I went in.

The en suite bathroom was lit by a small window in the opposite wall. The room smelled strongly of urine, and I could see that the lid and seat of the toilet were both up. Wrinkling my nose, I peered over – yep, the late occupant had relieved himself and not flushed. Charming. Mind you, after the amount of brandy he'd consumed, it was lucky that he'd even hit the target. Grimacing, I stepped quickly away, just in case his aim hadn't been entirely accurate…

I had a proper look around the bathroom and bedroom, but other than the small, badly placed writing desk against one wall (I would have put it in the middle of the wall, and it annoyed my fastidious nature that it was off-centre), everything you'd expect to see in a hotel bedroom and bathroom was present and correct. It was untidy, but that was down to the deceased; his clothes were thrown in a pile on the floor between the bathroom and the bed, his shoes half underneath the four-poster. And then of course there was the leather belt, encircling the bed post and the pile of bedding. Had he been playing some kinky sex game, like Debbie had suggested? And if so, who had he been playing it with?

I reached out and pulled the window towards me, deciding to leave it open a little bit to let that awful smell out and some fresh air in, then hurried out, shutting the door behind me and giving the ex-Saint Nick some privacy.

Chapter Eleven

I walked down the stairs, deep in thought. The revelation that Isaac was originally supposed to be in that room had thrown me. Did that mean *Isaac* was the intended victim?

It made sense. By his own admission, he must have made a lot of enemies in his life. He might be Mr Nice Guy now, but he'd been utterly ruthless in his business days and, although he'd set about putting things right, there could well be other people whose lives he'd unwittingly ruined, and who he hadn't caught up with. But the only person we *knew* had had reason to hate him – maybe reason enough to kill him – was upstairs, naked and impaled on an antique sword. And Isaac had (apparently) made things right with Steve anyway, so even he wouldn't have wanted Isaac dead; in fact, with the multi-millionaire philanthropist dead, Steve's son wouldn't get any help.

Who else could have wanted Isaac dead? Trevor could have been annoyed with him for refusing to invest in the hotel. But killing him wouldn't help Trevor's finances, so there'd be absolutely no point to the murder. What about James? He'd been acting a bit weird this morning – on edge, and quite unlike the cheerful, confident, flirtatious young man he'd been yesterday. And there was all that business (whatever it was) last night, in his room. But why would he want Isaac (or Steve) dead? They seemed to get on really well. He held a high position in the charity foundation, and there was nothing to suggest that he'd benefit financially or in career terms if Isaac died. And he just didn't strike me as a killer. He was charming, if a bit immature, but in my experience a lot of ex-public schoolboys were.

And there was still the issue of how someone had got into the room in the first place. The door would have been locked; it was the type that locked as you pulled it shut behind you. So Steve would have gone (staggered) to bed, shutting it behind him. How had the murderer got in?

Lily came out of the kitchen carrying a glass of water.

'You OK?' I asked her. She nodded.

'I know you warned me, but that was much worse

than I thought it would be,' she said. 'That was the first time I've seen a dead person.'

'Not a great one for your first time. Can I ask you, who knew who was staying in each room?'

'Me, Trevor and Pippa,' she said. 'Trevor and I worked out which rooms were ready to use, and Pippa helped me make up the beds. I showed you guys your rooms, but Isaac and Steve didn't know where they were sleeping until they went up to bed.'

'And then they ended up in each other's rooms...' I shook my head. 'No offence, the room you gave me and Daisy last night was lovely, but if you'd given me that suite I'd be moving in there permanently. Why would Isaac want to swap?' Lily of course had just as much idea about that as I did. 'Where are the spare room keys kept? Are they locked away?'

'The housekeeping keys?' Lily looked sheepish. 'No, they're not. Trevor keeps them in his bedroom at the moment. I know that's not very safe, but you have to remember we're not actually open as a hotel yet. We still haven't got a proper reception area set up. Half the doors didn't even have locks on them until last week – we only got them done so we could lock away the renovating stuff and all the tools while the party was on, in case any of the children got upstairs.'

'So anyone could have got hold of the keys, if they knew where Trevor kept them?'

'Well, no, not really. After Germaine got in and jumped on his bed, he locked the door of his apartment. And no one would have stolen them before then, because at that point we didn't know you were staying, did we? And only me and Trevor knew where he'd put them. Not even Pippa knew where they were until I told her this morning.'

'Right…' That didn't help me very much. I couldn't see Trevor or Lily having a motive to kill anyone. But then they'd both had opportunity, hadn't they? They both knew where the room keys were. And neither of them had an alibi; Debbie and Mum, me and Daisy, Isaac and Joshua – none of us had slept alone, and we all had someone to vouch for us being in our rooms all night. So, for that matter, did Bea and Liam (*except they're in it together*, I thought), and the Japanese girls. James, though, had slept alone, in one of the rooms near ours. Lily had spent the night on a mattress, in one of the downstairs rooms, while Trevor had slept upstairs in his private apartment.

Lily was looking at me curiously, obviously waiting for me to say something else. I hoped she hadn't realised that I was running the likelihood of her being a murderer through my mind. I cleared my throat.

'Why did you tell Pippa to go into the room this morning?' I asked.

'Breakfast was ready,' she said. 'And I wanted to

make sure everyone was fed and ready to get on the road in case we had more snow. We'd checked the news and they said the road across the moors was clear, so I thought you'd all be keen to get going – you wouldn't want to get snowed in for another night.'

'Why didn't you just call up to the rooms?'

'Not all the rooms have phones, and even the ones that do aren't hooked up yet. I told her to just go and knock, and if there was no answer to pop her head round the door and call out.'

I nodded. 'OK. Did Pippa tell you anything about what she saw? How she found the body?'

'No, she was in complete shock. We took her into the lounge to lie down, and I tried to ask her about it but she just wanted to be left alone for a bit. I didn't want to push her. She still seems pretty freaked out.'

'I'm not surprised, that would be enough to give anyone a turn. I think I do need to talk to her, though.'

'Just be gentle with her, will you?' Lily looked concerned. 'Pippa's been through a lot. She lost her husband a few years ago and had all sorts of problems with her son when he was little. She was already a bit nervy. God knows how this will affect her long term.'

'I'll be nice.' I smiled. 'I can be nice. But maybe you'd better come with me for moral support.'

Pippa was still in the kitchen, being talked at by Mum, who was perched on a stool by the kitchen counter, inhaling a packet of chocolate Hobnobs.

'So *of course* I got the doctor to look at it – such a nice young man – a proper looker – if I was twenty years younger—'

'Thirty,' I corrected absentmindedly. 'Mum, can you go and check on Daisy?'

'She's with Debbie.'

'Then you can check on Debbie while you're there as well.' Mum looked at me like I was mad, then her face cleared in understanding.

'Oh yeah, right you are, Guv,' she said, snapping off a quick salute. She turned on her heel, making sure to take the packet of biscuits with her. Pippa looked at me in helpless bewilderment.

'Don't mind her,' I said. 'She's getting on a bit.'

'Dementia?'

'God no, she's just really annoying, always has been. You OK to have a little chat?' Pippa looked like she was going to say no, but Lily pulled the stool over and sat down next to her. She took her hand.

'It's really important, Pip. Jodie knows what she's doing.' *I hope you're right,* I thought.

'All right. Although I'm not sure what I can tell you. I didn't see anything.'

'Sometimes we spot things that are significant

without even realising we saw them. We'll just have a chat while it's all still fresh in your mind, and see what comes up.' I smiled at her reassuringly. 'Now, can you tell me what happened this morning when you went up to the room?'

'You know what happened. I found him on the bed, like that.'

'I know, I know. Look, let's take it from the very beginning. Lily asked you to go and knock Steve up.'

'Not just Steve, Isaac and his little boy too. No one had seen either of them, so we thought they were still in their rooms.'

'Ah, OK. So did you go to the other room – the one on the upper floor – or just the Dyneley Suite?'

'Just the Dyneley Suite. I thought I'd do that one first, then the other room.' She gave a little shudder. 'But of course I didn't get that far.'

I leaned forward and put my hand on her arm. 'You're doing really well, being very brave. I know you don't want to think about it, but we need to know what happened.'

'You're not the police, though,' she said. 'I don't have to talk to you at all.'

'No, no you don't,' I said, 'but I'm only asking what they'll ask you. And I'm more sympathetic than they'll be.'

'If you go over it with Jodie first, it'll make it easier

when they talk to you,' said Lily. 'You'll know what you want to say. And she might even be able to talk to them on your behalf.' There wasn't much chance of that happening – Pippa was an important witness – but I wasn't going to put Lily right.

Pippa still looked reluctant, but I wasn't giving in.

'So you thought you'd check on Isaac and Joshua first. You knew they'd been given the Dyneley Suite?'

'Yes,' she said. 'Lily told me the night before where everyone was sleeping.'

'When you got up to the room, was the door locked or had it been left open?' She looked at me for a moment like she didn't understand what I was saying. 'When you came down the stairs, you had the key in your hand, yeah? And the door upstairs was left ajar. Was it already like that, or did you unlock the door and take the key out?'

'I…' She hesitated. *Oh for goodness' sake!* I thought. *It's not a trick question!*

'Was the door locked or unlocked?' I tried to keep the exasperation out of my voice. It was a simple enough question, and it might help the police work out how the murderer got in or, perhaps more to the point, how they got out again. If they were panicking or distressed – if the murder had been spontaneous, or maybe they'd acted in self-defence – they might not have thought to shut the door behind them in their eagerness to get away from the scene. If they'd been calmer – if they'd planned the attack – they might have taken care to shut the door, hoping perhaps that by the time the body had been discovered they would have already left the abbey. 'Maybe Steve had left the door open?'

'It was…locked.' She sounded like she was thinking aloud. 'Yeah…it was locked.'

'Definitely?'

'Yes. Yes, it was. I went up and the door was shut, so I unlocked it.' She looked at Lily. 'I'm sorry, the whole thing is so horrible, I can't remember all the details.'

'It's OK,' said Lily, patting her on the hand and looking at me with a *Go easy on her* expression on her face. I gave her a slight nod.

'What did you do then?' I asked, as gently as I could.

'I looked in and I saw him on the bed. And I noticed the smell.' She shuddered.

'Yeah, that was pretty bad… Did you turn the light on?'

'Why?'

'Well, it was quite dark in there. The police will take fingerprints off things like the door handle, the lock and the light switch, so if you did, they'll need to take your prints to eliminate them.'

'Oh, I see… No, I didn't. I thought, if Isaac had overslept, then it would be rude to turn it on and wake him up like that. I had the room door open wide and there was enough light from the hallway for me to see the shape on the bed – and the sword...' Her voice shook.

'It's OK, that's all I need to know,' I said. 'Thank you.' Lily patted her on the arm again.

'You've done really well. Why don't you come into the snug and join everyone else? It'll take your mind off it.'

'Maybe later,' she said, but I could tell she didn't really want to. I nodded.

'OK. Well, you know where we are if you need us.'

Debbie poked her head around the kitchen door. 'Are you done in here?' she asked.

'Yeah, why?'

'The Japanese girls have disappeared and no one knows where they are...'

I returned to the snug. James was sitting by the fire, looking tense. He had yesterday's newspaper in his hands and was apparently reading it, but I could see that he was just going over and over the same page, not taking it in, unable to concentrate. I really wanted to ask him about his midnight visitor, but not in front of Bea and Liam, who were on the other side of the room talking quietly between themselves. I just did not like those two at all.

'Where's Hina and her friends?' I said. James looked up, surprised.

'I don't know. They were worried about their car. Maybe they went outside to see if the damage was as bad as they thought it was last night?' I pointed to a pile of jackets on another chair.

'Their coats are still here. They wouldn't have gone outside without them. Didn't you hear what they were saying before they left?'

'I don't eavesdrop on people's conversations,' said James, and I wondered for a moment if he knew that I'd been listening outside his door the night before. He couldn't do. Could he? He gave a sudden rueful grin. 'Actually, I do, but not when it's in a foreign language that I have to concentrate on. I might sound fluent to you, but I'm not a native.'

'Fair enough. Let me know if you see them, will you? I think we all need to keep together.'

'Why?' Across the room Bea looked up, watching me with interest. I returned her gaze coolly.

'Because there's quite possibly a murderer in the house.' *And I haven't ruled you and your partner out yet*, I thought, but I didn't really suspect them of murder. I suspected them of *something*, but I wasn't sure what.

Debbie came into the snug.

'Found them?' I asked. She shook her head.

'They're nowhere downstairs. You don't think it was them, and they've done a runner?' she asked quietly.

'Why would a bunch of Japanese tourists kill Santa Claus? Do they even have Santa in Japan?'

'Blowed if I know,' she said. 'You're right, I can't see any of them being the murderer.'

'No. But let's not forget that *someone* here is, and until we know what their motive was, there's no way of knowing whether or not they'll strike again.' I looked at her seriously. 'We need to find them.'

'The girls or the murderer?'

'Both, preferably. But let's concentrate on the girls first.'

'Maybe we should get everyone together and set up a search party—'

'We can't, can we? Would you want to go and explore with someone who might be a killer?'

'I hadn't thought of that. OK, so what do we do?'

I smiled at her. 'What we do best. We go and have a nose around.'

———

Debbie had already searched the other rooms downstairs, so we made our way up to the first floor.

We'd just reached the top of the stairs when we heard footsteps behind us.

'Do you need some help?' It was James. Debbie looked at me meaningfully – *He could be the murderer!* – but despite his lack of an alibi, his night-time visitor and his weird mood this morning, I still couldn't see him murdering Steve. 'I thought I could act as an interpreter. You're looking for the girls, I assume?'

'Yes, we are,' I said. 'Thank you, I'm sure your language skills will be helpful.'

He smiled. 'Like I said, I'm not fluent, but I can make myself understood.' He joined us, Debbie looking at me again with an expression of *Are you sure about this?!* on her face. I gave her a slight nod.

'Shall we split up?' he asked.

'Yeah, let's.' Debbie was almost indecently hasty to get rid of him. 'Why don't you look upstairs?'

'Cool.' He turned and went up the second flight of stairs. Debbie turned on me.

'What are you like? What did you say to me downstairs? He could be the murderer.'

'I know, but I don't think he is. Anyway, if he tried anything, I reckon you and I could have him, no trouble. He went to a posh school, remember, whereas we grew up on the mean streets.'

Debbie snorted. 'The mean streets of Penstowan? It ain't exactly South Central LA.'

'No, it's worse. I've seen grown men fighting over the last pasty at Rowe's. It can get proper nasty, I'm telling you.' We stopped in front of a door. 'I don't even know if any of these rooms will be open. Lily said they'd locked the renovating stuff away, so…'

Debbie reached out and tried the handle of one of the suites. It turned. 'Maybe they unlocked them last night when they were deciding which rooms to use.'

We went inside. This room was larger than the crime scene, and lighter; the windows were taller, and the ceiling felt higher. This must be a part of the house that had been added later. The floor was bare wooden boards, and the few bits of furniture remaining had been pushed against a wall. Paint pots and a ladder were propped up in a corner, and it was pretty obvious that there was nowhere for a gaggle of Japanese girls to hide.

'This room's bigger than the first flat I had back in Manchester,' said Debbie, looking around. I nodded.

'Yup, I lived in a shoebox in South London when I first left home. You could have fit the entire apartment into this room and still had space left over.'

We checked the other suites. One was locked. Debbie told me it was Trevor's private apartment, which she'd been in the previous afternoon, rescuing the four-poster bed from Germaine's attentions; there was no way the girls could have got in there. The rest were much the same as the first, in various stages of renovation – apart, of course, from the suite at the end of the corridor, but neither of us had any desire to go in there again unless we really had to.

'I hope James has had more luck,' I said, as we shut the last door behind us. Debbie looked at me darkly.

'I just hope he didn't find them and do away with them all.'

'Why would he kill them? They were fawning all over him last night. He'd be more likely to try and sleep with them, I reckon.' I was joking, but I suddenly wondered if his visitor the night before had been one of the girls. Maybe they'd taken his flirting seriously? But then James had angrily turned them down. He didn't strike me as sleazy enough to actually take them up on the offer (if indeed they'd made him one of that sort), but he was nothing if not polite and well mannered, and I would have expected him to show a bit of good grace and gently let them down. Plus, while young women could be promiscuous (and good luck to them if that's what they wanted – the thought of stripping down to just my Marks & Spencer cotton undies with someone I didn't know sounded like a complete nightmare to me), for some reason I didn't think Japanese ones were. From the little I knew of the society (all gleaned from movies and fiction, so probably completely wrong), they were, if anything, a bit repressed, being very polite and concerned with status. I shook my head, suddenly disgusted with myself. I'd missed the most obvious point. The conversation I'd heard the night before – James's side of it, at least – had been in English, not Japanese. Even Hina only had a smattering of English, certainly not enough to try and seduce someone with. If it *had* been her (and even though I hadn't been able to make out the unknown visitor's half of the conversation, I'd heard enough to be pretty certain they'd been female), surely James would have let her down in her own tongue. I noticed Debbie looking at me. 'What?'

'You've been going through all these scenarios involving James either murdering or sleeping with someone in your head and dismissing them, haven't you?'

'Am I that obvious? I just think he's a nice bloke.'

'Jack the Ripper probably seemed like "a nice bloke" to anyone he wasn't murdering, that's how he got away with it.'

'The only reason you don't like him is because he's a bit posh. James is—' Our conversation was interrupted by a high-pitched scream from the floor above us. Debbie looked at me, an eyebrow raised.

'You were saying?'

We legged it up the stairs and into the corridor. With all the room doors shut and the overhead lights off it was dark, and the hallway was empty. I briefly wondered if the scream had actually been the ghostly howl of the so-far conspicuous-by-her-absence Grey Lady, but I was disabused of that daft notion as Hina came thundering around the corner where I'd hidden the night before and charged into us.

'Hina! What's the matter? What's happened?' I grabbed her by the shoulders and looked into her face. I thought for a moment that she was crying, but when she tossed her head back I realised she was laughing.

'Is she hysterical?' asked Debbie, drawing her hand back as if to slap her around the face.

'No she isn't!' I shook my head at her. 'Bloody hell, woman, you're a bit quick to throw your hands around, aren't you? No wonder Callum does as he's told.' I looked back at Hina, a serious expression on my face. 'Hina, stop. What's going on?'

She managed to stop laughing long enough to point behind her. I turned her around and practically frogmarched her along the corridor, round the bend and towards the short staircase up to the tower. As we reached it we were almost knocked off our feet by another girl careering down the stone steps. She was laughing so hard she slipped and nearly fell over. I put out a hand to catch her and stop her banging her head on the hard floor, although I'm (slightly) ashamed to admit that, what with their disappearing act and now all this irritating shrieking and laughing, the girls were starting to annoy me, and part of me wanted to let her fall over. That would shut her up.

'Where are the others? Have you seen James?'

Hina said something, and they both laughed, then pointed up the stairs. Debbie and I exchanged looks. 'Stay there,' I said firmly, with a *stay!* gesture and an expression that I like to think you wouldn't need to know English to understand, and marched up to the tower.

It was empty. I gave a big frustrated *aaargh*, and was about to leave when I heard a muffled banging noise coming from behind me. I turned slowly... there was nothing there...

'Jodie! Help!' I jumped and looked out of the window. James was outside, on the roof, scrabbling to get the window open. I grabbed the latch and wrestled it open – it was old, rusty and quite stiff, and I had to bash it with the side of my hand Bruce Lee-style a couple of times to get it to move – letting him and half a ton of snow inside.

'What the blazes...?'

'Those blasted women!' said James, hopping around, rubbing his hands together to try and warm up. If someone had done that to me, I'd have said something a bit stronger than 'blasted'. I reached out and started to rub my own, much warmer hands briskly up and down his arms, like he was a toddler or something.

'Hina and her friends shut you out there?' I asked in amazement. He nodded.

'I found them up here, playing hide and seek,' he said. 'I told them we should all go downstairs, but they said they were bored and that this was fun. Then one of them said she'd opened the window to look out, and her earring had fallen off into the snow. She seemed really upset, so I offered to climb out and get it – the roof's flat here, so I didn't think it would be difficult. And then the minx shut the window!' He shook his head in amazement. 'I love Japanese culture, but they do have a weird sense of humour.'

'How long had you been out there?'

'Only about a minute. I'm sure she'd have let me back in, but the window got stuck and she couldn't open it. It probably didn't help that she was laughing so much.' He smiled ruefully. 'I am a sucker for a damsel in distress. What an absolute idiot.'

'Not an idiot. It was really nice of you to help them. They shouldn't have done that, bored or not. Did you find all four of them?'

He shook his head. 'No, the other two are hiding in the rooms downstairs.' He grinned. 'I did give them a thorough telling off, about wandering around the house without permission. I probably deserved it for spoiling their fun.'

'Rubbish.' I dropped my hands and smiled at him. 'Come on, let's go and find the others and tell them off, too.'

Chapter Twelve

W e found the other two girls and marched them all downstairs, where I gave them a right rollicking, James translating. Their laughter stopped as I explained why we needed to all stay together.

'The man who died – we think—' Hina mimed clutching at her chest and keeling over. I shook my head.

'No. It was murder.' I then mimed back at her, grabbing an invisible dagger and plunging it into Debbie in a frenzy of stabbing, like something out of *Psycho*. Debbie played the part of victim a little too well, clutching at her 'wound' and staggering back before dying slowly, painfully, and, if truth be told, a bit cheesily. I made a mental note to tell her about the local am dram group, who were always looking for new blood. The girls all squealed and huddled closer together.

James said a few words and they all nodded, then he turned to me.

'They'll be as good as gold from now on,' he said. We all turned as Bea came out of the snug to see what was going on.

'Everything OK?' she called. James scowled, his good mood disappearing again.

'The police had better get here soon though, before we all go mad.' He pushed past her and went back into the snug, no doubt to resume pretending to read the newspaper. *Interesting,* I thought.

I made my way back to the lounge to relieve Daisy and Germaine of their babysitting duties, but they were both engrossed in the Christmas movie, where Nick Festive was in the process of admitting that yes, he was indeed Santa, and he was helping a grieving family rediscover the Spirit of Christmas. Isaac looked up and smiled as I sat down next to him.

'Any further on with the investigation, Detective?' he asked me in a low voice. I shrugged.

'More confused than ever,' I admitted. 'But that normally means I'm on the verge of a breakthrough.'

'Really?'

'Yes,' I said, hoping it wasn't obvious I was lying. 'Can I ask – why did you swap rooms with Steve last night? And who else knew about it?'

'Joshua and I went up to bed not long after you – I

think it was just gone ten? Poor little man was almost asleep on his feet.' Isaac glanced affectionately over at his son. 'But he really did not like that room. He thought it was spooky. Our place is a big, modern, glass and concrete box, nothing like this, so he's not used to old houses and all the creaks and noises they make. And apparently he heard Lily telling you about people being hung, drawn and quartered, and he wanted to know what that meant because it was obviously bad. So I did, which probably didn't help matters. Anyway, I couldn't get him to settle, so we went downstairs – I was going to see if any of the young ladies wanted to use it, and we'd sleep in here or something. But we found Steve in the kitchen, and he offered to swap with us.'

'So you slept on the floor above, in one of the en suite rooms?'

He nodded. 'Yes. Joshua was much happier and fell asleep straight away.'

'Was anyone else around when you and Steve agreed to swap? Did anyone hear you talking about it?'

He looked thoughtful. 'James came in when we were discussing it. He said Steve's room was next to his, so if we swapped he could give me a knock in the morning.'

I smiled. 'James doesn't have kids, does he?' He laughed.

'No. Joshua woke me up at six, wanting to build a

snowman. I heard you get up with the dog and he was quite keen to come with you, but it was just too cold.'

'You're not wrong, it was *freezing*,' I said. But I was thinking, *James knew...* So that, to my mind anyway, put him in the clear. He could (feasibly) have had a motive for killing Isaac, and could have ended up killing Steve by mistake as he was in what should have been Isaac's room, but if he'd known they'd swapped, that put paid to that theory. And actually, how could *anyone* mistake Steve for Isaac? Isaac was half the Santa impersonator's girth, and probably a good few inches taller. Even in the dark you'd be hard pushed to mistake one for the other. 'Did you hear anything else, earlier in the night? Any comings or goings? Voices?'

Isaac looked at me keenly. 'No... Why? Do you think someone on our floor had something to do with it?'

'No, I just—'

Germaine suddenly sat up, her ears pricked.

'What's the matter with your dog?' asked Isaac. But before I could answer, she'd leaped up and trotted out into the hallway, tail wagging as she headed for the front door.

'Probably just needs to relieve herself,' I said, following her. She gave a little whine and scratched at the wood. I reached up to open the door...

...and then jumped back in shock at the sight of Nathan standing in front of me, hand raised to knock. He jumped too, then laughed as Germaine launched herself at him (or at his legs, anyway), yapping excitedly. He bent down to make a fuss of her.

'Yes, I'm pleased to see you too,' he said.

'What are you doing here?' I gasped.

He grinned. 'Isn't it obvious? I came to rescue you.'

'Came to stop me poking my nose in, more like,' I said, but I was so pleased to see him. 'I didn't even hear you come up the drive.'

He gestured over his shoulder. Behind him stood a very fancy, very new-looking police car. I was surprised; he didn't normally drive a marked car. 'It's one of the new electric cars we've been trying out. Doesn't freeze up in the snow and it creeps up on criminals.'

I stood back to let him in, then prised Germaine off his leg and hugged him. 'Sorry, I know I shouldn't kiss you when you're on duty, but—' He laughed.

'It's OK, no one's looking...' But we were interrupted by Trevor and James behind us.

'Are you the police? Finally!' James looked relieved. Nathan turned, taking out his warrant card.

'DCI Nathan Withers from Penstowan CID. Are the officers from Carricksmoor not here yet?'

'No they're not,' said James, irritably. 'We need to get this over with so people can go home.'

'Absolutely, sir.' Nathan was always polite, but especially so to rude people. He was often so polite that they would suspect him of being rude himself, but there was never anything they could actually point to to prove that, which just made them confused and sometimes, even ruder. 'My colleague, DS Turner, is following and should be here very soon to take statements from everyone. If you could please listen out for him? Thank you.'

'What? Can't you at least get the ball rolling? This is taking ages—'

'Are you the owner of the house, sir?'

'No,' said Trevor, 'I am. Trevor Manning.'

'Mr Manning, if you could keep your house guests together, so that when DS Turner and the officers from Carricksmoor turn up they know where find everyone, that would be very helpful. In the meantime I need to inspect the crime scene. Ms Parker here can show me where it is.' Nathan gave Trevor and James his most polite smile, and stayed where he was until Trevor managed to shepherd a grumbling James back into the snug.

Nathan turned to me. 'Well, that one seems like a bit of a character.'

'James? He's all right, he's just a bit stressed. He's Isaac Barnes' right-hand man. Maybe that's what comes of working for a multi-millionaire.'

'Glad I'm a copper, then. Upstairs?'

We headed up the stairs.

'How's Matt getting here?' I asked. 'Why didn't he come with you?' Nathan's detective sergeant, Matt Turner, always accompanied him on cases, and I had the feeling that Nathan quite enjoyed taking the young officer under his wing.

'I managed to walk to the station, but he was stuck out at the family farm...' Nathan's cottage was in town, not far from the police station, but I vaguely remembered Matt saying that he lived in a barn conversion on his dad's farm, a few miles outside of Penstowan. 'He said they had to dig out their driveway, and then he'd borrow his dad's old Land Rover and meet me here.'

'I just hope it's not a diesel engine...'

We reached the top of the stairs. Nathan's nostrils twitched.

'Holy moly, that's not nice.'

'Yep, the smell is pretty bad. Just be thankful I turned the heating off in the room and opened the window.' I turned towards the Dyneley Suite, but Nathan touched me on the arm to stop me.

'Before we go in, catch me up on who's here. You, Daisy, Debbie and your mum – who else stayed overnight?' I went through the list of the abbey's snow refugees, Nathan's eyebrows getting higher and higher as I told him about the unexpected arrival of the Japanese eco-tourists and the enigmatic (and highly suspicious, to me at least) Bea and Liam. He sighed. 'Oh good, so we've got loads of possible suspects. I do love it when we've got at least ten people who could've done it. It makes my life so much easier than when there's just one person with a really obvious motive.' He looked at me hopefully. 'There *isn't* just one person with a really obvious motive that you haven't told me about yet, is there?'

'There's not even anyone with an *un*obvious motive,' I said.

'I suspected as much.'

I unlocked the door and stood back to let him in.

'You not coming in?'

'Am I supposed to?'

'No, but when's that ever stopped you? And I'm not going to tell anyone, am I?' He reached into his pocket and drew out two pairs of latex gloves, handing one pair to me. 'You know you want to.'

I smiled. 'Some couples go out for dinner, you know. Some go dancing, or to the theatre...'

'Yeah yeah, don't try and tell me you haven't already had a poke around in here. Tell me what you've come up with.'

We went inside. Steve's bulk was still covered by the sheet I'd thrown over him earlier. Nathan reached out and twitched it aside.

'Ooh, that's nasty…'

'The undignified position he ended up in, or the cause of death?' Coppers and emergency responders, in my experience, often end up with a slightly inappropriate sense of humour. When you're surrounded by evidence of the frailty of your own existence, or by the horror of humanity's worst behaviour, you have to be able to laugh to stop yourself falling into a black pit of existential despair, even if it's forced. Sometimes it helps. But not always.

'Both.' Nathan walked around the bed, studying the body closely – far more closely than I had been able to bring myself to do. 'That must be a very long sword. He wasn't exactly small, was he, and yet it's gone all the way through him. That'd take some doing.'

'It's weird, innit?' I said.

'A naked Santa impersonator with a sword sticking out of him? Yeah, it is a bit,' said Nathan mildly. I shook my head.

'No, I don't mean that. I mean, the way the body's been left. It's – unnatural.' I stared at him. 'And I know the whole thing's "unnatural", I just mean – there's something not right about the way he was killed. It's just – odd.'

Nathan looked at me keenly. 'I think I know what you mean…' He turned again to the corpse, then looked around the room. On the side table I'd spotted before lay a notepad and pen. Nathan took the pen and gingerly prodded at the pillow under Steve's face. 'These feathers – they've come from a gash in the pillow, which suggests some kind of fight, maybe? The sword's slashed through the pillow case, so someone was waving it around.' He moved his gaze along to the body itself, and I almost gagged as he poked at the cold flesh.

'What are you doing?'

'Looking at the site of the wound.' Nathan shuddered as he attempted to lift up the loose flesh of Steve's large, saggy belly, pressed against the bed. He grimaced. 'It looks like the sword is buried up to the hilt, although with all these pillows under him it's difficult to see properly. That really *would* take some doing.' He turned to me again, holding the pen up as if it were a sword. 'Imagine I'm trying to stab you through the chest—'

'Don't you get that pen anywhere near me!' I said, leaping back. It had touched a dead person. A *really* dead person. Eww. Nathan looked down it, then dropped it on the bed and held up his hand instead, grasping an invisible weapon.

'Imagine I'm stabbing you through the chest,' he said again, advancing on me. 'Bearing in mind that it's not as easy to stab a human being as people think, and the murderer would have to hit him with some force to get the sword all the way through him.' Nathan reached out and pushed me firmly in the chest. I staggered backwards, putting a hand out behind me to stop myself crashing into the wall. He leaped forward and grabbed me.

'Sorry. But I think I know why the position of the body looks odd.'

'Because he's fallen forwards,' I said slowly. 'And if someone had stabbed him in the chest, particularly with the force needed to drive it all the way through, he would have fallen backwards...'

'Exactly!'

'So that means...?'

'Buggered if I know. Yet.' He still had hold of me. 'Sorry I pushed you so hard. Are you all right?'

'Yeah, I'm Cornish, remember – we're tough.' Although I didn't feel very tough when I looked at the body on the bed. Here I was, in Nathan's arms; only last night I'd been dreaming about spending time with him in a room just like this, but the elephant (Santa) in the room put a whole new perspective on the matter. I shuddered. I'd settle for a romantic getaway in a tent after this, although maybe we'd wait until after the snow had melted. Nathan let go of me and I straightened up.

'So, I've been stabbed, right...' I grasped an invisible sword that was protruding from my chest. 'I stagger back —' I staggered back. 'I could, feasibly, bend forward, trying to yank the sword out of my body—' I demonstrated. 'So I could overbalance with the shock and blood loss, and topple forward...' I toppled forward, stopping myself before I did actually fall over. 'So that could account for how I ended up face down on the bed. Couldn't it?'

'Yeah...' Nathan looked doubtful. 'But if that's the case, where did the attack take place? There's no sign of any disturbance in any other part of the room, apart from around the bed where his clothes and that are on the floor, and the pillow feathers, of course. It must've happened right next to the bed, in which case, where's the attacker during all this? *On* the bed? That seems unlikely. I can't see that someone sitting on the bed would get enough thrust—' Nathan swung his arm back and mimed thrusting the sword into someone.

'No, you're right...' I looked at the corpse thoughtfully, so deep in thought that I almost wasn't even seeing him. I was trying to imagine how the murder could possibly have played out. 'OK, how about this? Someone is on the bed...'

'Who? Male or female? Why are they there?'

'I don't know, do I? Let's just say female, for argument's sake. There for some kind of assignation, which also explains how they got in – Steve let them in. Maybe he invited them up. Maybe he thought he'd got lucky when they knocked on the door. And that also explains why he's naked. Whatever. They're on the bed, maybe they didn't know what Steve was expecting—'

'And he was expecting…?'

'Sexy time.' I looked at Steve's bulk and his naked buttocks and shuddered. '*Kinky* sexy time. Have you seen the leather belt? Maybe he wanted to tie her up. Or her to tie *him* up.'

Nathan grimaced. 'Takes all sorts, doesn't it?'

'Anyway, maybe they – she – saw what kind of weird shenanigans he was planning, changed her mind and tried to get away, but Steve wasn't taking no for an answer. He went to grab her, she picked up the sword, and his momentum as he leaped on her did the rest. He impaled himself on the sword and his weight drove it right into him.'

'So who and where is this mysterious woman? And how did the sword get in here?' Nathan looked at the bed and shook his head. 'She would have been pinned under the body.'

'Not if she moved quickly enough,' I said defiantly, but he was right. My theory didn't really work. 'But then all of the women have alibis, anyway. The Japanese girls are all out of his league – sorry, Santa – plus they all slept together in the snug. And Bea stayed with Liam.'

'What about your mum?' asked Nathan, with a grin. I laughed.

'I wouldn't put it past her to arrange a secret assignation with a man, but I can't see her taking a weapon along, can you?'

'Maybe he was fighting her off…' I reached out and swatted his arm.

'Oi! That's my mum you're talking about. I mean, you're not wrong, but only I can say stuff like that about her. And Debbie shared a room with her, anyway.'

'What about your friend? The one who got you the gig?'

'Lily?' I frowned. 'I don't actually know where she slept. There weren't any more bedrooms, so she said she would sleep downstairs with the others, but I don't know where. But I can't see her wanting to get jiggy with Santa, and she's not a murderer. I've known her since school.'

'*Every* murderer has someone who's known them since school,' said Nathan. 'That doesn't mean anything. But OK, let's say it was none of the women. What about the men? I can't see someone like Isaac Barnes getting his hands dirty with something like this.'

'Isaac and Steve *did* argue,' I said, 'but by the time they went to bed it was all sorted out.' I told Nathan about Steve's son, and how his life had been ruined by Isaac. 'Isaac sent his PA an email last night, after the argument, setting out how he was going to help Steve's son. It proves that they'd made up. Plus he slept with his son, Joshua.'

'What about the owner? Manning?'

'Trevor? He wants to set this place up as a wedding venue. A grisly murder's not going to attract many blushing brides, is it? "Spend your first night as a married couple in the infamous Dyneley Suite, where a Santa impersonator from Plymouth met a sticky end." You wouldn't want *that* in your brochure, would you?'

'That's a fair point. Who else is there? Who was that stroppy bugger again, the one just now as I came in?'

'James.' I shook my head. 'Even if James does like other men, which I wouldn't bank on, going by the way he's flirted with most of the women here at some point over the last twenty-four hours, can you see him liking this particular man? He's young, successful, good-looking...'

'All right, no need to tell me how attractive he is.' Nathan narrowed his eyes. 'When you say he's flirted with *most* of the women, would that include you?'

'Of course it would. Have you seen me? I'm gorgeous.'

He laughed. 'Well yes, you are, and modest with it.' He looked at Steve's body. 'Yeah, he probably wouldn't be up for a spot of rough and tumble with Santa, would he?'

'He *did* get a visitor in the night, though,' I said. I told him about my impromptu run down the corridor and subsequent eavesdropping.

'Hmm... He wouldn't do *what*?' pondered Nathan. 'You think his visitor was female?'

'Yeah, I dunno why...'

'Well, bearing in mind that he's been flirting with every woman in the place...' he rolled his eyes at me, 'maybe one of them took him at his word.'

'And what? Knocked on his door, begging for him to ravish them, and he turned them down?' I tutted. 'Nathan, have you ever actually met a man?' He laughed, a little defensively.

'Hey, we're not *all* like that. In fact, I'd say most of my fellow men would be bloody terrified if a woman we'd only just met knocked on our bedroom door in the middle of the night and asked for a bunk-up.'

We looked at each other for a split second, then both burst out laughing. It felt good (if slightly inappropriate, vis-à-vis having a corpse in close proximity), and I suddenly realised how tense I'd been. We stopped laughing eventually, then Nathan clapped his hands together suddenly, making me jump.

'OK then, what have we got so far? Murder weapon.' He pointed to the bed. 'Check. Cause of death – double check. How did the murderer gain entry? Spare key?'

I shook my head. 'The spare keys were in Trevor's bedside drawer all night.'

'Do you know that for certain? Could someone have taken them out and put them back without him noticing?'

'No. Only he and Lily knew they were there.'

'OK. So the victim must have let them in. Secret assignation, like you said.'

'Not necessarily...' I looked around the room, my eyes resting on the mahogany window seat. I went over and examined the seat; the lid lifted up. I looked up at Nathan, excited. I couldn't believe I hadn't thought of it before. 'This house is full of secret rooms and hidden passageways.'

'Where?'

I rolled my eyes at him. 'I don't know, they're secret and hidden, aren't they? Lily showed us two rooms, one on the floor above – probably right over this room, actually – and another one downstairs, a priest hole. And she said that there used to be a passage between the butler's pantry and one of the bedrooms. I bet it was this bedroom! She said that one of the previous owners had filled the whole thing in when they redid the electrics and plumbing. They used it to run all the pipes through, and there wasn't enough room for anyone to get into it now. But what if there *was* room, for someone skinny? And where's the obvious place for it to come out?'

Nathan looked at me for a moment, then joined me in staring into the compartment under the window seat. It had an old blanket in it. He reached in and pulled it out, revealing a wooden panel underneath. We looked at each other, breathless.

'If it's like the priest hole, there should be an

indentation in the corner of the panel,' I said, my eyes roaming across the wood. I couldn't see anything. Nathan reached in and rapped his knuckles on the bottom.

A dull thud greeted us. We looked at each other.

'That sounds pretty solid to me,' he said, knocking on another spot, then another. 'Definitely doesn't sound hollow.'

'Bugger. I was so sure...' We both straightened up.

'OK, so the murderer didn't have a key, and they didn't use the secret passage from the butler's pantry—'

'Unless it comes out somewhere else. Maybe we should try it from the other end...'

'Or maybe we're back to Steve letting them in.'

'Which means it definitely *was* Steve who was the intended victim.'

Nathan looked at me sharply. 'What? Why wouldn't he be the intended victim?'

'Because Isaac and Joshua were originally meant to sleep in here, but Joshua was freaked out by all the tapestries and stuff, and it being all dark and creepy. They swapped rooms, but the first anyone knew of it was this morning.'

'But if the killer was after Steve, how did they know which room to come to?' Nathan looked perplexed. 'He must've told them. It must've been some assignation, like you said. Although it wasn't necessarily for hanky-panky.'

'He *was* stark flipping naked, Nath.'

'True… OK, so he arranged to meet someone, told them what room he was in, and let them in. Next thing: how did the sword end up here? Did it live in here? Was it an ornament or something?'

'No, it got tucked away in the butler's pantry when the kids were here for the party. It normally lives in a display case, but Trevor didn't want the little angels impaling each other with it during Musical Chairs.'

'Who knew it was in the pantry?'

'Everyone, just about. Well, probably not the latecomers. Definitely not the Japanese ones, I'd have thought, but I did hear Joshua talking to his dad about the sword when we were all in the snug after dinner – he was fascinated by it. The tourists don't speak enough English to understand, I don't think, but Bea and Liam could easily have heard.'

'Was it hidden? Locked away?'

'No, not really. We were keeping Germaine in there, out of the way of the party-goers, and I saw it just lying there on the side. Actually, I moved it up onto a high shelf, in case Joshua went in there on his own to see the dog. He's quite taken with her. But it wasn't hidden.'

'So the murderer got it from the pantry before they went to see Steve?'

'Or Steve could've taken it,' I said. 'Maybe they were planning to steal it or something.'

'Is it worth much?'

'No idea. It's very old, though, and it has got some history attached to it. It belonged to Elizabeth I's favourite priest hunter, Sir Richard or Sir Roger someone or other. In the right hands it might be worth something.'

'So if they were going to steal it, how did it end up there?' Nathan jerked his thumb over his shoulder to the shape on the bed. 'Going to be pretty hard to steal it or sell it now, isn't it?'

Chapter Thirteen

W e made our way downstairs. It was nice to have
Nathan with me to brainstorm with, but it
didn't feel like we'd made much progress. We still had no
idea who had killed Steve. Or why. Or how. Most of the
overnight inhabitants had alibis, in the form of room-
mates, and those that didn't had no obvious motive. But
one of those with no alibi, James, now stood at the front
door, arguing with his boss.

'We need to leave, now,' said James. He sounded like
he was almost pleading. Isaac shook his head.

'We can't, can we? The police are here now, or they
will be soon, anyway. All we have to do is make a
statement and then we can go. Let's just get it over with.'

'Everything all right, gentlemen?' said Nathan, polite
but firm.

'Yes, DCI Withers, we're just waiting for your colleagues to arrive,' said Isaac. 'Come on, James, come and sit down. What's got into you?'

James didn't answer, just licked his lips nervously. Nathan and I exchanged a look which said, *Guilty conscience?*

'What is it, James?' I said gently, approaching him and putting my hand on his sleeve. 'You've been acting strangely since you got up. Is there something on your mind?'

'No – no, I – having a dead body in the house is freaking me out a little bit, that's all.'

'Does it have something to do with your night-time visitor?' He looked at me, astonished. 'You can tell me, James. I told you, I'm not police anymore.'

'No, but he is.' James looked defiantly at Nathan for a second, then his shoulders dropped and he looked suddenly very small. 'Oh God,' he said, fixing me with a desperate look. 'I've been such an idiot, Jodie. I don't know what to do.'

'Then talk to me, James. I can help you. I can't believe you had anything to do with Steve's death—'

'No, no, of course not!' he cried. 'It's nothing like that…'

'How about we go and have a little chat, somewhere more private?' suggested Nathan. I looked over at the door of the snug, and sure enough Bea was standing there, pretending to look at something but clearly earwigging. And I *knew* that she was the one I'd heard knocking on James's door the night before.

James swallowed hard. 'OK. But Isaac should hear this too.'

———————

The library was empty, and the four of us had the room to ourselves. I still half suspected there was a secret passage somewhere behind a bookcase, and I wondered if the murderer was lurking there, eavesdropping. Because despite his obvious guilt and distress over something, I still couldn't imagine James killing anyone.

'I'm not a murderer,' he said, as if confirming what I'd been thinking.

'But you are guilty of something,' said Nathan, and he nodded.

'Only of being a complete fool.' He stood indecisively, in silence, for a moment. 'I don't know where to start.' I gestured to an armchair and sat down in one myself. The others followed suit.

'Who are Bea and Liam, and what have they got over you?' I asked. He looked at me, surprised.

'Bea's a journalist,' he said, and I saw Isaac stiffen next to him. 'Her real name's Belinda Walker, and she writes for the *London Post*.'

'That bloody rag!' Isaac looked furious. 'If I'd known, I'd have thrown them back out into the snow last night.'

'Liam's her photographer-slash-bodyguard, I think,' said James.

Nathan raised an eyebrow. 'Bodyguard?'

'Miss Walker's style of journalism is...combative, shall we say?'

'She pisses people off,' Isaac explained. As if to illustrate the truth of his remark, he looked and sounded suitably pissed off himself. I nodded.

'Gotcha. So why is she here?'

'The *Post* have been trying to dig the dirt on Isaac for years. They're not above making stuff up, paying people to lie, all of that, but every time they've tried it, Isaac's sued them.'

Isaac nodded. 'When I set up the foundation – I don't know if you remember this – I gave interviews everywhere, telling people that I'd made mistakes and that this was my way of trying to make it all right. I admitted that my past business dealings could have been handled better. Don't get me wrong,' he added quickly, looking at Nathan, 'they were all completely legal. But they weren't necessarily ethical. Even in my personal life, well, I was a bit of a rat.' He shook his head. 'The press have always liked to bring successful people down, to find scandals and dirt on them, and me opening the closet and showing them all my skeletons took the wind out of their sails, didn't it? They can't make a scandal out of something if I've already been open about it.'

'Belinda Walker has made it her mission in life to find something on Isaac,' said James. 'I genuinely think that's all she does. She's been pestering me for months.'

'You never told me that,' said Isaac, surprised.

James shrugged. 'She was just an irritant at first,' he said. 'You have enough to deal with, and I could handle her, so there didn't seem to be any need. But she kept going until she had something to use against me.'

'What did she find?'

James looked at us, frankly. 'I know what you all think of me – that I'm just some rich idiot schoolboy.' I started to refute that, but he shook his head. 'I saw the way you all looked when I mentioned having a Japanese nanny. I don't blame you. I look and act the part, don't I? But my parents weren't born into money. They're wealthy enough now, but, as my father is very fond of saying, every penny he has, he's worked hard for.' He gave a bitter little laugh. 'When I got this job he actually had the nerve to compare himself to Isaac, like he's some wonderful father and great philanthropist. But it's not true. The main reason I had a nanny, and why I went to boarding school, was because he and my mother were always working, and I was in the way. A son at Eton was just another status symbol.' He looked at me. 'I'm not saying this because I want you to feel sorry for the poor little rich boy, but so you understand what sort of relationship I have with my father.'

'Not a good one,' said Nathan, and he nodded.

'Anyway, one of the other things my father is fond of saying, is that you never get anywhere in life unless you're prepared to take risks. I've never been one to take risks, which is why he sees me as a failure.'

'The fact that you don't take risks is exactly why I hired you,' said Isaac. 'I know the charity's money is safe with you.' James looked for a moment like he might cry, and I felt sorry for him. I *had* thought he was a bit of a rich idiot, but underneath the veneer of confidence and good humour he was vulnerable, like everyone else. I was reminded again that money, although it may smooth out many of life's wrinkles, does not necessarily make you happy.

'My father likes to try and wind me up. I'm normally very good at ignoring him – which convinces him even more that I'm an idiot – but about three years ago I'd had enough and I took the bait.'

'What happened?' I asked.

'He gave me fifty thousand pounds and told me to risk it all.' We all looked at James, our mouths open. 'Yes, I know that sounds fantastic, but it was a test,' he said. 'He told me he'd made a lot of his money through high-risk, high-gain investments, and that I should try it. He told me to find something that would make the highest return possible on the money, and that whatever profit I made, I could keep.' He shook his head. 'I wasn't interested in the money, to be honest, but I wanted him to respect me for a change. So I agreed.'

'You invested the money?' asked Nathan. 'In what?'

'Although he'd told me to pick something risky, I wasn't going to completely gamble such a massive sum. That amount of money might mean nothing to him, but to most people it would be life-changing.'

I nodded. 'That could pay off someone's debts, or their student loan...'

'Yes, but I mean *literally* life changing. If you gave that money to someone overseas, it could literally buy them a house or an education or fund a hospital for a while. So I looked around for a worthy investment, and then, one fell into my lap. One I knew something about, and really believed in.'

Isaac groaned. 'Not Green Palms?' James nodded.

'What's "Green Palms"?' asked Nathan. Isaac and James looked at each other, then back at us.

'I invest in a lot of property development,' said Isaac. 'It's mostly eco-housing in this country, not much of a risk, short-term stuff but good returns. One of the developers I've invested with in the past told me about an eco-tourist resort they were building on Cayos Ondas, this little island off the coast of Nicaragua.' He saw my raised eyebrows and gave me a small smile. 'There are very few unspoilt, undiscovered paradise islands left in the world – undiscovered by tourists, that is – and Ondas is one of the few remaining. It's the sort of place that would appeal to very wealthy travellers, the type that see themselves as explorers and trailblazers, but still want a nice pool to sit and drink cocktails around.'

'And that's what you invested in?' I asked James. He nodded.

'Yes…but it wasn't really the hotel I was interested in, although it was going to be brilliant for the island's economy and bring lots of work for the locals. The developer was also going to build a brand-new school and medical clinic for the islanders. That was what swung it for me. You see, I spent six months on Cayos Ondas during my gap year, teaching the children there. It was such a magical place, with amazing people, and I wanted to help them.' He sighed. 'It would have been so good for them.'

'But it all fell through,' said Nathan, and both Isaac and James nodded.

'First of all, Hurricane Veronica tore through the islands, and devastated everything. Then there was a tsunami, which washed away everything within two miles of the beach.' James shook his head. 'It was terrible. The island was practically destroyed overnight. It's amazing the death toll wasn't higher than it was.'

'And it meant no more tourists,' I said.

'No more tourists. And no more development.' Isaac shook his head. 'We were in for a reasonable amount of money, and as a big investor I did get some of my money back, but we took a hit. What about you, James? I take it you lost everything.'

'Yes, every penny.'

'But your dad had told you to risk it, so he could hardly be annoyed about that…' I said.

'I didn't tell him,' said James. 'It was a test, and I'd failed. Again. But I assumed it was my money now, so I just fobbed him off and said that it was going OK. And then, a year later, he asked for his fifty thousand back.'

'But you didn't have it?'

'No! I don't have that kind of money saved up. I told him it was invested and I couldn't get it out, but he just gave me a deadline for when it had to be paid back.'

'Your father sounds like a real prince,' I muttered under my breath. James heard me.

'You could say that. Even when I said I didn't have it, he still insisted I pay it back. He said it was part of the lesson he was trying to teach me: not to gamble with more than you could afford to lose.'

'But it was his money! And he *told* you to gamble it!' Isaac shook his head. 'Some men don't deserve to be fathers.'

'You're right,' I said, thinking of Richard, Daisy's bloody useless and thankfully mostly absent dad.

'So what happened? Did you pay him back?' asked Nathan.

'I put my flat up for sale,' said James. 'It was in an expensive part of London and I couldn't really afford it, but my parents had given me a deposit on the understanding I bought somewhere in a pre-approved part of London – they couldn't have a son of theirs living in the "wrong" area, could they? They were horrified when I told them I was buying a place out in the wilds of zone 6. I thought they'd disown me when I told them I don't even have a London postcode anymore. I put my flat up for sale and I was going to pay him back out of the proceeds. But the deadline was approaching and the sale hadn't gone through, so...'

'What did you do?' asked Isaac, staring at him.

'This is what Belinda Walker has on me,' said James, not meeting his eye. 'Someone at the charity looked back over the books and discovered "financial irregularities"...'

Isaac shook his head. 'There's no "irregularities"!' he protested. 'I look at the figures regularly, and there's never been any money missing. I don't do the books, of course, but I keep on top of the numbers. Tell me you didn't do anything wrong, James.'

James now looked thoroughly ashamed. 'I took fifty thousand pounds from the charity's bank account, when we were paying out grants to some children's projects.'

Nathan stared at him, aghast. And now I really thought James was going to cry.

'It was only for two weeks, and I paid it all back!' said James quickly. 'With interest, as soon as my flat sale went through. I didn't steal it, I just borrowed it.'

'Without asking.' Isaac was thin-lipped, still glaring at him.

'Yes. Without asking.' James stared down at the floor, guilt written all over his face and in every sinew of his body, and, despite the fact that he'd done wrong, I felt sorry for him.

'He paid it back, though,' I said.

Isaac shook his head again. 'That's not really the point, is it?'

'So Belinda Walker knew what you'd done,' said Nathan quickly. I got the feeling he didn't want Isaac and James getting into what James had done, not while we were there; it wasn't relevant to the murder investigation. 'How was she trying to use it against you?'

'She was trying to blackmail me into dishing the dirt on Isaac,' said James. 'I told her no, but she kept on and on. She said she'd bury the story about me, if I gave her something on Isaac. She wanted me to throw him under the bus to save my own skin.'

'And did you?' asked Isaac, harshly. James looked shocked.

'Of course not! Apart from the fact that there *is* no dirt

on you, I wouldn't do it anyway. You're not just my boss, Isaac, you're my friend. At least,' he said, looking almost tearful again, 'you were. I'd never drop you in it to save myself.'

'That's why her and Liam were constantly bothering you,' I said. 'I noticed they kept following you around, sitting next to you when we were eating, and then you all disappeared after dinner.'

He nodded. 'They wouldn't take no for an answer. I was worried that they'd turn up at the party yesterday, which is why I was so keen to get away afterwards and get back to the hotel. But when I rang the hotel last night and said we wouldn't be back because of the snow, and to cancel our dinner reservation, the receptionist told me there had been a woman asking for me there.'

'Which is why you looked a lot happier about staying here overnight,' I said. 'You thought there was less chance of them catching up with you if they'd gone to Fowey, rather than here.'

'Yes. And then of course they turned up here anyway. I didn't know it was her at first – I'd never met the woman, just had her calling me, and of course she used a different name – but she took great delight in taking me aside after dinner and telling me who she really was.' He looked at me. 'She even came up to my room after we'd gone to bed, trying to twist my arm.'

I nodded. 'I couldn't sleep, so I got up to stretch my legs and I heard you talking to her.'

'Belinda told me this morning I had until lunchtime to come up with something, or she'd print the story about me. I was going to tell you in the car,' he said, turning back to Isaac. 'I didn't want you to read about it in the paper.'

Isaac stared at him for a moment, and then shook his head once more. 'I don't know what to think about this. You're my right-hand man, James. I absolutely trusted you.'

'I know,' said James, miserably. Nathan looked at me, and I knew he wanted to escape and get back to finding our killer. But I liked James, particularly now I knew why he'd been rude and grumpy this morning, and I hated the thought that his whole life could have been ruined, just because he was trying to pass some ridiculous test set by his father.

'Tell me about your gap year,' I said. James looked at me, surprised, and I could see Nathan's expression – he was thinking, *Oh God, Jodie, don't poke your nose into this!* But I couldn't help it.

'Really? Um, OK. Well, I spent most of it on the island. It's a beautiful place, Jodie, but so poor. The people there have nothing. The resort really would have helped the locals. And the kids! They were so full of life, just so – so joyful – I loved teaching them. They would really have thrived with a proper school. I had this vision of them all becoming doctors or teachers, or opening up businesses, staying on the island and contributing to it, rather than the intelligent ones leaving for the mainland as soon as they were old enough and the rest just stagnating.'

'That sounds wonderful,' I said. 'You're obviously very passionate about helping them.' I looked at Isaac. 'And your charity looks after disadvantaged kids, yeah? James sounds like just the sort of person you'd want running it, to me.'

'Not just kids,' said Isaac, petulantly, but he knew what I meant. He sighed. 'Yes, OK, all that gap-year stuff was one of the big things that set him apart from the other applicants. And we hit it off. We *are* friends, James. Which is why I can't understand why you took the money. Why didn't you just ask me? I'd have helped you.'

'My father thinks I'm useless. If I'd asked you for help, I'd have been proving him right, wouldn't I?' James looked at him, beseechingly. 'I *am* sorry, Isaac. I regretted doing it the moment I took the money, and I've felt guilty about it ever since. It's almost a relief that you know now, even if it does mean I'm out of a job.'

'Don't be dramatic. I'm not sacking you.'

'You're not?' James looked incredulous.

I grinned at Nathan and he rolled his eyes – me sticking my oar in seemed to have worked.

'There will be changes. But you're not being sacked. Or demoted. You're one of my son's favourite people, and that means a lot to me.' Isaac stood up. 'Right, let's go and find this bloody parasite Walker.' He strode out of the library.

Nathan and I exchanged looks and dashed after him, James, who seemed a bit dazed, following more slowly. Bea – or Belinda, as I now knew she was called – was loitering in the hallway, no doubt having attempted to eavesdrop at the library door. I couldn't imagine that she'd had much success, as we'd been sitting too far into the room. But that wouldn't have stopped her trying.

'Everything OK?' She smiled falsely, her eyes flicking between James and Isaac. Isaac strode over and took her by the arm, none too gently, and I felt Nathan tense beside me, ready to spring into action if it got ugly.

'I'm calling a press conference. And lucky you, you get the exclusive, Miss Walker,' he said, turning her and marching her into the dining room. Debbie and Mum came out of the snug at the sound of Isaac's raised voice.

'Ooh, has something happened?' asked Mum, following us to the door of the dining room. Nathan stopped her in the doorway.

'Sorry, Shirley, I think you might have to wait and

read it in the paper,' he said firmly. Mum pouted and went to speak, but I shook my head.

'Nope, not this time,' I said, although I too would have loved to go in and watch Isaac dealing with the duplicitous Belinda. His blood was up and I could only imagine the absolute roasting she was going to get. 'This has got nothing to do with us.'

Isaac, James and Belinda went into the dining room, followed thirty seconds later by a scuttling Liam, who had realised that stuff was going down. I shut the door, leaving the rest of us standing outside. Mum gave a grumpy *harrumph* as if I was constantly spoiling her fun, and wandered off. I didn't feel guilty, though. I knew that she was only heading into the kitchen to grab a glass and that, the moment Nathan and I left, she'd have it up to her ear, against the door, listening closely to every word Isaac said. She'd probably be committing it to memory, ready to relay it back to her friends at the next Wednesday OAPs' coffee morning.

Chapter Fourteen

However, our – I mean, Mum's – eavesdropping was interrupted by a commotion outside. Through a window we could see a police Range Rover heading up the driveway. Nathan smiled ruefully at me.

'Sorry, that's put paid to your investigating,' he said. 'I can't see them taking too kindly to you being involved.' I handed him my latex gloves and tried to look like I had no idea what was going on. Which was uncomfortably close to the truth.

We headed for the front door. Matt Turner was already there talking to Trevor and Lily as three uniformed and two plain-clothes officers entered. Matt looked up as we approached him.

'All right, Guv?' he said. He grinned at me. 'Might've known you'd be up to your neck in it.'

'You just got here?' asked Nathan. He nodded.

'Yeah, and the Carricksmoor lot were right behind me as I turned in the drive.'

Nathan took out his warrant card and approached the plain-clothes officers. 'DCI Withers from Penstowan. Was it you I spoke to on the phone?'

One of the officers nodded. 'Yes, sir. I'm DI Jones and this is DC Carver. Didn't think you'd get here before us.' He turned to me. 'You're Jodie Parker? The lady who called it in?' I nodded. 'Sorry we took so long to get here. You're not any relation to Eddie Parker, are you?'

'Yes,' I said, surprised. 'He was my dad.'

He smiled. 'My DCI reckoned it was too much of a coincidence. He started off at Penstowan, under your dad.' He turned back to Nathan. 'What have we got?'

'I'll show you the crime scene,' said Nathan. 'We've got a house full of suspects, just to make it more fun, if Uniform want to start taking statements from them.'

DI Jones nodded and turned to his officers, organising them. Nathan took me to one side and spoke in a low voice. 'Sorry, I know it probably feels like it's your case and now we're going to trample all over it, but you've done well, keeping everyone here and keeping the scene safe.'

Germaine had escaped from the snug and was sniffing around the newcomers' legs, basically getting in the way. Daisy appeared, looking for her, and I noticed (with a lovely warm feeling in my heart) the way her face lit up at the sight of Nathan.

'Nathan! What you doing here? How did you get here? Are the roads open, then?' She was practically jumping up and down with excitement. 'Did Mum tell you, we've all been investigating—' She either didn't see my frantic head shaking, or understand my throat-cutting gesture, as she ploughed on, '—me, Debbie and Nana? Did she tell you about the footprints in the snow?'

Nathan looked at me, exasperated, just catching the end of my throat-cutting. 'Don't tell me you deputised your twelve-year-old?'

'Thirteen actually, and no, she deputised me.' I told him about the footprints, and how Daisy had worked out that the killer must have been in the house overnight, and how they must still be there now. He nodded.

'That's very good police work,' he said to her, seriously. I loved the way he spoke to her, like a grown-up; a lot of childless people (and even some of those with kids) talk down to teenagers, patronising them, and it never ends well. 'I'll pass it on to the other officers so they know what we're dealing with. But now it's time for you to stand down, OK? Wait with everyone else and give your statement when they get to you, and then you should be able to go home.'

'What about you?' I said. 'Strictly speaking this is

Carricksmoor's patch, innit? But they've only sent a DI, so you're the highest rank here…'

'I don't know,' he admitted. 'I don't want to step on any toes, but I'm invested now. I'll have to play it by ear for the moment.' He gave me that gorgeous, slow smile of his. 'To be honest, I didn't really expect to do any work. I only came to rescue you.' *Awww!* 'And of course you did just have a sleepover with an unmarried multi-millionaire, and according to Matt the ladies think he's sexy, so…' I slapped his arm. 'I'm kidding!' He turned to glance at DI Jones, who had stopped briefing his officers and was waiting for him. 'I need to show him the crime scene. Wait down here, OK? I'll try and keep you in the loop but you know I shouldn't, really.' I nodded and he left with the DI, Matt following.

'Right,' I said, grabbing Germaine's collar as she swung past us, sniffing out the trail of the new arrivals, 'let's go and pretend we're normal innocent bystanders.'

We tried, but it wasn't easy. After crumbling under pressure and allowing my little gang to investigate, none of them had got very far before the Law had turned up and put paid to it. Daisy was still very proud of her footprints discovery, but in a way that only made it harder for her to sit back and let the police do their job.

She had the detecting bug. She really was a chip off the old block. I sincerely hoped she'd grow out of it...

Debbie also seemed restless. She went upstairs to offer her services as a medical expert, but the rather surly DC Carver dismissed her, saying that their own forensic medical examiner was on their way. She stomped back into the snug, muttering darkly under her breath about jobsworths, institutional sexism, and fragile male egos.

Even Mum seemed out of sorts. She'd found some more mince pies and stuck them on a plate for the uniformed officers, who were attempting to take statements from everyone, and was disconsolately munching her way through the festive treats herself without even attempting to flirt with them. When one of them stopped for a moment in the doorway, positioned right under the mistletoe, Mum's face lit up and I thought, *Oh God, here we go...* And then she just went back to eating her mince pie without even a mild innuendo, let alone any attempt to extract a Christmas kiss from the 'nice young man'. Maybe she was ill.

Two of the uniformed officers had taken Trevor and Lily out of the room – one to the library, one to the lounge – to take their statements, while the third was attempting to interview the Japanese girls. I could see by his face that he knew he was facing a hopeless, and probably pointless, task, but it had to be done. I thought about telling him that there was a fluent Japanese speaker in the house who could translate for them, but I decided against it; it kept him busy and feeling useful, which was more than could be said about myself at this point, and more importantly I wasn't about to interrupt whatever was happening in the dining room between James, Isaac and the despicable journalists. I hoped Belinda Walker would think twice about using such bullying tactics and blackmail in the future, although I doubted it.

'Well this sucks,' said Daisy, plopping into an armchair next to me. Germaine dropped onto her feet in sympathy. 'Now I know how you feel, when you can't keep your nose out of things.'

'Frustrating, isn't it?' I said. 'You just want to go and have a poke around, but you can't. But that's the way it is. The police have to do their jobs, and we have to do ours, which is sitting here, waiting for them to get to us, and then going home.'

'I know, but...' She sighed. Debbie joined us. She sighed, too.

'Oh for goodness' sake, what's the matter with everyone?' I said, shaking my head.

'I just realised how it must feel to be you,' she said, and Daisy gave a slightly bitter laugh.

'I know, right? How can they expect us to just sit here, like there's not a dead body up there and a murderer down here?'

'Because that's what normal people do,' I said. 'Normal people shy away from murder – and murderers, in particular. They don't start investigating because they're bored.'

Mum wandered over with her plate of food. 'Mince pie?'

'No, thank you.' I sat in silence for a moment, but I was aware they were all watching me expectantly. I groaned. 'What do you expect me to do? Smuggle you into the crime scene? Nathan's up there with CID, and any moment now Scene of Crime will turn up, and the Medical Examiner, and the people from the morgue will be along at some point to take the body away... I'm not sure there'd be any room left for three adults, a teenager and a dog.'

'There must be *something* we can do!' said Debbie. The other two nodded in agreement. 'How about we make up a plan of the house and mark on it where everybody was at the time of the murder?'

'CID wouldn't like that...' I said, but they could tell I was weakening.

'Bugger CID,' muttered Debbie.

'So we won't tell them,' said Mum. 'That's sorted, then. We need some paper, and a pen, and some clotted cream.'

'Clotted cream?'

'For the mince pies. They're a bit dry. Did you make them?'

'No I didn't! Bloody cheek.'

There was a writing bureau in the corner of the room, so Debbie went and rifled through it, returning triumphantly with an A4 writing pad and a couple of pens.

'What's the best way to do this?' she asked.

'I dunno – maybe use one page per floor of the house and draw out a map, then mark off the rooms and who was in them overnight,' I suggested. She nodded.

'Sounds like a plan.'

I laughed. 'It literally *is* a plan.'

———

So we drew out a very (very) rough outline of the ground floor, and added all the rooms and corridors we could think of: the back entrance and hallway, the butler's pantry, the kitchen, the downstairs toilet, all the areas that would have been unknown to the past lords and ladies of the house, being the domain of the servants. Then the grand front door, the hallway with the imposing staircase, the dining room, the lounge, the snug and the library. And, finally, the priest hole, which was hidden in the wall between the lounge and the butler's pantry. I wondered where the secret (but now supposedly blocked) passageway started in the pantry; if it went anywhere near the priest hole, or was there another passage off that hidden room that went to the Dyneley Suite? I shook my head – there was no way of knowing without getting into the priest hole and having a poke around, and the uniformed officer taking a statement in the lounge might have something to say if we went in and started prodding the wooden panelling. There was no way I was even going to mention it to the others, in case my enthusiastic (but wildly impractical) gang of amateur detectives came up with some hare-brained scheme to get in there and, worse, persuaded me to try it. Me, Mum and Debbie dragged our armchairs up close to the coffee table, while Daisy sprawled on the carpet with Germaine, who was very keen to help us as long as she could have her tummy rubbed while she did so.

'So, let's start with who slept down here,' I said. 'Hina and her friends were here in the snug when I went to bed, and I'm assuming that's where they stayed.' I remembered the gentle snoring I'd heard that morning, as we'd taken Germaine out; I was pretty certain it had come from this room. I don't know why but I'd immediately ascribed it to one of the Japanese girls, probably because it had been a delicate, almost melodic sighing noise that seemed to fit their slim, feminine appearances. Don't ask me how a snore can be feminine and melodic, but it can, particularly when compared to the polar opposite; my Mum's ear-splitting snorts and grunts. Those horrendous noises also really suited their originator, who was currently sitting opposite me, spraying pastry crumbs on the expensive-looking Persian rug. I hoped it could be dry-cleaned.

I marked the girls on the map. I only knew Hina's name; the others had been introduced, but I have trouble remembering names at the best of times, and when I can't even pronounce them there's more chance of you finding a sausage roll at a vegan wedding reception than there is of me committing them to memory. I marked down 'H' followed by three 'J's.

'Who else was down here?' asked Debbie, looking very seriously at the map. I smiled to myself; Debbie had been struggling to find a job (and herself) since she and Callum had moved down here with their kids, and with a nose for trouble almost as big as mine, she was clearly enjoying having a crack at this case. Maybe the two of us should set up a private detective agency? We could be Cornwall's answer to Cagney and Lacey.

'Belinda and Liam, and Lily,' I said. 'But I have no idea where any of them slept. Belinda and Liam were in here when we went and did our tour of the house before bed, but they'd gone by the time we came back. I assume they were harassing poor James, but I don't know where they ended up sleeping.'

'What about Lily?' said Debbie. Mum cackled but didn't say anything, despite me giving her 'a look'.

'She was going to drag some mattresses down here and sleep on one of them...' I started, but Mum cackled again. 'What? If you've got something to say, some marvellous insight, please tell us, oh wise crone, instead of cackling like you're about to ambush the Thane of Cawdor.'

'Reckon I know where she slept. *If* she slept. She looked proper tired this morning, didn't she?' Mum cackled again and it took all my strength not to grab my phone and ring the nearest Sunshine Home for the Elderly and Senile. But actually, as daft as my mum sometimes (often) is, she's definitely not senile, and she's occasionally even capable of great insight.

Occasionally.

'Tired but happy...' I looked at Mum, but before I could say anything Lily came back into the room, followed by the officer who'd been interviewing her. He smiled at the four of us and said, 'Who's next?'

'Me,' said Mum. 'I likes a young man in uniform. Likes 'em even more out of it.' She cackled again – honestly, I didn't make the mince pies so I have no idea what was in them, but the way she was going on, maybe they were akin to those 'special' brownies one of her friends had handed out a few weeks ago at the OAP coffee morning. Her grandson had made them just for her, to help with her arthritis pain, and she'd liked them so much that she brought them with her to share with the gang. The morning had ended with Mum's friend Janet demonstrating how to remove a bra without taking your top off, her other friend Nell being thrown out for harassing one of the male volunteer servers, and me getting a phone call to come and collect Mum, as she was fine but wouldn't stop singing 'Spanish Eyes' at the top of her voice. The officer looked a little bit alarmed but just smiled politely and gestured for her to head out of the room.

Lily sat down in the chair Mum had just vacated, looked at the map on the table, and said in a low voice, 'So, you haven't let the police stop you, then?'

'Nope. We're drawing up a plan of the house and marking up where everyone slept,' I said. 'So we can work out where everyone was at the time of the murder. I'm glad you're out, you can help us with the other floors.'

She was about to speak when James and Isaac entered. I looked up at them.

'Everything OK?' I asked. James gave a small nod, looking…not exactly happy, but less stressed than before.

'It will be,' said Isaac.

'Good. It would be a shame to let one mistake ruin everything,' I said, carefully, and Isaac nodded then too.

'Yeah, it would. It's not like I haven't made enough of

them,' he admitted. James smiled at me, looking more like his old self.

'Hey, James!' said Daisy. 'Watch this! Germaine! Say hello!' Germaine sat up, looking every inch the alert, working dog, and barked. James laughed and bent down to make a fuss of her.

'Good girl, Germaine!' he said, then went to sit down. Germaine followed him; she obviously realised he needed a bit of loving. Daisy sighed.

'I like James,' she said, then quickly added, 'Not like *that*, Mother, before you say anything! He's just nice.'

'You're right, he is,' I said. 'Germaine likes him, so he must be.' I turned back to Lily and said casually, 'Oh yeah, we need to mark you on here too. Where did you sleep last night?' I picked up the pen and sat poised with it hovering over the map. Lily blushed, and then giggled. *Oh my God, Mum was on to something*, I thought. And then I remembered Trevor putting his arm around her when she was upset, and then later, I'd thought he was going to put his arm round her waist but he didn't.

'I slept in Trevor's room,' she said, quietly but with a beaming smile.

'Ahhh, I see...' I smiled back at her. 'You'll be changing your relationship status on Facebook, then, will you?'

'Is this for your investigation or are you just being nosy?'

'What do you think?' Debbie said, sardonically. Lily laughed.

'I don't know. I mean, we're both single, and we get on really well, but we've always kept it strictly business, you know? I mean, he's my boss...' She was babbling, and beaming all over her face. 'But last night he invited me up to his apartment for a drink, to thank me for helping him out and to make sure I was OK, because it was quite a stressful day...' She flushed and leaned in close to me. 'I've been single for two years now, and *oh my God*, I don't remember it ever being that good.'

Just then Trevor walked in, his police interview over, and we all turned to look at him; the unlikeliest sex god in the whole of Cornwall. The poor bugger went as red as the late Santa's outfit, because it was so obvious what we were talking about, and Lily muttered, 'Oh my *God*!' again, and then we all looked at each other and got the giggles. Poor Trevor.

'Oh dear,' I said. 'I'm very happy for you both, but you'd better go and make sure the poor love's OK. And then come back, because we could use your help mapping out the rest of the house.'

She got up and trotted after Trevor, and I felt all warm as she touched his arm and reached up to kiss him. The smile that spread across his face was so genuine, you'd have to be made of stone not to go *awww*... A little bit of

Christmas magic, and I hadn't even had to steer the two of them towards the mistletoe.

'Ms Parker? Let's do you next.' I jumped as the officer who had been talking to Trevor approached me. I hastily pushed the map of the house away from me – I didn't want them to know what we were up to – and went off to give my statement, just like a normal, innocent bystander.

Chapter Fifteen

I told the officer everything that had taken place that morning, including my initial visit to the crime scene, where I had verified (with the assistance of our on-site medical professional Debbie) that the victim had indeed carked it. I mentioned that I had made sure that the room stayed locked and undisturbed, keeping the keys upon my person, but I sort of forgot (on purpose) to say that I'd gone back up there with Lily and had a better look round the room, and of course although I told him that I'd shown DCI Withers the room, I somehow neglected to tell him that Nathan had let me have a good poke around or that I'd helped him hypothesise how the murder had occurred. I was happy to be helpful, but there was no need to overdo it.

When we'd finished, the officer brought Daisy in so

that she could also make a statement with a responsible adult in attendance (I know what you're thinking, but I *am* very responsible when it comes to my girl). She excitedly told him about the footprints in the snow, and he wrote it all down but didn't seem terribly interested. She was crestfallen.

'Never mind,' I told her, as we left him and headed back to the snug. 'Nathan was really impressed, and he'll definitely take it into account. That's proper evidence, that is.'

When we got back to the snug, I noticed Bea – I mean, Belinda – and Liam sat in one corner of the room, talking heatedly between themselves. Isaac watched them with a smirk on his lips – I would have given *anything* to know how their discussion earlier had gone – but James made a point of ignoring them. He'd volunteered his translating services to the police officer who'd been struggling to talk to the Japanese tourists, and in spite of the terrible morning (and evening) he'd had, he now seemed to be enjoying himself immensely. James, I realised, was one of those people who liked to be liked, and needed to be needed. He thrived when he was making himself useful. It was why he'd offered to help me and Debbie search for Hina and her friends. Although he'd breached Isaac's trust, he was still a massive asset to the charity, and I hoped Isaac knew that; I hoped he would forgive James in time.

Lily was kneeling on the carpet, putting the finishing touches to the map on the coffee table. Mum was back from her interview – the police officer wrapping it up in super-quick time, I reckon – and back in the armchair, but Debbie was nowhere to be seen; probably giving her own statement. Daisy and I joined them.

'Is that the finished map?' I asked, quietly. 'All three floors?' Lily looked around surreptitiously and then nodded.

'Yes. I was just about to start marking out where everyone slept.' She showed me the ground floor, which I'd more or less finished before my statement. 'I asked Bea and Liam where they slept, and they said they were here, in the lounge, although I'm not sure I trust them now.' She pencilled in 'L + T' in one of the suites on the first floor, and blushed. *Awww!* 'So that's me and Trevor... Here's the Dyneley Suite...' She wrote 'S' on the map. I studied it.

'The suites are quite close together,' I said. 'You and Trev didn't hear any movement outside, or anything?'

'No, we were...' She blushed again. Mum looked like she was about to cackle again, but abruptly stopped and patted Lily on the arm.

'You were busy. We understand, love. He's a nice man.'

'Yes, he is.'

'So now you really *can* tell us how big his—'

'Mother, will you wind your neck in?' I rolled my eyes at Lily. 'Ignore her. No, I didn't expect you to hear anything, I just thought I should ask.' I pulled the other sheet of paper towards me – the top floor, where Daisy and I had slept. I pointed to our room. 'That's where we slept, with Mum and Debbie next door...' Lily marked us on the map.

'James was here...' She pointed to a room a couple along from us. 'And here's where Steve was *supposed* to have slept, but Isaac did instead.' She shook her head. 'Typical. We gave Isaac the best bloody room in the whole house, and he ended up sleeping in the worst one. We've not even finished renovating that bedroom, and the one person we're trying to impress ends up in it.' She looked up at us, sheepishly. 'Not that I didn't want to impress you lot too, I mean—'

'I know,' I said. 'Isaac told me. Trevor had talked to him about investing in the hotel. He'd already said no though, so the room wouldn't have made any difference. And he might be dead instead of Steve.'

She looked at me shrewdly. 'But surely the murderer was after Steve? Admittedly, a millionaire businessman seems more likely to have enemies than a Father Christmas impersonator, but...'

'How could someone possibly mistake Steve for Isaac?' said Debbie, suddenly appearing and sitting down next to me. 'Steve was twice the width and half the length of Isaac. Even in the dark—'

'And it couldn't have taken place in the dark, surely, because that room really *was* dark when I went in there this morning – during the night it would have been pitch black. How could you see to stab someone?' I shook my head. 'And then there's still the question of how the murderer got in, because you and Trevor,' I turned to Lily, 'were the only ones with access to the keys. Unless someone could have sneaked in while you were – er – busy?' She shook her head vehemently. 'No, OK, I didn't think so. What about this secret passage from the butler's pantry? I know you said it was blocked, but could someone have squeezed through it?'

She shook her head again. 'No, they couldn't. Honestly, the dog might get through but no one bigger. And anyway, it leads to Trevor's bedroom, not the Dyneley Suite. His room was originally used by Lady Devereaux, and we think the passage would have been used by her lady's maid.'

'Is there definitely no other way into the Dyneley Suite? Maybe from the secret book room? It's right above it, isn't it?'

Lily looked thoughtful. 'Maybe… And that room isn't locked. When we discovered it, we had to break the old lock to get into it, and we didn't replace it when we had the other doors done because we thought it was far enough out of the way that the party guests wouldn't find it. And we don't know what we're going to do with that room yet, either.'

Daisy sat up very straight in her chair, eyes shining. 'Does that mean...' she began excitedly, 'does that mean we can go and hunt for a secret passage?'

Lily and I exchanged glances, then grinned.

'Looks like it,' I said.

We waited until the three uniformed officers were busy taking statements from Bea, Liam and James, then me, Daisy, Debbie, Lily and the dog legged it out of the snug. Isaac and his son were playing a card game that Joshua had been given by the late Santa the day before, and the little boy was concentrating so hard on his hand of cards that he didn't even notice us leave. Isaac did, though, and looked intrigued, but didn't say anything. The Japanese girls were too busy checking their phones to see where the car breakdown truck was (I hadn't learned to speak Japanese overnight, but Hina kept saying 'AA', which sounded weird and foreign amongst their conversation) to pay much attention to us. Mum had decided to give it a miss and go and check on Pippa, who, I'm ashamed to say, I'd completely forgotten about. I hoped she hadn't been throttled by Steve's killer while we'd all been too busy to think about her, and that she'd cope all right with the police, who would definitely want to interview her – probably at some length – about finding the body.

'We are allowed to leave the snug, aren't we?' said Lily, as we crept to the foot of the stairs. 'By the police, I mean. They won't get annoyed with us?'

I shrugged. 'I'm sure they'd prefer us to all stay in one place, but they can't force us to. And it's your house. Well,' I added, 'almost.'

'One day,' said Debbie, and Lily laughed.

'It's been one night, ladies. One night.'

We quickly sneaked up the stairs, trying to be as quiet as possible. On the first-floor landing I paused, peering down the corridor towards the crime scene, but there were no CID officers outside, and the Scene of Crime people still hadn't shown up. I could hear voices though, Nathan's amongst them.

'Upstairs!' I hissed. 'Watch out for that bottom step.' We all avoided the bottom step, only to be rewarded by a loud creak when we stood on the second one. 'Ah, yeah,' I said. 'It was those *two* steps… Quickly!'

We rushed up the stairs, sounding like a herd of elephants, trying hard not to laugh because of course we'd all got the giggles. We made it, and then headed along the corridor towards the coldness of the old part of the house.

'Blooming 'eck,' said Debbie, gasping from trying to stifle her laughter. 'This is like a poor man's Famous Five, innit?' Germaine yapped. Debbie shushed her. 'Be quiet, Timmy!' Lily and I snorted with laughter, but Daisy was taking it far more seriously than the rest of us.

'Quiet, you lot!' she said, and we all shushed. Lily looked at me.

'Is that what you were like when you were in the Force?'

'It's what she's like now,' said Debbie, and we all giggled again. Daisy rolled her eyes but didn't tell us off again, for which we were all very grateful.

We reached the secret library and went in. Debbie was still giggling, but she stopped immediately at the sight of the walls lined with ancient books.

'Holy mackerel!' she gasped. 'These look proper old…'

'They are,' said Lily. 'Don't touch them! They're very delicate.'

I looked around the room. Every wall was covered in books, and it didn't look to me like anything had been moved, but I honestly wasn't sure how I'd tell. They weren't covered in dust or cobwebs or anything, which would have been a sure-fire way to see if anything had been disturbed. As if she'd read my mind, Lily said, 'Pippa and I have been in a few times to dust, but we haven't dared move more than one or two.'

'Well, I think we *are* going to have to move some of them,' I said. 'If there's the entrance to a secret passage in here, we won't be able to see it with all the books in the way.'

Lily took a deep breath, then reluctantly said, 'OK… but be careful!'

We decided to all work on a wall each, gently removing the books from the middle and lower shelves. The doorway downstairs into the priest hole had been small and low down, so it was a reasonable (but not necessarily correct) assumption that any other doors would be the same. Although, I suddenly realised, the other hidden door had been in a wooden panel, and this room was lined with grey stone. Maybe we were barking up the wrong tree…

We'd only been at it for five minutes when Daisy gave a shout. 'Oh my God! Look! There's something here!'

I rushed over and studied her section of wall. One of the stone slabs looked slightly set back from the others in the wall, and there was a definite draught coming from around it. If it *was* a hidden passage into the Dyneley Suite, and someone *had* used it in the middle of the night, it would have been awkward but by no means impossible to remove the books and squeeze through the gap between the shelves. I pushed the stone, but it didn't move.

'It's never that easy,' said Daisy, who had suddenly

become an expert on hidden rooms and secret doorways. 'You never just push. You have to find the right spot and just sort of lean on it...' She reached up and pushed in the corner of the stone. It *still* didn't move. We tried the other corners, all four of us leaning over and pushing and shoving, but to no avail. I shook my head.

'Sorry, sweetheart. I think it's just a wonky stone...' She sighed in disappointment, stood back and sat down on the sturdy wooden shelf on the opposite wall, where Debbie had removed a row of books.

'I was so certain...' she said, and then we all stopped in shock as the stone moved, grinding slowly backwards.

'Well that's a turn-up for the books,' said Debbie.

'I don't suppose anyone thought to bring a torch?' I said, already knowing the answer.

'There's one on your phone,' said Daisy.

'Is there?'

'You are *such* a technophobe. Here.' She held her hand out and I passed over my iPhone.

'Why can't we use yours?'

She snorted. 'I'm not letting you take *my* phone down a deep, dark secret passage full of spiders. Can you unlock it?'

I unlocked the phone, then she swiped upwards from the bottom of the screen to show the Control Centre shortcuts. 'Have you never used this before?' she asked.

'No. It's come up a few times by accident, but...'

She shook her head. 'Technophobe,' she muttered again, then held out the phone to show me. 'Look, there's a torch icon. Just tap it.' She tapped it and a bright light immediately shone from the back of my phone. 'Tap it again to turn it off.'

The others were watching with interest. 'Did you know about that?' I asked. They both murmured, 'Yeah... of course...' but I didn't believe them. I took a deep breath and leaned in to get a look at the gap in the wall, shining the phone's torch into the darkness.

There was a handle, rusted with age and disuse. But that didn't mean it *hadn't* been used, once, last night. I reached my hand into the gap, bracing myself in case the hole was full of spiders.

'Argh!' I cried, frantically trying to pull my hand out of the hole. The others shrieked and ran forward, tugging at my arm, but I stopped screaming and laughed, pulling my hand out and holding it up to show them I was OK.

Debbie reached over and slapped me. 'Oh, you silly sod!' she said, crossly. Daisy shook her head at me.

'I'm disappointed in you, Mother,' she said, and I laughed.

'Sorry, I couldn't resist. There's nothing in there except cobwebs. A lot of cobwebs.'

Daisy gulped. 'And a very large spider...'

'What? Where?' I twisted around violently, trying to

spot the large arachnid clambering up my arm, but Daisy just laughed. The others joined in.

'Serves you right,' she said.

'*Touché.*'

I stuck my hand back in the hole, grasped the handle and pulled. To our huge surprise, a section of the wall to the right, where Lily had been working, swung open, book-filled shelves and all. Lily jumped out of the way as the secret door revealed the opening to a long, dark passage. A waft of cold, stale air drifted into the room, making it even less inviting but (conversely) more exciting.

'Bingo!' cried Debbie. 'Now *that* is proper Famous Five stuff.'

Germaine ran over and stood at the threshold, growling and shivering.

'So that's not at all unnerving, is it?' I said. 'Stop it, Germaine! Someone grab the dog. I'll go and look, the rest of you wait here.'

'Not bloody likely,' said Debbie. 'I'm right behind you.'

'And I'm in front of you!' said Daisy, but I grabbed the collar of her sweatshirt and hauled her back.

'Nope. No way. I'm going first, in case it's dangerous. Let me check it out, then you can come in too.'

'But—' she started. Lily stopped her.

'She's right, we don't know what's in there. I thought

you were worried about losing your phone? And spiders?' Daisy couldn't really argue with that, but Debbie had no such fears and I couldn't stop her following me in.

'I feel like Indiana Jones without the whip,' she said, as we entered the passage. I gulped.

'Yeah... If you see an idol on a stone plinth, or anything that looks like it could release a massive round boulder, don't touch it, yeah?'

———————

It was dark, despite the bright light coming from my phone. And narrow – very narrow. Neither Debbie nor I were particularly lithe these days; I definitely ate more and exercised much less than I had during my time in the Force, and Debbie and her family liked food a little more than they should. We'd have to be careful, in case we got—

'No no no!' said Debbie, behind me. I whirled around, inadvertently shining the torch in her face.

'Keep your voice down!' I whispered. 'We're right above the crime scene. What's the matter?' My heart was pounding, my head full of booby-traps and poisoned spears (honestly, *Raiders of the Lost Ark* had a lot to answer for).

'I'm stuck.' Debbie's idea of 'keeping her voice down'

just meant she talked at something approaching a normal volume.

'What? It's not that narrow.'

'It's not my fat backside,' she hissed, 'it's the heel of my boot. There's a grate or something down here and it's stuck.' I shone the light down, and it wasn't a grate, it was a ruddy big hole in the floor. *Uh-oh*, I thought. Even without the (probably non-existent) booby-traps, how safe actually was this secret tunnel?

'Can you get your foot out of your boot? I'm sure we'll be able to pull it or prise it out of the hole if you take your foot out.'

'Shine your phone over here, I need to undo the laces…' Just then we heard voices – male voices. They were coming from below us. I held up my hand to shush Debbie and listened closely.

'You brought a civilian in here, sir? Was that wise?' DI Jones sounded respectful, but, at the same time, horrified. I couldn't blame him. I assumed I was the civilian.

'Jodie Parker isn't a "civilian", she's an ex-officer and a consultant. She's worked on several cases with me where she's had specialist local knowledge. I really think it would be worth talking to her,' said Nathan calmly. He wasn't defensive; he was the highest rank in the room, and they basically had to do what he said, even if they didn't like it.

'Even so, sir… And anyway, what specialist

knowledge can she have in this particular case? Is she an expert on breaking into locked rooms? I thought she was a chef.' Sarcastic git. I decided I disliked Carricksmoor CID intensely.

'No, but she was actually here when the murder occurred, and spoke to all the suspects before and after the murder, so I'd say that counts as specialist enough, wouldn't you?' I could imagine the expression on Nathan's face; that calm one he used when delivering news he knew you wouldn't like or agree with, but that you couldn't do a damn thing about (I hasten to add he'd never had the opportunity – or nerve – to use it on me). 'Unless you've had a sudden breakthrough you haven't told me about? No? In that case, DS Turner, go and find Ms Parker for me and bring her up, will you?'

'Damn damn damn!' I muttered furiously under my breath. There was an opportunity to actually get brought onto the case, even if only briefly, and here I was, stuck in a secret corridor behind a mad woman tugging at her trapped foot. I hopped from my own foot to foot, not sure if I should get the hell out of that passage before the police caught us, or finish exploring it, because I might not get another opportunity.

'Look, don't worry about me, leave me behind,' said Debbie, dramatically.

'Are you sure?'

'No I'm not bloody sure! You were supposed to say, "No, Debbie, don't be stupid!"'

'Sorry. "No, Debbie, don't be stupid." Is that better?' I turned round again, shining the light down the passage. I made my decision. 'Look, I'm going to really quickly go and have a shufty and see where this goes, then I'll be back.'

'What?! You can't—'

'Think about it. If they find us up here, they'll properly shut us down. Even Nathan won't be able to defend us. This is our only chance to find out whether or not this is how the murderer got in. Call Lily, see if she can come and help you.'

'If you leave me here in the dark, Parker, I swear to God—'

'Don't be such a drama queen. Back in a minute.' I quickly picked my way further along the tunnel, ignoring her hisses of 'Jodie! Jodie Parker, you come back here right now!' I could see light, just up ahead.

I soon found out where the light was coming from. The passage ended at a window, surrounded by very solid-looking masonry. There were no draughts or suspiciously off-kilter stone slabs, no wooden panels, and no doorways down into the bedroom below us. It was just another secret room; it didn't lead anywhere. *Bugger*, I thought, and turned back.

I'd just reached Debbie when I heard a voice again,

but this time it wasn't from below, it was from the room beyond the passage.

'What the bloody hell...?' Nathan sounded amazed, but not entirely shocked. Like, this was a surprising turn of events, but not unexpected, given who was involved. He sighed. 'Where is she?'

'Stuck behind Debbie,' I called.

'Oi!' said Debbie. 'I told you, it's not my fat backside.'

'I know it's not, you've got a lovely backside,' I said, soothingly. 'Now let's get your foot out of that hole...' Suddenly a strong pair of arms appeared on the other side of her, grabbing her leg and tugging at it. Debbie shrieked in surprise, her boot heel coming free of the hole with a *pop!*, and she staggered back into Nathan in a very undignified fashion. He gently pushed her upright, and she patted her hair down and rearranged her clothing.

'Thanks, Nath,' she said. 'Now let me out of here.' She pushed past him and fled. Nathan looked at me and grinned.

'Don't ask,' I said. He shook his head in mock exasperation.

'You don't seriously expect me not to?'

'All right, but let's get out of here first...'

We headed back out into the light of the secret library, where Debbie stood massaging her foot, and Lily and Daisy had already started putting the books back on the shelves.

'Where did it end?' asked Daisy excitedly. 'Does it go down to the crime scene?'

'No,' I said. 'It just ends in another priest hole, this time with a window.'

Lily started. 'A window? A proper, big window like the others on this side of the building?'

'Yeah, why?'

She shook her head. 'Of course... We had a curtain company come round to measure up. They said we had thirteen windows on this floor, but when we went into the rooms and counted, there were only twelve. They said they'd counted from the outside, as they'd arrived, but they must've miscounted.'

'But they obviously didn't,' said Nathan, looking around the room. He fixed the others with a stern glare. 'Cool secret room, but no more exploring, OK?' he said, then winked. 'Not until the Carricksmoor lot have gone, anyway.' He looked at me and gestured to the door. 'After you.'

We left and headed down the stairs.

'I take it you heard us talking?' he said. 'Because we heard you. Couldn't work out where all the shrieking was coming from at first. I can't believe you left Debbie in the dark on her own.' He grinned at me again and I knew he absolutely could believe it, and that he'd have done the same.

'I wanted to see if the passage led down to the crime scene,' I said.

'But it doesn't.'

'No. It's just a secret room.' I laughed. 'Listen to me! "Just" a secret room. There are so many in this house, you get blasé about them. Are you any closer to working out how the murderer got in? Or are you still working on the theory that the victim let them in?'

'That's what DI Jones reckons. It doesn't feel right to me, not after we talked about it earlier, but until we get something else to go on…' He shook his head. 'If he hadn't been naked at the time of death, it would make more sense – it could have been anyone in the house. But who would he be letting in, with no clothes on?'

'I don't know,' I said. 'I don't know anything about Santa's sexual proclivities. And then there's the matter of alibis. Who was sleeping with who.' I stopped and reached into my pocket; I'd folded up the three sheets of paper with the plan of the house on them. 'Here. My crack investigation team put this together, but I don't think we're going to get any further now, are we? So you might as well have it.'

He quickly studied the map of the first floor. 'This suite here's quite close to the crime scene. If there was any kind of argument or struggle, then L and T – that's the owner and your friend Lily? – they would have heard something, surely?'

'No, they were…busy.'

'Busy? What were they doing in the middle of the nigh—? Oh, right, *busy*, OK…'

'*Very* busy, according to Lily, so maybe there was a struggle, but they just didn't hear it. And no one on the second floor would have heard a thing over Mum's snoring.'

'Was she doing her hippopotamus-with-sinus-trouble impression again?'

'Debbie had a nightmare about someone coming after her with a chainsaw.'

Nathan nodded. 'I can understand that. I've heard Shirley when she's fallen asleep in the armchair after dinner. I can only imagine how loud that must sound in the dead of night…' He studied the rest of the maps. 'Where's what's-her-face? The woman who discovered the body? Where did she sleep?'

'Pippa? She went home. She lives down the end of the drive, in the old gatehouse.'

'What time did she leave?'

'Hmm, it must've been just after six. Certainly no later than six-thirty, because we were eating by then. She was leaving as Bea – I mean, Belinda Walker – and Liam turned up. Lily invited her to stay for dinner, but she wanted to go home. I don't blame her, it had been a long day.'

'Did she have much to do with the victim?'

'No, not really. She didn't have much to do with anyone, to be honest. She's quite shy. Strikes me as a little nervy and neurotic, but Lily told me she's had a hard time of it, so that might be a bit harsh.'

'And she didn't come back to the house until this morning?'

'No. I was already up with Daisy and the dog. She got here about eight thirty, I think. It was her footprints Daisy spotted, remember? One set heading down to her cottage, made last night after it stopped snowing, and one set heading back up this morning. Technically, I suppose she *could* have come back in the night, and then followed the same set of prints back up here in the morning, but it would be pretty tricky to get your feet exactly into every single footprint, so it only looked like a single journey. And besides, her footprints led to the front door, which was still locked and bolted on the inside when I got up this morning.'

'She couldn't have got in, then.'

'No. And, anyway, what motive could she possibly have to kill anyone? She's a cleaner at a minor country house in the middle of nowhere.'

DI Jones cleared his throat behind us.

'So, some of the other guests have mentioned that Isaac Barnes had an altercation with the victim last night, and he seems to be the only person who knew which room he was sleeping in.'

'Apart from James,' I said. DI Jones looked at me.

'Yes, I'm aware of that—'

'Only you said Isaac was the "only" person who knew, and he wasn't,' I explained. I could almost feel Nathan next to me, thinking, *Let it go, Jodie*... But I hadn't forgiven Jones for being sarcastic about me earlier.

'James McAllister doesn't have a motive.' Jones ignored me and spoke to Nathan, even though it was actually me he was replying to.

'He doesn't have an alibi, either,' said Nathan, mildly. 'Mr Barnes does. His son was with him. But you're right, we do need to speak to him anyway. Take him into the dining room. Give me five minutes and then I'll join you.' He waited for DI Jones to leave, then turned to me. 'Time to go home, Jodie...'

Chapter Sixteen

I moaned, but Nathan was right. There was no point me staying; I'd already been more involved in the investigation than I should have been, and if I annoyed DI Jones any more he could easily make trouble for Nathan about it. Mum, Daisy and Debbie all needed to get home, and the police had finished taking statements from all of us, so there was no excuse. Belinda and Liam were already bundling their coats on, watched with great hostility by the rest of us, and with one final glare at James, they thanked Lily and Trevor for their hospitality (to which Trevor gruffly responded that he'd have thrown them out in the snow, had he known who they were), and left.

Matt Turner had heard from Sergeant Adams back in Penstowan, who had taken his orders from Nathan the night before very seriously and had been continuing to pester the Highways Agency for information, despite finishing his shift a few hours ago. The roads across the moor had all been cleared, although it was still better to avoid the narrow country lanes and stick to the bigger A roads where possible.

'We'll go via Bodmin and then onto the A39,' I told Nathan, as we finished packing everything back into the van. 'It's longer, but I reckon it'll be safer.'

'Just drive carefully,' he said, 'and text me when you get there so I know you've got home OK.'

'I will,' I said, giving him a peck on the cheek. 'But all this is academic if the Gimpmobile won't start...'

He laughed. 'You have *got* to stop calling it that.' But the outline of the decal on the side – placed there by the previous owner, who had owned a saucy fetish shop in staid Tavistock – still showed through the paintwork, even after a complete respray, and (unfortunately) 'Gimpmobile' was the only apt name we could think of.

I walked around to the driver's side and got in, Nathan stopping next to the open door, ready to look under the bonnet of the van if need be. 'OK, cross your fingers, eyes, legs, pray to whatever gods you believe in, here goes...' I turned the key, and...it started first time, the engine purring as if to say, *What were you worried about?*

'Bloody hell,' said Debbie, clambering in next to me through the passenger door. 'I weren't expecting that.'

'Nor was I!' I leaned out of the door, pulling Nathan towards me for a proper kiss goodbye as Daisy, Mum and Germaine all climbed in and squashed up next to Debbie. 'I'll text you when I get home. Message me when you leave, yeah? It'd be nice to see you properly tonight.'

'*Im*properly's more fun,' said Mum, getting ready to cackle again, but Daisy sighed.

'Oh, Nana, we can't take you anywhere.'

'*Au Cointreau*, Daisy love,' said Mum. I thought about correcting her terrible French pronunciation, but decided against it. 'You can take me *everywhere*, as long as you take me twice. The second time to apologise.'

'Sounds about right,' I said.

Nathan laughed and shut the van door, then waved us off as we drove slowly out of the courtyard, past the police cars, Matt Turner's old Land Rover, and a shiny BMW which I assumed belonged to the medical examiner, who had arrived as we were getting our stuff from the kitchen. Trevor had roped in a couple of police officers to help him clear the driveway of snow, and he gave us a cheery wave as we passed him. But I didn't feel cheerful.

'I cannot wait to get home and give my babies a hug,' said Debbie. 'They'll hate it, but I don't care.'

'Callum'll enjoy it,' I said, and she laughed.

'My big chunk of love…' She gave a big dramatic sigh and laughed again, then looked at me. 'What's the matter with you?'

'We didn't solve it, did we?' I said, feeling unsatisfied.

'No, but we had a right crack at it. It was fun! And we did only have a couple of hours.' Debbie was being reasonable. I hated it when I was in a mood and she was reasonable.

'I know, but…'

'And we got to find a secret room!' said Daisy, her eyes shining. 'That was so cool. How many people can say they found a secret room?' Germaine barked, in clear agreement. 'We could have been the first people to see that room for hundreds of years! Just think, you and Debbie could literally have been walking in the footsteps of some priest, in hiding from the Queen's men. Or a monk, or a nun or something—'

'A nun on the run,' said Mum.

'I know,' I said, but there was still the vague feeling at the back of my mind that I'd missed something.

We reached the gatehouse. Pippa was outside, scraping snow off her car. I pulled up alongside her.

'All right, Pip? You off out?'

She nodded. 'Yes. I thought I'd pop into St Austell, do some Christmas shopping to take my mind off…everything.'

'Be careful, the roads are still slippery. Merry

Christmas, Pippa.' Behind me, my little gang all sang out, 'Merry Christmas, Pippa!' She smiled.

'Merry Christmas to you, too.' She stood and watched as we drove away. In the rear-view mirror I saw her turn and go back inside the house.

I passed the Japanese girls' hire car, which was still stuck in the ditch waiting to be rescued, then turned the van gingerly into the lane, skidding slightly on the packed ice. The road itself looked pretty clear, though. I would just take it very, very slowly. A telecom van was parked at the side of the road, a cold-looking engineer working on the telephone-line box on the grass verge. *So THAT'S why the phone wasn't working,* I thought. There must be a line down somewhere. It had had nothing to do with the murder after all; it really was just a coincidence. For some reason that made me feel even more dissatisfied. I pulled over slightly to make way for a van, a private ambulance which I assumed was heading for Kingseat Abbey and the remains of the dear departed Saint Nick.

My phone pinged with a text message. 'Can you read that for me?' I asked Debbie, wriggling slightly so she could get her hand in the pocket of my puffer jacket. She grabbed the phone. 'My passcode—' I started, but then stopped when I realised she'd already done it. 'How did you know what the number was?'

She rolled her eyes. 'Daisy's birthday, yeah? And you

a copper, as well...' She read the message. 'It's from Lily. You know the book she was looking at? Well, it does mention a secret passage from one of the bedrooms, and she reckons, going by the age of the book, it's referring to the Dyneley Suite. But it doesn't say where the entrance is, or where it goes.'

'Bugger...' I said. 'I wonder if she's told Nathan...' I had a sudden vision of Nathan, at the crime scene with me earlier that morning, before anyone else had arrived. Picking up the pen and prodding the flesh on Steve's tummy... I slammed on the brakes (not a good idea when the road was icy, but I got away with it) and turned to look at the others. 'Oh my God, I am so stupid.' I tugged off my seatbelt. 'Deb, you can drive this, can't you?'

'Well, yeah...'

'Can you take everyone home? I'll get a ride back with Nathan.' I took my phone out of her hand, then pulled my woolly hat from my other pocket and rammed it down over my ears.

'Mum, what are you doing?' Daisy looked a little concerned, but again, like Nathan earlier, not *that* concerned because I had form for this sort of thing.

'It's fine, sweetheart. I just know where the entrance to the secret passage is. And yes,' I said quickly, interrupting all three of my companions as they opened their mouths to speak, 'I know in theory I could ring

Nathan and tell him, but the phone signal's dodgy and, to be fair, I just don't want to.' I leaned across Debbie and gave Daisy a kiss. 'Be good for Nana.' I looked at Mum. 'And, Nana, be good for Daisy. Germaine, just be good. Debbie, do what you like. Laters.'

I leaped out of the van, leaving them open-mouthed. I was very glad that we hadn't got that far down the road, as it was freezing and I was already regretting walking back rather than driving. But the lane was quite narrow, and I didn't fancy my chances of doing a three-point turn without ending up sliding into a hedge. I looked back as the van started up again and gave them a big wave that they probably couldn't see, and walked on.

The entrance to Kingseat Abbey was a bit further on than I'd thought, but I was soon passing the gatehouse. Pippa's car was still outside, but there was no sign of her. She must have decided not to go shopping after all. I thought that was wise. It wasn't the weather to be going out on the roads, not unless you really had to.

I slogged my way up the drive, remembering how the Gimpmobile had struggled up there the day before. My breathing sounded almost as laboured as the engine had, the cold air getting on my lungs and making me cough. I pulled the zip of my jacket up as far as it would go and stuffed my hands in my pockets, but I was relieved when I reached the house.

I banged the heavy iron knocker, which made that loud but very satisfying *BOOM* against the wooden door. Lily opened it so quickly that I jumped.

'Woah! You nearly gave me a heart attack!' I gasped. 'Were you just passing the door or something?'

'No, I was waiting for you to come back,' she grinned. 'You took longer than I thought.' She peered over my shoulder. 'You walked?'

I nodded. 'I left Debbie to drive, I wanted to get Daisy home. I know where the entrance is.'

'To the secret passage? Where is it? In the Dyneley Suite?'

'Yes. I'm positive.' I frowned. 'Or at least I was when I jumped out of the van and started walking. Where's Nathan?'

'Jodie?' Nathan came out of the dining room, followed by Matt. 'What's happened? Has the van broken down? Are you all right, you look frozen...' He rushed over and took my hands, rubbing them to warm them up, and I allowed myself a little swoon – a swoonette, if you will – before getting down to business.

'No no, it's fine, Debbie's driving everyone home. I know how the murderer got into the room.'

DI Jones came out of the room. He didn't look very pleased to see me. 'I thought you'd gone? Sir, I thought we'd cleared Ms Parker and her group and sent them home?'

'Why don't you carry on interviewing Mr Barnes?' said Nathan, in a tone of voice that made it clear it wasn't a suggestion. 'Ms Parker and I have things to discuss. Possible new evidence.' Jones didn't move. 'As you were, DI Jones,' said Nathan firmly. Ooh, I loved it when he pulled rank and got all bossy...

DI Jones glared at me and went back inside. Matt Turner gave a snort, then looked at Nathan. 'Sorry Guv, I know we're all s'posed to be on the same team and that, but the Carricksmoor lot are a bunch of—'

'Yes, I know. Give me Davey Trelawney and even Sergeant Adams, God help me, any day of the week.' Nathan shook his head. 'And I really never thought I'd say that... So come on, Ms Parker, what have you got for us?'

'Well, DCI Withers, DS Turner... I'm an idiot. We need to go up to the crime scene now.'

'Forensics are still in there, Guv. And the ME.'

'Leave them to me.'

We headed up the stairs and down the corridor to the Dyneley Suite. Inside, the Scene of Crime team were tagging blood spatters and crimson feathers from the slashed pillow beneath the unfortunate Santa. The female medical examiner was getting something out of her kit. She looked up as we entered, but didn't say anything.

'Merry Christmas,' said Nathan, sardonically. 'This one's a real gift, isn't it?'

'Isn't it just,' she said. 'Interesting wound.'

'Interesting, in what way?' I asked.

'The angle of entry. The sword went in here…' She pointed to an area just beneath her own collarbone to demonstrate, 'nicked a lung, then out through the middle of his back. Like this.' She held her hand up at an oblique angle, pointing down.

'That *is* interesting,' said Nathan, bending low over the body to have a closer look. 'I could see before that it hadn't gone straight through, but *downwards*? That puts a new spin on things.'

'Does it?' I asked. I had a vague idea of what they were getting at, but it was just that: vague.

'So the murderer didn't just pull their arm back and stab the poor bugger,' said Matt. 'Instead of—' He mimed pulling his arm back, holding an invisible sword, and thrusting it out into an equally invisible unfortunate victim. 'It was more—' He thrust his invisible sword downwards. He looked at Nathan. 'That's really awkward, Guv. The attacker would have to be a lot taller than the victim to do that.'

'Yes…' said Nathan, thoughtfully. He looked at the

ME. 'Any idea of time of death yet? When can we get this poor sod out of here?'

'Give me a chance, DCI Withers,' said the ME. 'I've only been here five minutes. It's going to be difficult to pin down, as the window was opened, I'm guessing by whoever discovered the body, to let the smell out.'

I nodded. 'Yeah, that was me, sorry. But to make it even more hard to gauge, the heater had been left on all night, and I didn't realise until a couple of hours after he was found, when the smell got really bad...'

'Not to worry. It'll be as exact as I can make it, but we can never say it's completely accurate. I was about to take Santa's temperature.' She held up a large thermometer. 'He very considerately died in the perfect position.' We watched in horrified fascination as she turned towards his naked buttocks. I wrenched my gaze away.

'Rather you than me,' said Nathan, grimacing. He turned to me. 'Can you show me this passage?' He snorted. 'Bearing in mind where the ME's about to shove that thermometer, maybe that's not the best choice of word. Do you need me to clear the room? There's a lot of people in here.'

A lot of people to be embarrassed in front of if I'm wrong, I thought, but I wasn't wrong, I could feel it.

'If you could just move some of this stuff away from the wall...thank you...' One of the SOCO team moved a box of bagged evidence away and stashed it on the other side of the room. I stared at the wooden panel, and the floor beneath it, and I knew I was definitely right.

'What is it?'

I pointed to the desk. 'That really annoyed me earlier. It looks so wrong. Why would you put a piece of furniture there? It's not in the middle of the wall.'

'No...' Matt Turner looked doubtful. 'Maybe – don't take this the wrong way, Jodie – maybe you're just a little bit OCD and it hadn't occurred to the owner to move it into the middle? Maybe they liked it there?' But Nathan was looking at me like I was a genius (which I am).

'You're right. They've obviously taken a lot of care over this room, the decor, the design...' He waved his hand towards the figure on the bed. 'Obviously that spoils the ambience a bit...that desk just isn't right.' I pointed down to the thick rug on the floor. It didn't cover the whole room – there was a gap around the edge, showing off the grey flagstones – but the front two legs of the desk stood on it.

'Look at the rug. Further along – where the desk *should* have been, I reckon – there are two indentations in the rug.'

'Where the front legs of the desk would be. They must've stood there for a while, if they've made a dent in the carpet.'

'Exactly. That's where the desk normally stands, not where it is now. Someone moved it.'

'Why?' asked Matt, but we all knew. Nathan bent down to study the panel.

'You said that the priest hole entrance had a worn bit in the corner, where you pushed it to open the door...' He shook his head. 'There's nothing like that here.'

'Maybe because it was never used as much as the priest hole, maybe that one just got worn down over time. And then, of course, the secret room upstairs had a completely different opening mechanism. They weren't necessarily all built by the same person, or at the same time, so why would they all work the same?' I bent down to look at it as well. 'Or maybe, most of the time, it got opened from the other side...'

Matt leaned forward to look at the panel too. I became aware that everyone else in the room had stopped what they were doing and were watching us, incredulous. I could feel my cheeks going red. I *was* right, wasn't I? I turned slightly to address them.

'If anyone else has any better ideas...' I said, but my feet caught on the edge of the rug as I turned, and I fell back. I stuck out a hand to save myself and heard a gentle *click* as the panel slid open. Nathan, Matt and everyone else in the room (apart from the corpse) looked at me, amazed. I smiled. 'Told you so...'

'I never doubted you for a minute,' said Nathan.

Matt grinned. 'Gotta admit I did…'

I stood up, taking my phone out of my pocket and turning on the torch – I felt very proud of myself for being so technologically advanced, before I saw that Nathan and Matt had already done the same. I took a deep breath and bent down again to get through the door, but Nathan put out a hand to stop me.

'I think I should go first, don't you?'

I snorted. 'Yeah, in your dreams. I worked it out, I'm going first.' Nathan shook his head.

'What am I going to do with you?' he said, exasperated. *I could give you a few ideas,* I nearly said, but then I banished those thoughts from my mind, as this was neither the time nor the place, and apart from that, the corpse on the bed was a bit of a passion killer. 'Go on, then. Matt, you stay here. If we're not back in twenty minutes, bring some back-up.'

'Yes, Guv,' said Matt. He shone his phone into the dark hole behind the panel and then straightened up with a smile. 'Rather you than me. I hate enclosed spaces…'

I stepped through the door, bent low to avoid the panel above it, then straightened up, shining my torch around. Bang in front of me was a wall, and I realised we must be in the narrow gap between the wood panelling in the bedroom, and the smooth plaster wall in the corridor. To my right there was another wall; to my left, the passageway continued for another couple of feet. Nathan followed and barged straight into me, reaching out to grab me as I nearly slipped over.

'Sorry, I should've got out of your way,' I said, but he shook his head.

'No, it's a good job you didn't. Look.' He pointed the beam of light from his phone down to the floor, and half a step in front of me the floor disappeared. 'You'd have gone down there. Be careful...'

We edged closer and shone our torches at the gap in the floor, revealing that it wasn't in fact a hole but a steep slope downwards. The passage must come out somewhere on the ground floor, which meant that anyone in the house that night would have had access to it. If they'd known it was there.

We carefully made our way down. The passage meandered and zig-zagged somewhat – it obviously couldn't just go straight down, or we'd have slid all the way to the bottom of it, like we were on a helter-skelter or something – and I tried to work out where it would end, but the twists and turns disoriented me. At one point we came face to face with a brick-built stack, and I thought of the stone chimney that connected the priest hole with the lounge; it would make sense for there to be another way out of there, in case of discovery. But no. The tunnel abruptly cut away from the chimney (if that's what it was) and kept on heading down.

'Does this house have a cellar?' asked Nathan.

'I don't know,' I said. 'Probably. I think most houses of this age would have, but Lily never mentioned one.'

'Well, I think we're definitely below ground here,' said Nathan. 'We've been going down for a long time now, and the air feels musty.' He was right; it smelled earthy, and it was cold. I was glad I'd kept my jacket on, but poor Nathan just had a thick jumper.

The tunnel took another abrupt turn, but now I could see it stretching out straight ahead of us. Nathan stopped and shone his phone torch at the ceiling. 'Look.' There were lights above us, pretty old, by the looks of it, but still electric. They led onwards, all through the tunnel. 'Either this passage isn't as old as it looks, or it was in regular use at one point in the not-so-distant past.' He studied the light fittings. 'Was this house used during the war? These look like they're from the thirties or forties to me.'

'I don't know. A lot of the old places down here were used as convalescent hospitals for shell-shocked soldiers, so maybe…' We carried on walking. 'We must be well out of the house by now, mustn't we? I don't know if we're heading towards the road or the other way, towards the old stables. That would seem like a good place for the passage to come out.'

Nathan shook his head. 'I think we've gone further than that.'

We walked on. The tunnel began to slope upwards, almost imperceptibly at first, and then suddenly there was a wooden door in front of us. We stopped and looked at each other.

'I hope it doesn't only open from the other side,' I whispered.

'Me too,' said Nathan. He was whispering as well; we didn't know what was on the other side of the door... He pointed to a brass handle protruding from the wood. 'We're in luck. But I'm definitely going first this time.' I nodded, suddenly very nervous as well as excited to see where the passage would end.

Nathan reached for the handle. I waited for it to be stuck, for it to be just another red herring in this twisty murder case, but it turned easily. We looked at each other, both holding our breaths, then he opened the door and we stepped through.

We were in a ground-floor bedroom. It was small, but full of character. The walls were papered with a chintzy patterned wallpaper, the sort I'd normally hate, but it suited this room, with its ornate, stone-arched windows which looked out into the garden. There was a double bed, covered in a blue and white floral duvet cover, and white-painted wooden furniture. It was so *normal*, so completely at odds with what I'd been imagining – some Gothic torture chamber, maybe, or at the very least a run-down, dingy outbuilding. Not this bright, neat bedroom with its Laura Ashley curtains and Ikea chest of drawers. I turned; the door into the secret passage was part of a built-in wardrobe, with three doors. I opened one of the other doors, in case there was another passage behind it, but it was just a cupboard, empty but for the naked coat hangers dangling from a rail. I shut both doors. The door of the bedroom itself was ajar, opening out into a hallway.

I turned to look at Nathan enquiringly, but he put a finger to his lips, then pointed to the end of the bed. On the floor there was a holdall or overnight bag, packed so tightly that the zip wouldn't do up. There was a photo in a frame sticking out of it. I crept over to it and pulled out the picture. It was a young man in a soldier's uniform, in his mid-twenties by the look of it. I stared at it in astonishment, then held it up for Nathan to see.

'Is that Isaac Barnes?' he whispered, surprised. I shook my head.

'He was never in the Army,' I said, quietly. 'But it looks just like him…'

Just then we heard movement outside in the hallway. Nathan grabbed me and pulled me to one side of the bedroom door, his arm across my chest – either to protect me or stop me leaping out, I wasn't sure which.

Pippa walked in, dressed warmly, ready to go out. She reached out and picked up the holdall, then turned to scan the room; the classic gesture of someone moving out, or at least going away for a while, making sure they hadn't left anything behind. Her gaze eventually reached us, standing by the doorway, and she froze.

'Hello, Pippa,' I said, conversationally. 'You changed your mind about going shopping, then?'

'Er, yes,' she said, her eyes darting guiltily across the room to the door of the passageway. She was obviously trying to work out if we knew about it or not. But how else would we have ended up in her room?

'Mrs Shaw? We haven't met. I'm Detective Chief Inspector Nathan Withers, Penstowan CID.' Nathan always used his full title when he wanted to intimidate someone. 'Decided to go away for Christmas instead, did we?'

'Yes. This business has really upset me.' I had to hand it to her, most other people in her situation would have completely crumbled and admitted that the game was up, but she was determined to go down fighting. Or talking, anyway.

'Maybe going to spend some time with your son?' I said, and the look on her face told me we had her.

Chapter Seventeen

Nathan called Matt – the mobile phone signal had definitely improved alongside the weather – who appeared through the secret door about two minutes later, having already got more than halfway down the passage. We'd obviously taken longer than we'd realised. He handcuffed Pippa, which I was going to protest against – she wasn't exactly a big, burly gang member or anything – before I remembered that she'd driven that sword into Steve with enough force to go clear through him. Although I still didn't understand how or why. Nathan went outside and found Pippa's car full of suitcases; she'd obviously been planning to disappear with all her worldly goods and possessions.

We thought about taking her back to the house through the grounds, but it was so cold and Nathan wasn't dressed that warmly, so we marched her back through the passage, emerging onto the crime scene to be greeted by faces that were even more incredulous than when we'd left.

'Where's DI Jones?' asked Nathan, propelling a surly Pippa into the room. 'Is he still interviewing Mr Barnes?'

'Just finished, sir,' said DC Carver, who was watching us with amazement, and still a touch of hostility. 'We know Isaac Barnes argued with the victim—'

'And made up with him minutes afterwards – yes, we know,' said Nathan impatiently. 'We needed to document that of course, but he was never really a suspect.'

'Wasn't he?' Carver looked confused. Nathan swept past him, leading Pippa by the arm. Matt and I grinned at each other and followed. Solving cases was always a real rush, but getting one over on Carricksmoor made it even more satisfying.

We followed Nathan as he led Pippa gently but firmly down the stairs and into the dining room, where Isaac still sat, looking annoyed. James was talking to him in a quiet voice, obviously trying to placate him, but I could tell that Isaac was furious at having been questioned at such length when the email to his PA surely cleared him of any wrongdoing.

Isaac looked up as we all walked in, surprised to see us.

'I thought you'd both gone home?' he said to me and

Pippa, his eyes widening as he spotted the handcuffs around her wrists. He looked up at Nathan. 'What's going on?'

'I really must protest, sir—' DI Jones began, but Nathan stopped him.

'Thank you, DI Jones, but I've got this now,' said Nathan. Jones fumed, but didn't say anything. Nathan turned to Isaac. 'Do you know this woman?'

'I can't say I do, DCI Withers,' said Isaac, looking at Pippa. She writhed against the handcuffs.

'You're denying me *again*?' She shook her head. 'Why does that surprise me?'

Isaac's face changed, his expression of utter bewilderment showing sudden, horrified comprehension.

'Philippa?' He stared at the furious woman in front of him, incredulous. She nodded.

'I can't believe you didn't recognise me,' she spat. 'After all, I've hardly changed.' Her tone of voice made it obvious that she was aware exactly how much she had.

'You look—' he started, and for a horrible moment I thought he was going to say 'older', but thankfully he wasn't completely stupid. He changed tack, shaking his head and looking at her wistfully. 'It's been thirty years, Phil. We always used to call you Phil, didn't we? Or Phyllis, because we knew it wound you up. With everyone here calling you Pippa, it just didn't click...'

'You're old friends, then?' I said, but it was obvious they'd been more than that. The photograph in her holdall proved that.

'Yeah, we went to school together. The three musketeers...' Isaac was still staring at her like he couldn't believe what he was seeing.

'Three?'

'Yeah. Me and my mate Mark. Mark Sykes. Phil was Mark's girlfriend. I heard you got married.' Pippa nodded, her eyes never leaving Isaac's face, which was clearly making him very uncomfortable. 'I was really sorry to hear about him passing away. I would've come to the funeral, but by the time I knew about it, I'd missed it...' Isaac turned to Nathan. 'I still don't understand what's going on. Why is Phil – Pippa – in handcuffs? You surely can't think she killed Steve? Why on earth would she do that?'

'That's what we want to know,' I said.

'It was very clever, using the secret passage,' said Nathan to Pippa. 'We'd completely discounted you, because you left the house well before the murder and came back well after it, and during most of that time the doors were locked. And the snow meant that we could see that no one had approached the house overnight. We were convinced that it had to be someone who'd stayed here overnight.'

'Secret passage?' DI Jones looked bewildered. I'd

almost forgotten the poor bugger was still in the room. 'What on earth are you talking about?'

'From the crime scene,' I said. 'We followed it and guess where it came out? The gatehouse. Where Pippa here was getting ready to do a runner.' I turned to her. 'How did you know about the passage?'

'I've worked here for years, long before Trevor bought the place,' she said. 'I was a carer for the previous owner's mother, Mrs Wolstencroft. They moved me into the gatehouse so I could be close to her, and after she died they put in a covenant that meant I could live there for as long as I liked, even if the house was sold to new owners. Mrs Wolstencroft slept in that bedroom, and she told me about the passage. She told me that it had been built to smuggle priests out of the house, but that Thomas Dyneley – *his* ancestor – had kept his mistresses in the gatehouse, and used the tunnel to sneak them into his bed.' She sneered at Isaac. 'Things never change, do they? Rich men use poor women, and it's always the women who end up paying.'

Isaac looked confused. 'What are you talking about?'

'Don't pretend you don't know,' she hissed, but he shook his head.

'I really *don't* know what you're talking about. Have I done something to hurt you?'

Nathan and I exchanged looks. *Time to mention the young man in photograph*, I thought.

'How old's your son, Pippa?' I asked. 'Is he still in the Army?'

'He's twenty-nine,' she said, staring at Isaac. Isaac stared back, dumbfounded, and I could see realisation finally dawning.

'Wait – you're not saying—' Stunned, he looked at James, who was sitting next to him, then turned back to Pippa. 'Your son – are you really saying he's mine? I didn't know – I had no idea...'

'I believe you,' said James. He turned to Nathan. 'Are you sure she's telling the truth? No offence,' he added hastily, looking at Pippa as she threw a murderous glance in his direction.

'He looks a lot like you, Mr Barnes,' said Nathan. 'He's got your chin.'

'How did it happen?' I asked. 'And how come you didn't know?'

Isaac sighed deeply. 'It was the night before I left for London. We all went to a mate's birthday party—'

'We?' asked Nathan.

'Me, Phil and Mark.' He turned to Pippa with a sad smile. 'You and Mark were meant for each other. I couldn't compete with him. He was a good bloke.' He shook his head. 'I knew you knew I fancied you, but when you said you had a leaving present for me, I didn't think you meant...' His voice trailed off, and we all knew what that leaving present had been. 'I shouldn't have done it, but I was leaving and I had no intention of coming back, and I thought, as long as he never found out... Did Mark know? Did he know that he wasn't the father?'

Pippa shook her head, but looked doubtful. 'No. At least, I never told him. We did try for another baby, but it never happened, and all the time Lee was looking more and more like you... I don't know. Maybe he guessed. But he never mentioned it.'

'So,' said Nathan, 'all the time we've been assuming that poor old Santa was the intended victim, we've been barking up the wrong tree, haven't we? It was Isaac you were after, not Steve.'

'I get that you might have a bit of a grudge against Isaac for getting you up the duff as a teenager,' I said, 'but what I *don't* get is why you would want to kill him now? What good would it do you? If it was me, I'd be suing him for child maintenance back payments, although even that seems a bit harsh, as he obviously knew nothing about it. And your son's all grown up. What's the point of dredging all this up?'

'The *point*,' shot Pippa, and I took a step back, because she appeared to be on the verge of becoming completely unhinged. Nathan took a warning step towards her. Up to this point, she hadn't seemed very dangerous, but the blood-soaked Santa Claus impersonator upstairs said otherwise.

Pippa took a breath to calm herself. 'The point is, he *did* know. I told him.'

Everyone turned to look at him as Isaac gasped in disbelief. 'When? I haven't heard from you since that night. I heard *about* you, I knew you and Mark got married and had a baby after I left, but you never told me the baby was mine.'

'Liar.' She stared at him, her face a mask of calm hatred. But the rest of her obviously wasn't quite as calm, because she wobbled and put out a hand to steady herself against the wall. Nathan reached out and pulled over a chair, gesturing to her to sit.

'Tell us your side of the story, Pippa,' he said, firmly but gently. She took another deep breath.

'I knew I was pregnant, a few weeks after you left,' she told Isaac. 'And I knew it was yours, because Mark and I had never done it. You were my first.'

'Oh God,' said Isaac, looking even more wracked with guilt. 'If I'd known, I wouldn't have gone along with it. Your first time should have been with Mark, not me.'

'That was my choice. I knew you would never come back, and anyway, although I fancied you, I didn't want to be with you, I wanted Mark. So I slept with him and told him the baby was his.' She looked up at the faces of everyone watching her. 'What? I was sixteen years old, what else was I supposed to do?'

'Tell the truth?' suggested DI Jones. James shot him an exasperated look.

'Easy to say when you're not the one holding the baby,' he said, and I had to agree with him.

'Mark was a wonderful husband and a brilliant dad. We never had much money, but we were happy. We used to see you in the paper, see how successful you were, and Mark was so proud of you, even if you never bothered with us anymore. I knew I'd picked the right bloke to bring up my son. He wasn't selfish like you.' Isaac hung his head in shame, and James reached out to touch him on the arm. I remembered our conversation in the kitchen the night before, although that now seemed like it had been weeks ago. Isaac had been selfish, throughout his life, and he knew it. But he'd tried to make amends. Surely if she had contacted him, he would have helped her?

'Mark died when Lee was fourteen. We had no savings or life insurance – we'd barely been able to get by as it was, let alone put money away – and without his wages, I couldn't afford to pay the mortgage. We were on the verge of being kicked out of our home. I didn't know what to do.' She looked up at Isaac and smiled grimly. 'And then there you were, on the news, having just paid off this woman who said you'd knocked her up at a tech conference a couple of years before. You'd been denying it was yours, and then suddenly you agreed to settle out of court, so you must've been lying. You gave her some ridiculous amount of money, like half a million or something. All I wanted was twenty grand to pay off my mortgage. That's all I was asking for, some help to keep the roof over our son's head.'

Isaac looked at her, his face a picture of misery. 'Oh God, Phil, if I'd known...'

'You did know! I wrote to you!'

'When? I never got any letter.' Isaac pulled up a chair and sat next to her. 'I swear to you, I would have helped you if I'd known, of course I would.' He sighed. 'If you'd told me when you got pregnant, I—'

'What? You'd have come back to rescue me?' said Pippa, her voice heavy with sarcasm. Isaac shook his head.

'No, not if you didn't want me to. But I would always have made sure you had money.'

'After you settled with this other woman – I bet you had all sorts of people saying you'd done this or that, trying to get money out of you?' Nathan asked. He nodded.

'I did. All these women coming out of the woodwork, saying we'd had affairs or one-night stands.' He sighed. 'Like I told you last night, Jodie...' I saw Nathan prick up his ears; was he feeling a bit jealous, maybe? 'I wasn't a nice person in those days. I was young and rich and a cocky little bugger, and a lot of women seemed to like that. So yeah, I probably *had* slept with some of them, but most of them I didn't know. Some of them were accusing me of having sex with them in cities I'd never even been to. They didn't even try to make their lies very convincing. But I never saw anything from Pippa.'

'You told me you had a crack legal team, who used to – how did you put it? – insulate you from fall-out. If someone tried to sue you for your actions in the boardroom, your legal team would make it all go away.' I was thinking aloud, but it made sense to me. 'Maybe they tried to make your actions in the bedroom go away, too?'

Isaac stared at me. 'You mean there could have been more women out there, saying stuff like that, and they never even told me about them?'

'There could even be more babies out there,' said DI Jones. Isaac looked horrified while Nathan shot Jones another exasperated look.

'That's not up to us to speculate about, DI Jones.'

I turned to Pippa. 'Did you get a reply to your letter?' I asked. She nodded.

'Yeah, I got one all right. Telling me that Mr Barnes completely refuted my allegations and that he didn't recall ever meeting me. They said it was up to me if I wanted to pursue it, but if I made my allegations again they would take me to court for defamation or something.'

'But surely you could have had a DNA test done? You could have proved it?'

'Lee had just lost his dad – his *real* dad, not the sperm donor. I didn't want to go to court and have him find out about Isaac. I didn't want him thinking it had all been a lie.'

'So you left it at that?' asked Nathan.

'I did try again. I wrote back and explained that I was a very old friend from Cornwall, but they sent me some legal letter telling me I had to leave Isaac alone.'

'A cease and desist letter?' I asked, and she nodded.

'Phil – Pippa – I am so sorry,' said Isaac. 'I honestly had no idea…'

'We lost the house,' she said matter-of-factly. 'The house where my son had grown up, where I'd had happy years with my husband, where all my memories of him were. We got put into emergency housing. I got very depressed and they took my son away from me.' She wiped at her eyes, and I felt tears coming to mine, too. This poor woman had made mistakes (not the least of which was lying under a sheet in a bedroom upstairs, waiting for the ambulance to take him away), but she had suffered a lot, too. Some people might judge her for hiding her son's true parentage, but she'd been little more than a child herself at the time. Teenagers do stupid things, and most of the time they don't get caught out; but when they do, how are they supposed to cope? Teenagers don't have a team of lawyers and legal experts to get them off the hook, not like millionaire businessmen do.

'What happened then?' I asked gently.

'I got lucky.' She snorted. 'God knew I was due some good luck. I got the job here, with the gatehouse to live in. I got my Lee back. But he'd been with foster parents for almost a year by then. It was the worst year of my life.'

'So why didn't you just confront Mr Barnes when you saw him yesterday?' asked Nathan.

Pippa looked at us mutinously. 'I was going to, but when he turned up, swanning around like he's the Messiah, like money cures everything... It wasn't that he didn't give me the money I needed all those years ago – how would that money help me now? I already lost my home. But when he wouldn't even admit to knowing me, because I'm just some ordinary woman from Cornwall, a cleaner for God's sake, not a fancy businesswoman or glamorous actress – you can shake your head, Isaac, but I've seen photos of you with your girlfriends, they're all young and blonde. You were my first, and you couldn't admit you knew me. Or worse, you didn't even remember me.' She turned to me. 'I wasn't going to kill him. I just wanted to scare him, or shout at him, I didn't really know what I wanted.'

'But you took the sword,' said Nathan. 'That sounds like premeditated murder to me.'

'No! It wasn't like that – I was just going to leave it in his room. I wanted to freak him out.'

'It's a symbol of his family's betrayal...' I said, and she nodded. Nathan looked confused. 'Lily told us about the history of the sword. Isaac is related to the family who lived here in Elizabethan times. They worked here. They dobbed in the owners for being Catholic, and were given the house as a reward. That sword was also given to them, to remind them of the great service they'd done the queen – it was used to behead the owner. But it was also a constant reminder of their betrayal, and eventually it drove the head of the family mad.'

'You wanted to remind me of my betrayal?' asked Isaac. Pippa nodded. 'But I didn't even know I'd betrayed you!'

'I got the idea about leaving the sword after Lily told everyone the story about it,' said Pippa. 'I'd already taken it out of its glass case earlier, to keep it away from the kids at the party. It was easy to tuck it under my coat when I left and went home.'

'That still doesn't explain how the sword ended up sticking out of the victim's chest,' said Nathan.

'Or how you could mistake him for Isaac,' I said. 'He was twice the size of him.'

Pippa shook her head. For the first time she actually looked remorseful.

'I didn't kill him. I don't know how the sword ended up in him, I honestly don't. I never meant to hurt anyone, least of all that poor man.'

'What did you do, Pippa?' I asked gently.

'I was just going to leave it on the desk, so Isaac would see it when he woke up,' she said. 'When I made up the room that evening, before I left, I moved the desk away from the secret door, so I could get in without making a noise. I waited until three in the morning, so that Isaac would be asleep. But when I got there, the bed was empty and the bathroom light was on, and I thought, if I could leave it in the bed, it would be even better. It would be more disturbing.'

'You left a sword in my bed, knowing that my eight-year-old son was sleeping there as well?' Isaac looked at her in disgust. She hung her head.

'I know, I know. I didn't care about you but I would never hurt a child. I thought about leaving it under the bedclothes, but I was worried that you wouldn't see it, and your little boy would get in and cut himself on it – it's still really sharp. I thought it would be really dramatic if I left it sticking out of the bed, so I stuck it in the pillow. I didn't want to slash the mattress because it would cost Trevor more to replace. But the hilt of the sword was so heavy that it made it fall over.'

'So you tried standing it up the other way…' I said. I could kind of see now what she'd done. 'Was it you that tied the leather belt onto the bed post?'

She nodded. 'I didn't have much time to think about it. The belt was on the floor next to the bed – I stood on it, and I thought I could use it to tie the sword to the bed post or something. But I couldn't get it tight enough, so the sword *still* wouldn't stand up, and I could hear Isaac – or Steve, as I now know it was – finishing in the bathroom. There was a big pile of pillows and blankets on the bed, so I held the sword upright and stabbed a couple of pillows onto it…' She demonstrated, using her hand in place of the sword.

'Like a kebab?' I said. 'You skewered the pillows onto the sword and then left it standing upright, with the hilt at the bottom and the pointy bit sticking up, weighed down by the pillows?'

She nodded. 'I wrapped a blanket round it, too, to help keep it in place. It only had to stand up long enough for Isaac to see it when him and Joshua left the bathroom. And that's how it was when I left it.'

'With the sheets pulled back so the sword was in full view?' asked Nathan. I could see by his face that he was imagining it too. She nodded.

'Yes, I swear. I was sure that Isaac would keep the bathroom light on at least until Joshua was safely in bed, so I was certain they would both see it.'

'But you were wrong.' Isaac shook his head, his eyes never leaving her face. 'What if whatever happened to Steve had happened to Joshua?'

'I could never have lived with myself—'

'You don't think maybe that would be worse than not paying child maintenance for a son I never even knew I had?' Isaac's normally calm and controlled tone of voice was rising. James put his hand on Isaac's arm, but he shook it off. 'I'm fine. I'm not going to lose it over her.'

'I wouldn't blame you if you did,' said Pippa in a quiet voice, quite unlike the one full of spite and vitriol she'd used earlier. I realised now that she'd been in a state of shocked denial since discovering Steve's body, and the enormity of what she'd done was only now coming home to her.

'OK, so you left the sword in a highly dangerous place,' said Nathan, reasserting his authority over the conversation. 'So what happened? How did Steve end up dead?'

'I think I might know,' I said. 'But we need to go and look at the crime scene again, I think.'

Nathan and I went back up to the Dyneley Suite, DI Jones following somewhat sullenly behind us. Nathan leaned in close to me.

'This would be a lovely place for a romantic night away, wouldn't it?' he murmured. I laughed.

'I thought that too, until Steve got himself killed. I think I'd rather find somewhere without a dead body in the next room...'

We reached the landing, then had to stand to one side as two men, sombrely dressed in black trousers and polo shirts, wheeled a trolley along the hallway towards us, their cargo a large black body bag that stopped our light-hearted banter in its tracks.

'Poor Steve,' I said. 'He didn't deserve such a nasty end.'

'No one does,' said Nathan simply. 'Come on.' We let the mortuary men pass us, then headed for the crime scene.

The ME had packed away her things and was chatting to the forensic team. She smiled at Nathan.

'I'm all done. I'm putting time of death between 2 a.m. and 6 a.m.'

'That fits in with what we've been told,' he said. She looked surprised.

'You've got the guy already? You don't hang around, DCI Withers.' She pulled off her latex gloves and balled them up, throwing them into a rubbish bag just outside the door. 'I look forward to seeing you at the post-mortem.'

'I think I'll be passing that particular pleasure on to

DI Jones,' said Nathan. Jones, who had been talking to one of the SOCOs, looked up at the sound of his name. The ME nodded, picked up her bag and left.

'So come on then, Ms Parker,' said Nathan. 'Tell me what you're thinking…'

'I'm thinking we need to retrace Steve's steps,' I said. I walked over to the door of the en suite bathroom. 'He was in here when Pippa came in through the secret passage.' I went in and stood in front of the toilet.

'Please tell me you're not pretending to stand there and pee like a man,' said Nathan behind me. He really did know me too well.

'Gotta get in the zone, haven't I?' I said. I pretended to zip up my fly.

'He was naked,' pointed out Nathan. 'No flies to do up.' I unzipped my invisible fly.

'Better?'

'Oh, *miles* better.' Nathan grinned at me. 'So he's finished pointing Percy at the porcelain, what now?'

'He's got the light on, remember,' I said, turning and walking back to the door. 'And he's drunk, and he's probably taken a sleeping pill. Debbie reckons they're really strong ones, too. So he's pretty out of it. He might even have been to sleep, then got up for a pee. You know when you do that thing, where you stagger out of bed, half asleep, not wanting to wake up properly because you're going back to bed in a minute? He might even have kept his eyes half shut so as not to fully wake up.'

I stood in the doorway. From here, I could see the head of the four-poster bed, but the post that the leather belt had been tied to was mostly obscured by the lamp on the bedside table. And apart from that, the sword itself had been propped up just off the centre of the bed. 'He wouldn't have seen the sword or Pippa messing about on his bed from here,' I said, 'even if he'd stopped to look at it.'

'If he was that drunk, and if he was sleepy from the pills, he wouldn't have been very alert or observant,' said Nathan. 'Which also explains how Pippa was able to faff about with the sword and the belt and everything without him hearing her.'

I reached up and turned on the bathroom light. An automatic extractor fan clicked on with it.

'The noise of the extractor fan would have covered any sound she made, as well,' I said. 'And that light is really bright. Imagine finishing in here, turning the light off…' I turned the light off, 'and then stepping back into the bedroom, where the light was off.'

'It was already dark in here, with the heavy curtains and everything, but after being in the brightness of the bathroom, it would have been absolutely pitch black.' Nathan looked at me. 'He must have blundered right into the sword.'

'Yeah, you're right.' I looked at the floor between me and the bed. 'Look, down here,' I said. Steve's discarded clothes were still in a heap on the floor next to the bed. 'His shoes have been kicked under there.'

'He had big feet,' remarked Nathan.

'And big shoes. Big enough to trip him up and send him flying onto the bed.'

'And onto the sword.' Nathan turned to me. 'His own weight would have completely flattened the pillows and driven the sword right through him.' He looked at the blood-stained sheets and shook his head. 'Poor bloke. What a horrible way to go. It would have taken a little while for him to bleed to death.'

I shuddered, feeling suddenly tearful. Poor Steve. He'd only come to Kingseat Abbey and donned the red Santa suit because he wanted to help his son.

Nathan looked at me and pulled me in for a hug, much to the bemusement of DI Jones, who'd been loitering close enough to hear what we were saying.

'Are you OK? I know you've seen plenty of dead bodies, but when it's someone you were talking to only a few hours ago...'

'I just... I was thinking about what must have been going through his head. Fear and bewilderment, and pain of course, but he'd also have been worrying about his son...' I felt my eyes watering. 'Being here on his own, knowing that he was dying, maybe trying to pull himself off the sword but unable to – not that it would have made much difference to the outcome, probably, but...' I buried my face in Nathan's shoulder and he pulled me closer. He spoke over the top of my head.

'DI Jones, I think we're done here. If you can arrange transport for Pippa Sykes back to Carricksmoor, I'll be taking Ms Parker home. She's helped us enough for today.'

'Yes, Guv,' said DI Jones. I waited for him to make some sarky comment, but he didn't.

'Get the Scene of Crime guys to pack up the victim's belongings and take them back to the station for his family to collect. And liaise with the owner, Mr Manning, about getting this room cleaned. Give them the number of your usual crime scene cleaners.'

'Yes, Guv.' I pulled away from Nathan and looked up to see Jones watching me. He gave me a reluctant smile. 'Well done, Ms Parker. My DCI back at Carricksmoor said if you were anything like your dad, you'd be one to look out for.'

'Thank you, DI Jones,' I said.

Chapter Eighteen

We stood in the hallway, watching through the open door as DI Jones and DC Carver led Pippa out to one of the waiting Range Rovers. A shocked Lily had followed them, and I was pleased to see Jones show a little bit of humanity and let her hug Pippa before gently ushering her away. He unlocked Pippa's handcuffs and helped her into the back of the car, then climbed in next to her as Carver got in the front and started the engine.

'They'll treat her OK,' said Nathan. 'She's not a murderer, even if she did cause someone's death.'

'What do you think will happen to her?' I asked. He shook his head.

'No idea. Prison, certainly. Low security though, I

would think. She's not exactly of sound mind, is she? She needs help, not just punishment.'

'Poor Pippa.' I sighed.

'Jodie?' We turned to see Isaac standing behind us.

'How are you?' I asked him.

'I'm not entirely sure.' He gave a small smile. 'Feeling guilty, even though I genuinely didn't know about Lee. He's in the Royal Artillery, based in Salisbury, apparently.' He looked bewildered. 'And he has no idea who I am.'

'Will you tell him?' asked Nathan. He nodded.

'I asked Pippa what she wanted me to do. She's going to be away for a while, isn't she? She asked me to visit him, explain things.' He sighed. 'Part of me's dreading it, but part of me thinks it'll be nice for Joshy to have a big brother. If he wants anything to do with us.'

'It'll work out,' I said. 'What will be, will be. Does Joshua know what's happened? With Steve, and Pippa and everything?'

'No.' We all turned as James appeared from the kitchen, Joshua on his shoulders, clutching a chocolate Santa. 'No, and I don't want him to know, either, not until he's older.' He smiled as James said something and Joshua roared with laughter. 'I've decided to forgive James, as well,' he said, looking at me. 'You were right, Jodie. We all make mistakes. He's a good man. With a bit of guidance, he could be a great one.' James reached us.

'Are we OK to go?' he asked. Nathan nodded. 'Thank you. Sorry if I was a bit rude before. I was a bit stressed out. No excuse for being impolite, I know, but... Sorry.'

'No problem, sir. Just be careful about borrowing money in future, yes?'

'I am *never* borrowing *anything* again,' said James vehemently. Isaac patted him on the shoulder.

'Let's forget all about that now. It's nearly Christmas Day! Joshy is excited, aren't you son?'

'Yes, Dad,' said Joshua, looking at Nathan shyly. Nathan smiled, making my heart flutter. He really would make a good dad.

'I hope Santa brings you something nice, Joshua,' said Nathan.

'I hope he brings me a dog like Germaine,' he said eagerly. I grinned at Isaac.

'Oops. Sorry...'

We watched Isaac and James say goodbye to Lily and Trevor, then get into Isaac's Porsche SUV. Matt Turner appeared with the stragglers from the forensic team, helping them with their equipment and bagged-up evidence. And then the breakdown truck turned up, with the girls' hire car on the back, to give them a lift all the way back to their hotel in London.

'What are you thinking?' asked Nathan.

'I was thinking, it just goes to show how important fathers are,' I said. He looked at me, surprised. 'Think about it,' I said. 'Steve was only here because he was worried about his son. He only took the job on so he could confront Isaac about him and get some help. He did that, but it cost him his life.'

Nathan nodded. 'At least he knew that his son would be OK.'

'I hope he did. Isaac reckoned he was steaming drunk by the time he went to bed. Then there's James. His father sounds like a real piece of work. Imagine living your whole life, knowing that your dad thought you were a failure? Trying to prove himself to his dad nearly cost James his job and could've ruined his future. I mean, I always wanted to make my dad proud of me, but I never, ever had to worry about disappointing him. I knew that he'd love me, whatever I did.'

'He *was* proud of you,' said Nathan. 'Your mum was talking to me about the way you and him were so similar, and she said he was even more proud of you than you realised.' He took my hand and squeezed it.

I smiled. 'What about your dad? I don't know much about either of your parents.'

'They ran a pub in Crosby,' he said. 'My dad taught me how to make a pint last all night, so I wouldn't look like a lightweight in front of my mates but I wouldn't get a hangover, either.' He smiled as he thought about Mr Withers senior, who I hadn't met yet but – if we were serious – I would someday. 'The best thing my dad taught me is that it's all right to cry.'

'Really?'

'Yep. I remember one Sunday evening, watching *Little House on the Prairie*—'

'I loved that programme! And *The Waltons*.'

'Yeah, we watched that too. Anyway, in this particular episode, this bloke's wife had died and they were trying to take his son away from him. My dad was in pieces, the soppy old bugger. Mum gave him a hug – she was completely dry-eyed, if I remember right – and told him it was just telly, and he laughed and wiped his eyes, but he wasn't embarrassed. And he was a big man, my dad, used to throwing drunks out after last orders. And I thought, *If it's all right for him to cry, it's all right for me.*'

'Aww, that's so sweet...'

'They gave up the pub a couple of years ago, when it started getting a bit too much for them. They're semi-retired now, but they do a lot of voluntary work. Dad goes to the RSPCA a couple of times a week, and walks the dogs. He's always loved dogs, but a pub wasn't the right place to have one. Mum says she's waiting for him to bring a couple home with him. She helps out at the local hospital, visiting the new mums in the premature baby unit.'

'As long as she doesn't take one of *them* home with her...'

We watched as the Japanese girls climbed into the cab of the breakdown truck, shrieking with laughter. Lily and Trevor said goodbye to them through the window and waved them off. 'Everyone knows how important mums are,' I said, 'but dads... Isaac hated his dad, and that's what made him leave home and make something of himself, but it also nearly ruined the way he brought up his own son. He was lucky to recognise that when Joshua was born. And of course Pippa's husband – how could he not have known that their son was actually Isaac's? He looked so much like him. But even if he did suspect, it didn't matter, he still loved him and looked after him.'

'Do you ever worry about Daisy? Not seeing her dad, I mean.'

I shook my head firmly. 'No. I did at first, but she doesn't need him. He's useless, anyway. She's always been surrounded by great male role models. My dad was a fantastic grandad, and of course Tony was always around, every time we came down here to see my parents. We might not be related, but he's definitely her Uncle Tony.' I smiled and looked at Nathan, feeling a bit shy all of a sudden. But I had to say this. 'And then of course there's you.'

'Me?' Nathan looked surprised, but (I was happy to note) dead chuffed.

'Of course. She sees the way you treat me, with respect, and kindness, and consideration. You never talk over me, or make me feel like I'm stupid, like Richard did. You're helping me show her what a proper relationship looks like. She won't settle for some arsehole like him now. She'll want a partner who treats her the way she *should* be treated.' I gazed at him, knowing that I probably had a big soppy grin on my face, but not caring. 'The way you treat me.'

Nathan smiled and reached out to gently touch my cheek. 'You know why I treat you like that, don't you?'

'Because you're scared of me,' I said, thinking, *Ooh, this is getting real now, act like a clown, quick!*

He laughed. 'A little bit, yeah. I prefer to call it having a healthy regard for my own skin.' He pulled me towards him, his arms slipping around my waist and his eyes staring deep into mine. 'That's not the only reason, though. It's because...' He took a deep breath. *Say it!* I thought. So I did.

'I love you, Nathan.'

He let out his breath. 'That's what I was just about to say!'

'That you love yourself? That's a bit narcissistic, innit?' He laughed again and shook his head, pulling me into the doorway of the snug and positioning me under the mistletoe.

'Will you just stop messing about and let yourself be kissed, woman?' he said. So I did.

Jodie's tried and tested recipes #4

Frangipane Mince Pies

Aah, Christmas! Is there anything better than the festive season? At what other time of year can you sit around in a tasteless jumper and pyjamas, eating a Terry's Chocolate Orange for your breakfast, without attracting reprobation, censure and disapproval? I mean, OK, I did go through a phase of doing this every weekend when I first left home, and Debbie says she did the same (but with raisin and biscuit Yorkie bars) when she was a student nurse, but other than that – oh, and of course at Easter, chocolate eggs are definitely an acceptable alternative to cornflakes – but other than that...

Christmas is a special time, a family time, and the food we celebrate it with in the Parker household is special, too. Roast turkey with all the trimmings – pigs in blankets (sausages wrapped in bacon, not *actual* pigs in *actual* blankets – weird), Yorkshire puddings (not *actual* puddings, although I think they may really have originated in Yorkshire, and not strictly traditional at Christmas, but we love them), sage and onion stuffing, roast potatoes and parsnips...all smothered in gravy. Some people go for a ham or a joint of pork as well, but that's just greedy. But tasty.

And after that, a flaming Christmas pud, rich and fruity (how Mum says she likes her men), served with lashings of brandy butter, custard, or ice cream (for the non-traditionalists), or all three (for those of us who *love* dessert).

Because Christmas dinner is usually served early afternoon (if you're proper English, it should be done and dusted by 3 p.m., when the Queen's speech comes on the telly), by about seven in the evening you'll probably start feeling peckish again, despite, no doubt, nibbling on that tin of Quality Street or Ferrero Rocher the neighbours brought round. And that's where cake comes into it.

We do *the best* festive cakes in Europe. The Italians have *panettone*, a sweet, fruity bread that's so light you can actually eat a HUGE slice without feeling like a total pig. I can, anyway. The Germans – well, the Germans have pretty much got Christmas treats sewn up, what with gingerbread, *stollen* (one of my favourites), and *lebkuchen*. If you ever get the chance to go to a Bavarian Christmas market (or a branch of Lidl, in December), do it, but wear an outfit with a bit of give in it. Lycra and elasticated waists are the way to go.

But for me, it's not a proper Christmas until someone gets out the mince pies. These days, the supermarkets get them on the shelves in blooming *October* (next to the Halloween stuff!), so Christmas starts early for us, because I am *addicted* to them. My mum used to make them with puff pastry, and they would puff up so much they would practically explode in the oven, but they were delicious. It's much more traditional to make them with sweet shortcrust pastry, but I recently found a recipe that tops both of these and, even better, can be used all year-round with different fillings. Try this recipe and you'll be addicted to them, too!

If you want to be *really* fancy (or show off), or you fancy yourself as the next Mary Berry (there can be only one), you can make this whole thing from scratch. Or you can be the next Jodie Parker and cheat/save yourself the time and hassle by using shop-bought pastry and mincemeat. Note for non-UK residents: mincemeat actually has no meat (minced or otherwise) in it. Back in the olden days, it did have minced/ground beef in it, heavily spiced, with added fruit, but at some point in time people went, *Oh my God, minced beef and fruit IN THE SAME PIE? What are you, INSANE?* and started leaving out the meat. So it's basically just a mix of dried fruit with sugar and spices. The shop-bought stuff is pretty good, so unless you want the faff of making it yourself, cheat. But I've included a recipe at the end for fruit mince if you want to have a go (it's nice if you've got the time and inclination, because you can change the ratios of the fruits if you prefer more of one than the other).

Shop-bought pastry is pretty damn good too these days, and (if it's a consideration), most of it is vegan (in the UK – can't vouch for anywhere else). Again, if you want to make it yourself (and pastry-making is a good skill to have, and it's not actually that hard) there's a recipe at the end.

OK, so here we go...this makes about 15–20 pies, depending on the size of your cupcake pans. Or you can make one large pie.

Let's begin...

1. Pre-heat the oven to 190°C.
2. Line a cupcake baking pan with sweet shortcrust pastry. Remember to grease it first to stop the pastry sticking, or you'll be hacking out your finished pies with a knife, sobbing, because they (and you) are in pieces and they just smell so damn fine... (Yeah, I've been there, my friend.) You can use butter or vegetable oil (don't use olive oil, because it will change the flavour of your pastry). Another tip is to then lightly dust the pan with flour. The easiest way to line the pan is to find a mug or plate that is slightly bigger than the pan, and cut around it – this should give you the perfect-sized piece of pastry for your pie's bottom. Remember, with pies (as with your own bottom), BIGGER IS BETTER! Because you can always trim it. Although my own bottom (and Debbie's, truth be told) has so far resisted all my attempts to shrink it.
3. Fill the pastry-lined pie pans with fruit mince, or your preferred fruity filling. Fresh raspberries or blueberries go particularly well with this recipe. You can even add a thin layer of jam to the bottom first. Don't fill the pans to

the top – remember to leave room for the frangipane mixture.

4. Cream together **140g soft butter or margarine** with **140g caster sugar**.

5. Add **85g self-raising flour**, **100g ground almonds** and **2 large eggs** and mix thoroughly until creamy and smooth. You can also add ½ **tsp almond extract** to really bring out the nutty flavour if you have it, but don't worry about it if you don't, it'll still be delicious.

6. Top the fruit tarts with the almond and flour mixture, and smooth to the edges. Top with **flaked almonds**.

7. Bake for 20–25 minutes, until golden brown, and until the almond mixture is cooked through (insert a skewer into it, and if it comes out clean it's done). It's easier if you use a shallow cupcake tin, rather than a deep muffin pan, as the mixture cooks through quicker.

8. Leave the pies to cool in the pan for 5 minutes before taking them out and cooling them on a rack. (Or eat them while they're hot. You might get indigestion, but it's worth it. Yes, I've been there too.) Serve with a dollop of cream for extra yumminess.

Sweet shortcrust pastry

This makes about 1kg of pastry, but you won't need all that for the mince pies. You can freeze what's left over or use it to make jam tarts or something.

This is a really rich, sweet pastry, using eggs – so unlike shop-bought, it's not vegan. But it is delicious...

1. Rub together **500g plain flour**, **100g icing sugar** and **250g butter or margarine** until the mixture resembles fine breadcrumbs. At this point you can add extra flavours if you want to, like a little bit of **lemon or orange zest** (both work really well with the fruit mince and the almond frangipane topping).
2. Add **2 large eggs** and a splash of **milk** – enough to bring it together into a firm dough.
3. Wrap in clingfilm and leave to rest in the fridge for 30 minutes. Try not to handle the dough too much, as it can result in tough pastry. When you come to roll it out, either do it on a lightly flour-dusted surface (and dust the rolling pin, too, to stop it sticking), or place the pastry between two sheets of grease-proof baking paper. This stops you inadvertently adding more flour to the pastry and making it dry.

Fruit mince

This is a basic recipe for fruit mince. You can adjust the quantities of fruit, according to your own personal taste. This recipe includes alcohol, but you can leave that out and make it child/lightweight drinker/recovering alcoholic friendly.

Finally, there's not a massive amount of preparation involved, but you do need to make this ahead of time, to give the fruit a chance to marinate and allow all the flavours to come together.

This mincemeat (if you store it properly – more on that later) can last for up to a year, although it doesn't in our household; anything that doesn't end up in a mince pie gets stirred into a good-quality vanilla ice cream come New Year.

1. Mix together **400g dried fruit**. Traditionally this would be a mix of sultanas, currants and candied mixed peel, but you can use what you like really. Dried cranberries would be nice, and very Christmassy.
2. Peel, core and finely chop **1 apple** (cooking or eating, either is fine) and add to the dried fruit,

along with the grated zest and juice of **1 lemon** and **1 orange**.

3. Add **175g shredded suet** (I prefer to use vegetarian but beef is fine – it won't taste of beef, I promise you!), along with **225g brown sugar** and **2 tsp mixed spice**. If you want to add a few other things to taste, like extra cinnamon or some nutmeg, go ahead, but don't overdo it.

4. Give everything a good stir, cover with a clean tea towel and leave overnight for all the flavours to infuse.

5. The next day, preheat the oven to 110°C. Cover the dish with foil and leave in the oven for around 2½ hours. Then take it out and leave it to cool, stirring from time to time to distribute the fruits and spices evenly.

6. Once it's cool, add **4 tbsp brandy** (if using) – this will help preserve the mincemeat for longer, but if you're going to use it quickly and you just want to loosen the mixture up, you could add a dash of orange or apple juice.

7. One more stir! Then put the mincemeat into previously sterilised jars, cover with a waxed paper disc, and screw on the lid.

A note about sterilising jars

Make sure you wash the jar and the lid with hot soapy water and rinse thoroughly first. Then dry them in the oven at 120°C for 10–15 minutes.

Be aware that when you take them out of the oven, they will be hotter than a certain DCI standing under the mistletoe…

Acknowledgments

They say it takes a village to raise a child. Well, it's not much different when it comes to book babies. A huge number of people have helped bring *A Cornish Christmas Murder* into the world…

It was a relatively short but occasionally painful pregnancy. Thank goodness for my birthing partners, fellow writers and amazing women *Carmen Radtke, Jade Bokhari, Sandy Barker, Andie Newton* and *Nina Kaye*. They saw me through the early stages, stopped me giving into weird cravings, and persuaded me not to give my book baby the type of 'unusual' name that would lead to it being teased or getting beaten up in the playground.

During my labours, I was ably supported and pushed on by my husband, *Dominic*, and son, *Lucas*, who kept me going with the regular application of generous amounts of tea, chocolate and hugs.

And when it was time, the skilful literary midwifery of my editor at One More Chapter, *Bethan Morgan*, brought the book into the world. Her advice helped me cut the umbilical cord, before she sent it off to have its little booky fingers and toes counted by a crack copyediting and proofreading duo, *Simon Fox* and *Nicky Lovick*. And then our talented book cover designer *Lucy Bennett* came up with a beautiful outfit for it to wear.

Present throughout was the reassuring, calm presence of bookish fairy godmother, my agent *Lina Langlee* at The North Literary Agency, even while she dealt with her own little flesh and blood (and undeniably far cuter) bundle of joy. Many thanks as well to the wonderful community of fellow writers, book bloggers, tweeters and Instagrammers who helped me announce the new arrival.

I may have pushed the baby analogy a little far (you think?!), but writing and releasing a book really can feel like giving birth, and it was made that much easier by having this fantastic team behind me. Thank you all!

Read on for a preview of *Murder on the Menu*, the first sparklingly delicious chapter in Jodie's story...

Still spinning from the hustle and bustle of city life, **Jodie 'Nosey' Parker** is glad to be back in the Cornish village she calls home.

Having quit the Met Police in search of something less dangerous, the change of pace means she can *finally* start her dream catering company and raise her daughter, Daisy, somewhere safer.

But there's nothing quite like having your first job back at home be catering an ex-boyfriend's wedding to remind you of *just* how small your village is. And when the bride vanishes, Jodie is drawn into the investigation, realising that life in the countryside might not be as quaint as she remembers.

With a missing bride on their hands, murder and mayhem lurks around every corner...

But surely saving the day will be a piece of cake for this not-so-amateur sleuth?

Murder on the Menu: Prologue

I'm not superstitious. I never have been. I make a point of walking under ladders and I positively encourage black cats to cross my path. My old partner on the beat, Helen, used to laugh and tell me that I was tempting fate, like I was standing there glaring at it, fists raised, going, *Come on then, is that all you've got?* But I wasn't, not really. I've never tempted fate; I just can't help poking at it. If I see something wrong, I can't resist getting involved.

I'm not superstitious, but I do have a few rituals, which is more to do with avoiding bad karma or Murphy's Law. Lots of coppers do. Stuff like, when you go out to a café or restaurant, always sit facing the door, so you can see everyone who's coming in and going out (which makes life difficult when you're out for a meal with another police officer, because if you can't get the right table and neither of you gives way, you end up sitting next to each other). Or not polishing your shoes before a Friday or Saturday night shift because if you do you're bound to run into a drunken hen party trying to stab each other with their stilettos outside a nightclub at 3am, one of whom will definitely unload seven Bacardi Breezers and one doner kebab all over your shiny black footwear as you get her in the van. That kind of thing.

The other ritual I have is always leaving a good-luck card for the new occupants whenever I move house. I've moved house *a lot*. There was the skanky bedsit I lived in when I first relocated to London. I loved it because it was the first place which was *mine* (even though it was rented) and I had become a grown-up and my life was just getting started and it was all so exciting. I was away from my parents and following in my dad's footsteps without being in his shadow for once. All this despite the bedsit having hot and cold running mould and a wicked draught from the one solitary window, and a landlord who refused to get anything repaired until I told him I was a copper. And then he *still* didn't repair anything; he just put the rent up by another hundred quid a week until I moved out. There were the shared houses – often with other police officers from the same nick – which kind of made sense until we all ended up doing different shifts, so it didn't matter what time of day it was, there was always someone trying to sleep and someone else waking them up as they came home and someone getting ready to go out. That had been particularly stressful. There was the nice flat I finally found myself in, just before I met Richard; it was small but perfectly formed, and quiet. I bought a cheap poster print of a famous painting of the coast near my home town in Cornwall and I would sit there, in the peace and quiet of my lovely flat, staring at the picture and thinking about the way the light reflected off the sea back home, and I would cry because I was so flipping lonely and homesick when I wasn't actually at work, but I wasn't about to give in and go back and admit I'd been wrong to leave.

And then there was this place. This was the first house I'd ever actually owned – *we'd* owned, me and Richard – and although it wasn't perfect, it was full of memories. Memories of Richard carrying me over the threshold after we got married, banging my head on the door frame as he did so. *That* was bad karma and should have made me wary of what was to follow. Of bringing our daughter Daisy back from the hospital after a long-drawn-out labour that put me off having any more children, at least for a year or so, and by then Richard had gone off the idea anyway. It was a few more years before I found out why.

The good-luck card lay on the kitchen counter, which had been cluttered with cookbooks and gadgets the day before but was now empty. They were inside a box, inside the removal van, which had already left. The picture on the front was of a lovely country cottage made of stone with climbing roses around the door. It was ironic because it looked nothing like this house but wasn't too dissimilar from where we were moving to. I picked up the pen and composed in my head what to write.

Good luck in your new home. I hope you are as happy here as I was.

...Or as happy as I was before I found out that my stupid useless can't-keep-it-in-his-pants husband was cheating on me.

I hope you are as happy here as I was once I got him out of this house and our lives, before he moved in with his new girlfriend ten minutes away, but STILL constantly let his daughter down by turning up late when he'd promised to take her out (if he turned up at all). If we're living miles away he can't let her down anymore, as she won't expect anything from him (she already knows better than to do that, but she's only twelve so she can't help hoping).

I hope you are as happy here as I was when I could still afford to pay the mortgage, before he started kicking up a fuss about paying child support and before I left the job that I absolutely loved but which (after a particularly nasty incident) my daughter didn't. I could see her point. If anything happened to me she'd have to go and live with her dad, who, as I think we've already established, is a total waste of space, oxygen, and the Earth's natural resources. So I left and retrained and now we're both ready to start again somewhere else.

I hope you are happy here spending an absolute fortune on this cramped house with its tiny garden, noisy neighbours, and busy road outside while I'll be paying considerably less for somewhere bigger with a lovely view of the sea and neighbours who are more likely to wake me up at 6am with their loud baaing than at 3am with their drunken return from a club.

Hmm. Maybe I was overthinking it. I opened the card and wrote inside it.

Good luck.

It was definitely time to go home.

Murder on the Menu: Chapter One

Funny how things turn out. I only went in to buy a sofa.

Penhaligon's was one of those old-fashioned family-run department stores – the type that once upon a time every town had but which were now disappearing (and with good reason, to be honest; most of the stock looked like it had been procured in the 1950s and came at such an exorbitant price you were forced to step outside and double-check you hadn't inadvertently wandered into Harrods by mistake). But Penhaligon's had persisted, remaining open through world wars, recessions, and the rise of internet shopping. The zombie apocalypse could hit Cornwall (*I know, I know, would anyone even notice?*) and Penhaligon's would *still* be there, clinging stubbornly to its prime spot on Fore Street, serving the needs of both locals and the undead brain-hungry horde (or 'holidaymakers', as they were otherwise known).

I wouldn't normally have bothered with Penhaligon's, but we'd been at our new house for four days now and Daisy and I were sick of sitting on my mum's old garden chairs – they were literally a pain in the backside – so as I was passing I ventured inside.

It hadn't changed much since the last time I'd been there. It had barely changed since the *first* time I'd been there forty years ago. But I was pleasantly surprised to see that someone had given the furniture department a bit of a makeover and there were a few lounge suites that looked like they'd actually been designed sometime after the fall of the Berlin Wall (as opposed to before the building of it).

I sank gratefully into a big, squashy sofa, stroking the fabric appreciatively and reaching for the price tag. The figures made me suck in my breath in mild horror (along with an unfortunate fly who was just passing), but the words 'Next day delivery!' had an immediate soothing effect.

I stood up to get a better look at it and jumped as a voice boomed across the shop floor at me.

'Oh my God, Nosey Parker! Is that really you?'

I turned round, already knowing who it was. Tony Penhaligon, great-grandson of the original Mr

Penhaligon, old classmate and sometime boyfriend (we went out for two weeks in 1994, held hands a bit, kissed but didn't – *ewww* – use tongues), stood in front of me, a big smile on his face. Like his family's shop, he also hadn't changed all that much over the last forty years and every time I looked at him I could still see a hint of the annoying little boy with the runny nose who had sat next to me on my first day in Mrs Hobson's primary class. But he had a good heart and it was nice to see a friendly face.

I did a double-take as I took him in properly. Hang on a minute; he actually *had* changed. The last time I'd seen him, on one of my trips back to see my mum, he'd been sporting a dad bod, a paunch brought on by too many pasties and pints. But that was gone and he was looking rather trim. Also gone was the unflattering store uniform of white polo shirt and black chinos, replaced by a sharp, well-tailored, and expensive-looking suit. A little voice in the back of my mind went, *I'd blooming well let him use tongues now*, before I shut it up with a contemptuous internal glare.

'It's been a while, Tone. I haven't seen you since—'

'New Year's Eve, three years ago.'

I laughed. 'You've got a good memory.'

'Last time anything exciting happened here. Did you stick to your resolution?'

'That was the first Christmas after I broke up with

Richard,' I said. 'I think I probably made a lot of drunken resolutions that year.'

Tony grinned. 'Yeah, there were one or two. Tell me you've stuck to the main one though? "Avoid idiot men"?'

'Oh, *that* one I live my life by these days. What was yours?'

He shook his head. 'I never announce my resolutions. That way nobody knows whether I followed it up or not.'

'And did you?'

'Nope. But it doesn't matter now anyway. So what're you doing here? Visiting your mum? I heard she'd been ill.'

'Buying a sofa,' I said.

'You do know we don't deliver to London,' he said.

'That's just as well because I don't live there anymore.'

He looked surprised. 'Since when? Are you back, then?'

'Yeah.'

I could see that he was dying to ask me more but the thought of pushing it too far and losing out on his commission was too much for him. Plus, he knew that if I was sticking around he'd get it out of me eventually.

'So what do you think of the sofa?'

I sat back down. 'Honestly? It feels like my backside

has died and gone to heaven where it's being caressed by the wings of an angel.'

He laughed loudly. 'Do you want a job in our marketing department? I always said you should be a poet, not a copper.'

'I'm not either anymore,' I said, fishing in my bag and handing him one of my new business cards.

'"Banquets and Bakes",' he read. 'What's this?'

'My new business,' I said. 'I've just started up—'

'Wait, are you a chef now? Do you do weddings?' Tony looked at me hopefully.

'Weddings, christenings, bar mitzvahs, you name it. If people want to eat there, I can cater for it.' I *hoped* I could anyway; I hadn't actually had any clients yet, but in theory…

'This is brilliant!' cried Tony. 'It's … what's that word? Serentipidy?' I thought about correcting his pronunciation but decided against it; it would only make both of us feel bad. And anyway, he was waving across the shop floor to a woman who was stalking proprietorially around a display of crystal glass vases. 'Cheryl! Come over here! I've found a caterer!'

He held out my business card as Cheryl approached. She read it, then looked me up and down, clearly not overly impressed with what she saw. Which was fair enough as I had really only popped out to get some teabags in between coats of paint and was looking more like the Michelin Man than a Michelin chef.

'We're getting married,' said Tony proudly, and I could understand why. Although the expression currently occupying Cheryl's face was reminiscent of a bulldog sucking a lemon, she was (probably, in the right light) quite attractive, and she had to be ten years younger than him, even if she did dress a bit like Dynasty-era Joan Collins. I couldn't remember the last time I'd seen shoulder pads that size outside of the Super Bowl. It also explained the dapper suit that Tony was currently sporting, as well as his newly svelte figure.

'Congratulations,' I said. He deserved happiness. Tony's first wife had left him for her driving instructor, the betrayal made all the worse by the fact that Tony had paid for the lessons and she hadn't had the decency to leave him until she'd passed her test (after three attempts), done a motorway safety course and a defensive driving course, and was halfway through getting her HGV licence. The driving instructor hadn't lasted long and, according to my mum, who knew her mum, she now drove tankers up and down the country with just her dog – a Pomeranian called Germaine – for company.

I hoped he was going to ask me to do their catering – I needed the money – but at the same time I wasn't sure I wanted to risk cocking up his nuptials. Oh, well, I would just plan everything really, really carefully.

'Our caterer let us down and the wedding's next weekend,' he said.

Next weekend? Holy—

'I was just saying to Jodie' – he turned to his fiancée, indicating me with a wave of his hand –'I was just saying, it's serentipidy—'

'Serendipity,' she corrected, smiling at him condescendingly. *Hmm.* 'So – Jodie, was it? – what are your credentials? How many weddings have you done? We've got a very upmarket venue – Parkview Manor Hotel, do you know it? – and lots of guests coming from all over the country.'

I opened my mouth to confess that I hadn't actually done any weddings but if they were this close to their wedding day, good luck finding someone else as willing (or as desperate for the money) as me. But Tony beat me to it.

'Her credentials are, she's an old friend and ex-copper, and you don't get better references than that,' he said. Cheryl pursed her lips but didn't argue, aware that if she didn't want to end up feeding her upmarket guests pasty and chips in the very downmarket Kings Arms in Market Square, she didn't have much choice. I smiled.

'I'll do it for whatever the last caterer was going to do it for, if you throw in the sofa.'

So that was how I found myself, six days later, standing outside the imposing entrance to Parkview Manor Hotel. It was early evening, the day before The Wedding of the Century™; many of the guests were staying overnight and Tony had (against Cheryl's wishes, I thought) invited me to join their welcome drinks. I tugged down my dress; I'd put weight on since leaving the force, and even more since doing my catering course, and my going-out clothes, which I didn't get the chance to wear much, were all starting to get a little snug. My shoes were already pinching my toes. They were hardly Jimmy Choos but they were the only ones in my wardrobe that weren't made by Nike or Dr Martens. I comforted myself with the thought that I'd be in the kitchen tomorrow and back in my eminently more sensible jeans and trainers, took a deep breath, and entered.

The hotel foyer was very plush and wouldn't have looked out of place in London, rather than in the Cornish countryside. Marble covered every conceivable surface and I got the feeling that if I stood there gawping for too long I'd get marble-ised as well. There were lush, exotic ferns and birds-of-paradise dotted all over the place, and the plant-killer in me (I have brown thumbs) immediately suspected they were plastic. I surreptitiously stroked a leaf as I passed (thereby condemning the poor unsuspecting fern to an early grave); they were real and all very well cared for.

I vaguely recognised the woman behind the reception desk. Although I hadn't lived in Penstowan for almost twenty years, I'd grown up and gone to school here, and seventy-five per cent of the inhabitants were either old classmates, siblings of classmates, or parents of them. She smiled and inclined her head slightly towards the sign that said, 'Penhaligon and Laity Wedding Party', with a photo of the happy couple and an arrow pointing towards a function room. It was forebodingly quiet, with very little in the way of music or chatter floating into the foyer.

Inside the function room, there were a few guests standing at the bar chatting, with Tony holding court. He was clearly very excited about his upcoming big day, chattering away with a boyish enthusiasm that was quite endearing. It was still fairly early so presumably this wasn't it; Cheryl had said they had guests coming from all over the country so maybe they just hadn't arrived yet.

'Nosey!' called Tony. Now *that* was less endearing. I really needed to have a word with him about using my childhood nickname. I plastered on a smile and tottered over, grimacing at the blister that was already threatening a little toe.

But I never reached Tony and his chums because

everyone's attention was suddenly drawn to the doorway of the function room. The double doors had been thrown open and Cheryl stood there, smiling beatifically at the assembled guests. She was dressed to the nines in a fitted cocktail dress of deep scarlet silk, while her hair had been seriously coiffured and hair-sprayed to within an inch of its life. She was still rocking that 80s kind of vibe, but there was no denying that she did it well. My cheap chain-store dress and ugly shoes felt even more uncomfortable under her gaze and I could not wait to go home and put my pyjamas on.

She paused for a moment longer, milking her dramatic entrance, then opened her mouth to speak.

Her words were lost as she suddenly disappeared from view, bulldozed and tossed to one side by a screeching harpy in a khaki boiler suit.

Murder on the Menu: Chapter Two

For a split second nobody moved; we were all wondering what the hell had just happened. And then came the sound of bitch-slapping from the foyer.

I yanked off my stupid uncomfortable shoes and ran outside to see Cheryl lying on the ground, her hands thrust upwards and attempting to choke the madwoman sitting astride her – a madwoman who was still managing to wheeze threats at her.

'Mel?' Tony arrived seconds after me, and stood staring in astonishment.

'Is that really Mel?' I said, amazed. I hadn't seen Tony's ex-wife for years, and the last time I had she'd possessed a head of wonderful red curly hair. The harpy's hair was bleached blonde and cut very short and spiky.

'You can't marry him!' the harpy screeched. 'You don't love him! I won't let you ruin his life!'

'*You* already did that, you cow!' snarled Cheryl, who was having trouble breathing under Mel's not inconsiderable frame. I had to admit she had a point.

This was entertaining but getting out of hand. No one else was going to stop it – they were all still too gobsmacked – so I waded in. I've had the training, after all.

'All right, ladies, that's enough,' I said, as I tried to prise Cheryl's fingers away from Mel's throat. When that didn't work – she had a strong grip for someone with such well-manicured hands – I chopped her hard on the inside of the elbow with the side of my hand, making her yelp and let go. Then I dragged Mel to her feet and positioned myself between the two women.

I glared at Tony and the crowd (who were mostly male) gawping at us.

'It's all right, lads, don't bloody help or anything, will you,' I said, rolling my eyes. Tony shook himself and helped Cheryl to her feet.

'She can't marry him!' cried Mel, straining to get to the furious and not-so-blushing bride-to-be again. I shook her and made her look at me.

'Mel,' I said. 'Mel! Calm down. Do you remember me? Jodie?'

She looked at me and slowly recognition dawned.

'Aren't you the one who went off and joined the police? What are you doing here?' A look of relief washed over her. 'Are you investigating them? Are you—'

'Just calm down,' I said. 'I'm going to let go of you so we can talk properly, okay? I don't want a repeat of whatever that was.'

'I want the police here RIGHT NOW!' shouted Cheryl. She was understandably shaken, but I couldn't help feeling she was almost enjoying being the centre of attention, or help noticing that her lacquered hair had barely moved under the onslaught. She must've sprayed it with liquid Kevlar.

Tony looked at me helplessly. I seem to have that effect on men; at some point in our relationship they always look at me helplessly. I sighed.

'Let's not be hasty, Cheryl,' I said. She glared at me but I carried on before she could start shouting at me. I don't normally take an instant dislike to people but I really could not warm to her. 'It's the night before your wedding, all your guests will be arriving tonight, and you're meant to be having a party. Do you really want to spend the evening at the police station? It'll take hours for them to take statements. Your whole night will be ruined.'

Tony looked at me gratefully and I forgave him for being a helpless wuss. My kind heart will be the end of me one day.

'Jodie's right,' he said. 'Let's just go and have a drink and forget about it, yeah? No harm done.'

Cheryl looked for a moment like she was going to open her mouth and unleash such a stream of verbal abuse that it would make a navvy blush.

"Ello, 'ello, 'ello, what's going on here then?' The man's voice stopped Cheryl in her tracks. We all turned to stare at the small group of guests who had just arrived in the foyer and were looking on, bemused, obviously wondering if they'd missed the evening's entertainment.

I took in the appearance of the man who had stolen what was, by rights for an ex-copper, my line. He was in his early sixties, dapper and well dressed in casual but expensive-looking clothes. A Ralph Lauren polo player gambolled discreetly on the breast pocket of his shirt and the chunky diver's watch on his wrist did not look like a cheap knock-off from the local market. He radiated self-assurance and good humour, particularly if it was at someone else's expense. Behind him stood another, younger man, good-looking in a cocky kind of way – the sort of bloke you knew deep down you couldn't trust, but who could probably persuade you otherwise just long enough to get into your knickers. A sardonic smile, almost a sneer, crossed his face as he looked at Cheryl, who had gone uncharacteristically silent.

'All right, Chel?' His voice had a mocking, slightly

belligerent tone to it. 'My name weren't on the invite but I'm sure you didn't mean nothing by it.'

'We did send you one,' said Tony awkwardly. 'The post round here…'

The older man smiled – he was clearly very amused both by Tony's obvious discomfort and by the tableau in front of him – and inclined his head towards Mel.

'Is this the floorshow? I don't think much of your strippergram.'

Oh, so he was a dick. Good to know up front.

'That's really not helping, Mr…?' I said, in my best police officer's voice. These things never leave you.

'Laity. Roger Laity.' He held out his hand to shake, but my hands were still occupied with holding onto Mel. 'Uncle of the blushing bride.'

'Well, Mr Laity, if you and the rest of the group could make your way into the function room, rather than stand there making funny comments, that would go some way towards salvaging your niece's party, don't you think?'

He looked at me appraisingly. I got the impression that he expected me to blush or falter under his gaze but then, he really didn't know me. He turned away and patted Tony on the back condescendingly: *you can stand down now, son, the real man of the family has arrived.* Tony looked like he wanted to wash and possibly disinfect the spot his uncle-in-law-to-be had touched, and I felt a rush of sympathy for him. All he'd wanted was a nice wedding.

'Come on, babe,' said Tony, tugging at Cheryl.

The bride-to-be bestowed a murderous glance on Mel, who deserved it, to be fair, and on me, who didn't, and then allowed Tony to take her hand and lead her away. But she stopped and turned to me, hissing, 'Get that ... that *thing* out of my sight or I really will call the police!'

We waited while Tony, Cheryl, and their guests left the foyer and then I led a now docile Mel out of the hotel and into the grounds. We found a bench in a secluded spot near a pond full of koi carp, and sat down.

'So what was all that about?' I asked. Mel looked remorseful.

'I'm so sorry,' she said, miserably. 'I tried to talk to her but she brushed me off and I just got this rush of blood to the head.'

'That was quite a rugby tackle,' I said. We looked at each other, the image of Cheryl and her hair flying into the air running through our minds, and both stifled giggles.

'You don't like her either, do you?' asked Mel.

'I hardly know her,' I said, and she laughed gently.

'That's not a no, then,' she said, and I laughed too.

'No, it's not.'

We sat quietly for a moment, letting her calm down and marshal her thoughts.

'I don't think she loves him,' Mel said finally. 'She's going to ruin his life.'

'At the risk of sounding judgemental…' I started.

'I know, I know, I already ruined it.' She sighed. 'I didn't do it lightly. And I did love him. I just fell in love with someone else as well.'

'Your driving instructor.'

She looked at me, surprised. 'I keep forgetting that everyone knows everyone's business in this town. Your mum and my mum—'

'They both go to the OAPs' coffee club at the church hall on Wednesdays,' I said. She nodded.

'Of course. Anyway, I fell for my instructor but I still loved Tony. I wasn't stringing them both along, I just didn't know who I wanted to be with.' She sighed again. 'If it's any consolation, I chose the wrong one. She did to me what I did to Tony.'

I looked at her miserable face. I remembered how I'd almost instantly fallen for Daisy's dad – PC Richard Doyle, to give him his official title, or 'that cheating swine' to give him the unofficial one my mum always used – spotting him across the room at a team briefing. He'd just transferred to the station and I had to show him around. I ended up showing him a lot more than that after a few drinks in the pub after work. I hadn't known he was married at first, and I didn't care about his wife when he left her because it meant he'd chosen me. I'd been a lonely workaholic and I wasn't letting him go. Doubtless the woman he left me for – who I was sure was just one of many sad extra-marital conquests – twelve years later didn't care how I felt, either. It had felt like he'd ripped my heart out and stamped on it. And stamped on Daisy's, too, because when he left me he left her as well.

There wasn't a finite amount of heartbreak in the world. It didn't make any difference how many people suffered from it, it didn't lessen the sting. I sighed.

'Of course it's not a consolation, not to anyone. Not even to Tony, because he's not like that.' I picked up a piece of gravel and tossed it into the pond, watching the ripples spread out. I turned back to Mel. 'But what makes you think she's going to ruin his life?'

'She's not marrying him for love,' she said firmly.

'What makes you say that? What's she marrying him for?'

'Money.'

I laughed. 'He hasn't got any, has he? I mean, I know the shop's still going after all these years...'

She looked at me steadily.

'The shop?' I said. 'You think she wants the shop?'

Mel shrugged but didn't say anything. Why would

Cheryl want the shop? It can't have been that profitable; I was amazed it was still going. Smaller shops were closing all the time in seaside towns like Penstowan.

I looked at her thoughtfully. 'You said to me earlier, was I here investigating them. Investigating who?'

'The Laity family,' said Mel without any hesitation. 'Are you?'

'I'm not a police officer anymore,' I said. 'I'm just doing the catering.'

'Oh.' She looked disappointed.

'I'm still nosey, though,' I said. I had to admit that my childhood nickname had become quite apt during my years on the force. 'Why should the Laity family be investigated?'

She looked around nervously. 'My cousin works for the council. Let's just say, that family have got plans for Penstowan that not everyone will agree with.'

'What sort of plans?' I asked.

'Everything okay?'

I looked up into Tony's concerned face. He looked anxiously from me to Mel, a worried smile on his face.

'Tony! I'm so sorry...' started Mel, looking like she might cry.

'Do you want me to leave you to talk?' I said, standing up. Emotional scenes are not my thing. But they both looked horrified at the idea. Mel grabbed my hand.

'I just wanted to make sure you were okay,' said Tony.

'I know it must be hard for you, seeing me move on and be happy—'

'Oh, for Christ's sake, Tony, this is not a bloody love triangle with you in the middle!' she snapped. He looked affronted, then annoyed.

'Oh, so you just decided to rock up and ruin my wedding for a laugh?'

Mel got to her feet and it was in danger of all going off again. I jumped up and stood between them.

'Tony, thank you for checking on us; everything is fine. Mel is going to go home now so you get back to your party and I'll be in for a drink in a bit.' I really needed a drink after all this. To think I'd been expecting to be bored. I gave him a little shove towards the hotel and took Mel's arm.

We left him standing there with his mouth open, catching flies.

'So what were you going to say?' I asked Mel, when we were out of earshot. But she shook her head.

'No. Balls to him. If he wants to marry her, let him get on with it.'

We were almost in the car park by now. She disentangled her arm from mine and stopped.

'Thank you for stopping me make an even bigger idiot of myself,' she said. 'I appreciate it, honestly.' She looked over at an old and slightly battered Vauxhall that was parked on the other side of the gravelled drive. A small, furry, and undeniably cute face peered out of it, nose sniffling at the window. 'I left my dog in the car. She must be hot.' Mel must have seen my disapproving expression; the window was open a tiny crack, barely enough to let any air in, and it had been a hot day. 'I can't leave the window down any further than that or she gets out,' she explained, and chuckled. 'She's so clever, she throws all her weight at the top of the window until she forces it down, and then wriggles out. I should have called her Houdini. I'll just let her out for a pee and then I'll be off.'

She went to leave but I grabbed her arm to stop her.

'If you ever want to talk...' I said. 'I'd give you my business card but I left my bag in the bar.'

She smiled softly. 'Thank you. If you've moved back to Penstowan I'm sure we'll run into each other.'

I watched as she opened the car door and made a fuss of Germaine, faithful companion and would-be canine escape artist. Then I went back to the bar.

I thought I should probably stick around long enough to have a glass of wine, and then I would make my excuses and leave. It really wasn't my kind of party. But there was someone else missing from the bar too: Cheryl.

Tony saw me enter, brought me a glass of champagne, and steered me over to the window.

'So, do you think she'll come back?' he asked.

I gulped at my champagne. 'Who, Cheryl?'

'No, you muppet. Cheryl's having an early night. Mel. Will Mel cause any trouble tomorrow?'

'Oh, right. No, I don't think so.' I shook my head. 'And anyway, if she does turn up, I'll be right over there in the kitchen, preparing vol-au-vents and making dinner for a hundred people. I will have access to a lot of sharp pointy things.'

'You could do your awesome ex-policewoman ninja stuff again.' Tony laughed. 'That was so hot…'

I gasped in mock horror and slapped him. 'Anthony Penhaligon! You're practically a married man!'

He smiled. 'I know,' he said. 'I'm very lucky.'

'Hmm,' I said non-committally, sipping at my drink.

'You don't like my wife-to-be much, do you?' he said.

'I hardly know her.' I was painfully aware that was the exact thing I'd said to Mel. He laughed.

'That's not a no, is it?' He stared out of the window for a moment then turned back to me. 'I know Cheryl can be a bit…' *What? A bit of a fricking nightmare?* 'A bit high maintenance. But she's not had an easy life.'

I thought about the things I'd gone through over the last few years.

'Lots of us have had a hard life—' I started.

'She lost her parents when she was fifteen.' *Oh crap.* 'That's how she ended up with her uncle. I don't know what her parents were like – they didn't live round here – but her uncle and his lot...' Tony shook his head and lowered his voice. 'They're not very nice people. So cut her some slack, yeah?' He touched me gently on the arm. 'I'm glad you're back, Jodie. I'd really like you and Cheryl to be friends. Will you try?'

'Of course,' I said. And I meant it, for him.

I finished my drink and left the bar. Should I go up and talk to Cheryl? Part of me wanted nothing more than to just go home and relieve my mum of her babysitting duties – Daisy liked to think she was a grown-up, but she was still only twelve – but the concerned (or nosey) part of me thought that maybe I should pop up and check on her.

I stood outside her room, hesitating. Maybe I shouldn't disturb her if she wanted an early night. But I could hear movement – a lot of movement – from the other side of the door. So I knocked.

There was silence. To my mind it was a guilty silence – like someone had been caught doing something they shouldn't. Don't ask me how a silence can be guilty, but it can. I just have this instinct...

Just as I was becoming convinced she wouldn't answer the door, she did, opening it a crack. She had a smile on her face which dropped as soon as she saw me.

'Oh, it's you,' she said.

'Just checking that you're all right after that little incident earlier,' I said sweetly. I can do sweet.

'I'm fine,' she said. Through the crack in the door I could see a suitcase on the bed with a mess of clothes half in and half out.

'Getting everything ready for your big day?' I said. 'Packing for the honeymoon?'

'Yes,' she said, attempting to close the door a little tighter. I had a horrible feeling that packing wasn't what she was doing.

'Look, we may have got off on the wrong foot,' I said. 'If you want to talk—'

'Not really.'

'Okay.' I was relieved. 'Tony's a really good guy, you know. He deserves to be happy.'

Her face dropped. *Uh oh.*

'I know he does.'

'So if you've got any doubts…'

She looked at me for a few seconds, then plastered on a fake smile.

'No doubts at all,' she said. 'Thank you for your concern.' And with that she shut the door in my face.

I went home and went to bed, first looking in on Daisy, who had given up waiting up for me and gone to bed, and on my mum, who was staying in the spare room. I'd mentioned her moving in with us permanently as she was getting on a bit and I worried about her being on her own (especially since she'd been diagnosed with angina a few months ago, which had helped persuade me now was a good time to move back), but she'd been almost indecently hasty to reject that idea, saying that she valued her privacy and she could hardly bring a man home if her daughter and granddaughter were there.

I turned the light off and stared at the ceiling before finally falling into a restless sleep. My dreams were filled with 80s hairstyles, rugby tackles, and dickheads in Ralph Lauren, and somewhere in the middle of it Tony saying he'd deliver the sofa tomorrow. Except of course he wouldn't because it already had pride of place in my living room and tomorrow was his wedding day.

I woke the next morning and saw the text from the groom, and in my sleep-fuddled state I thought, *He's arranging a time to deliver the sofa.*

When I opened it, I was unsurprised to read that the bride had disappeared.

Don't forget to order your copy of *Murder on the Menu* to find out what happens next...

Don't miss *A Brush with Death*, the second irresistible instalment in the Nosey Parker series...

When a body turned up at her last catering gig it certainly put people off the hors d'oeuvres. With a reputation to salvage, **Jodie's** determined that her next job for the village's festival will go off without a hitch.

But when chaos breaks out, Jodie Parker somehow always finds herself caught up in the picture.

The body of a writer from the festival is discovered at the bottom of a cliff, and the prime suspect turns out to be the guest of honour, the esteemed painter Duncan Stovall.

With her background in the Met police, Jodie has got solving cases down to a fine art so she knows things are rarely as they seem.

Can she find the killer before the village faces another brush with death?

You will also love *A Sprinkle of Sabotage*, the third side-splitting entry in the Nosey Parker series...

A film company is coming to the Cornish village of Penstowan, and the whole community turn up to be cast as extras, even **Jodie 'Nosey' Parker**.

Determined to join in with the fun and ignore any dramas, Jodie intends to make the most of this time with her mum and daughter and hopefully see their names in lights...or really small writing on the credits page.

But right on cue, the company's caterer is sabotaged and Jodie must step up. It soon becomes clear that someone is out to spoil the filming...

With actors behaving out of character and the house literally being brought down, breaking a leg is the least of their worries.

Can Jodie save the day once again, or will it be their final curtain call?

**And look out for *A Body at the Bake Off*, the next
unmissable case in the Nosey Parker series...**

When popular TV baking contest 'The Great British
Baking Roadshow' rolls into town and sets up temporary
home in the grounds of Boskern House, a historic stately
home near Penstowan, **Jodie's** boyfriend, Nathan, who
also happens to be the local DCI, hatches a grand plot to
surprise her.

Teaming up with Jodie's daughter, Daisy, and her mum,
Shirley, they secretly enter Jodie into the beloved
competition.

But, as ever, peril lurks just behind every corner...

When the body of the production assistant is found in the
grounds of the house, lying on a bridge over the river
Ottery, Jodie is drawn into another high-stakes case with
both her reputation and her life once again on the line.

Can Jodie expose the culprit before the show is ruined?

ONE MORE CHAPTER

YOUR NUMBER ONE STOP

FOR PAGETURNING BOOKS

One More Chapter is an award-winning global division of HarperCollins.

Sign up to our newsletter to get our latest eBook deals and stay up to date with our weekly Book Club! <u>Subscribe here.</u>

Meet the team at <u>www.onemorechapter.com</u>

Follow us!

 @OneMoreChapter_

 @OneMoreChapter

 @onemorechapterhc

Do you write unputdownable fiction? We love to hear from new voices. Find out how to submit your novel at <u>www.onemorechapter.com/submissions</u>